AT THE RUSTLE OF MOVEMENT, THE SENTRY WHIRLED

Calvin James aimed his Uzi and squeezed off a burst. One bullet spanged off a wire link in the fence, raising sparks and blue coils of electrical flames that crackled along the metal. The remaining slugs slammed into the sentry's skull, punching him backward to the ground.

Given the all-clear, Manning emerged from the tall grass to kneel by the fence. He removed a square of plastique from his pocket, placed it at the base of the post and set the timing mechanism to a detonator. Then he grabbed his rifle and raced for the tree line.

The explosion was barely audible. Fire spit from the end of the cable as it whirled away from the post, and sparks sputtered as the cable was severed.

Manning removed a small chain from his pocket and tossed it into the fence. No sparks. The fence was no longer electrified.

They were in.

DON PENDLETON's

MACK BOLAN.

STONY MAN IV

A GOLD EAGLE BOOK FROM

WORLDWIDE.

TORONTO • NEW YORK • LONDON • PARIS
AMSTERDAM • STOCKHOLM • HAMBURG
ATHENS • MILAN • TOKYO • SYDNEY

First edition February 1992

ISBN 0-373-61888-3

Special thanks and acknowledgment to
William Fieldhouse for his contribution to this work.

STONY MAN IV

Printed in U.S.A.

STONY MAN IV

PROLOGUE

August 19, 1990

They had arrived. Kaborya watched the men descend the gangplank at the port side of the cargo ship. Thin and pale, they'd spent years in prison, excluded from sunshine and restricted to meager diets and poor food. Many were scarred, and some had fingers or fingernails missing; a few limped, favoring a damaged leg or foot; some wore cloth patches over empty eye sockets. Yet the passengers seemed cheerful as they marched from the vessel. They smiled, revealing broken and missing teeth, as they chanted passages from the Koran.

Kaborya had expected to see a collection of dour and grim figures arrive at the port of Aden. These men seemed joyous in spite of the obvious suffering they'd endured. Naturally they were certainly happy to be released from prison, but this didn't explain their display of enthusiasm as they marched from the cargo ship.

Kaborya stroked his clipped beard as he observed the men. He'd been told the Iranians had undergone a drastic alteration in attitude and behavior while held prisoners of war in Iraq. Kaborya had seen footage of other Iranian POWs released by Saddam Hussein. He hadn't been impressed by the file of freed prisoners

who chanted praise for the dictator as they crossed the
border to Iran. They were going home. The fact they'd
formerly fought Iraqi forces and spent years incarcer-
ated by the enemy wouldn't prevent them from cheering for Hussein if this hastened their departure for
home. They wouldn't have cared that their release had
been initiated due to Iraq's concern about a possible
confrontation with the United States military. Hussein wanted to bury the figurative hatchet with Iran
because he faced a potentially far greater opponent
and hoped to make an ally of his former foe.

However, the men who arrived in Aden weren't going home. They'd left the inclement prison cells to
travel to Yemen. The POWs knew there'd be no hal-
cyon utopia when they arrived. Indeed, they'd soon be
part of a bold covert war, far more ambitious and
ruthless than anything conceived by the mind of the
late Ayatollah Khomeini.

Major Karim Hawran appeared on deck at the top
of the gangplank. Although dressed in a shabby jacket
and wrinkled cotton trousers, Hawran behaved as if
clad in full dress uniform. Tall and athletically lean,
he stood fully erect and surveyed the pier as if he
commanded everything in sight. His hawkish features
seemed arrogant yet intelligent.

A person's face wasn't necessarily an accurate ba-
rometer of one's personality, but Kaborya knew this
wasn't the case with Hawran. The Iraqi major was
supremely confident in his own abilities. The fact that
he'd traveled from Iraq aboard a shipful of Iranian
POWs who had formerly been captives of the government he represented, was proof of Hawran's cer-
tainty that his efforts to convert the loyalties of the

prisoners had been successful. The fact Hawran had survived the journey revealed that this confidence was justly founded.

Kaborya knew Hawran well enough to appreciate the Iraqi's intelligence and skills. The major was a well-educated man, and a superb strategist. He had acquired expertise in many unusual fields. Many of his theories seemed farfetched to Kaborya, yet Hawran had been able to deliver everything he claimed he'd do. At least thus far.

Major Hawran marched down the gangplank, accompanied by Sharif Mohandra. A giant by Iranian standards, Mohandra was more than two meters tall, and his physique resembled that of a circus strongman. The similarity was enhanced by the man's bald pate and thick black mustache. He was a striking contrast to other Iranians, but Mohandra had been Hawran's first convert, his "top Iranian."

The big man had become the major's trusted aide and co-commander.

Hawran instructed Mohandra to remain with the other Iranians and to wait on the pier until ordered to do otherwise. The major then headed for the row of large, canvas-shrouded trucks parked near a harbor warehouse. He easily recognized Kaborya from a distance, as the man was a Palestinian and wore a checkered *keffiyeh*.

After exchanging the requisite traditional Arab greetings, the two men embraced briefly. Hawran and Kaborya weren't close friends and didn't particularly like each other, but the display of brotherhood was for appearances. The Iranians and the other men positioned by the trucks had to believe wholly in the unity of all members of their cause.

"I was afraid you might have trouble passing through the blockade in the gulf," Kaborya remarked.

"The Americans and their infidel friends are only stopping oil tankers and vessels they suspect may be transporting troops or weapons," Hawran replied. "That's why we used cargo ships and fishing trawlers."

"So more of your men are coming?"

"Two hundred and twenty-three total. You didn't think we could do this?"

"I had my doubts," the Palestinian admitted. "To be honest, I feared one of these Persians would cut your throat and throw your body overboard once you were at sea."

"The men are mine, Kaborya," Hawran declared with obvious pride. "I personally supervised their interrogations and conditioning when they were prisoners of war. I broke them down and rebuilt them for our purposes."

"And you trust all two hundred and twenty-three?" Kaborya asked, a note of doubt in his voice.

"Originally I worked with more than five hundred possible candidates for my program of reeducation," Hawran explained. "The majority proved unreliable for our needs. I screened the Iranians for years. I studied them and tested them until I was certain of every single man chosen for the mission. They are totally devoted to me and our holy war."

"They were formerly completely devoted to the Iranian holy war commanded by the Ayatollah," Kaborya commented with a frown. "How can you be so sure of their loyalty now?"

"Because I didn't try to erase the qualities that made them embrace a holy war. Indeed, I used these character traits to my advantage. One doesn't enlist the aid of a fanatic by tearing down everything he believes in. That sort of transvaluation in a man's personality leaves him a hollow shell. I appealed to the beliefs that made them ideal choices for our plan and reshaped those that might pose problems."

Kaborya nodded. He understood some fundamentals about behavior modification, crudely referred to as brainwashing. The Palestinian knew Hawran was an expert in this subject.

"It appears you've accomplished everything you said you would," Kaborya stated, "but we might have some trouble establishing the training camps here in Yemen. Things are changing in this country. There was a coup in 1986, and the support from the Soviets has dropped off since the *glasnost* policies changed how Moscow does business abroad."

"The same thing happened with Iraq," Hawran said bitterly. "The Russians only supported us because they thought they could turn Arab states into satellite countries as they did in Eastern Europe. Now they aren't even holding on to those."

"That's causing problems for those of us who have been expatriates at the desert training bases here in Yemen," the Palestinian added. "We've been training revolutionaries for missions against the enemy nations of Israel, Western Europe and the United States. Some of our people have been fugitives from their own countries since the mid-1970s. They're still wanted by the authorities in their homeland and can't return as long as the present repressive governments remain in power."

Hawran didn't comment about the status of these "revolutionaries" or the "repressive governments" Kaborya referred to. The Palestinian's harried friends were in fact international terrorists from a dozen different countries, most of them Western democracies. The terrorists were remnants of such Marxist outfits as the Baader-Meinhof gang, the French and Italian Red Brigades and the Japanese Red Army. They were idiot dreamers who still believed they could somehow pull down entire governments, crush capitalism and establish a Panglossian society based on Communist socialism.

Of course, the Berlin Wall had fallen and both Germanies united under a democratic government. Communism had fallen apart in Poland, Czechoslovakia and elsewhere. Even the Soviet Union was undergoing changes of democratic reforms. The leftist radicals of the so-called revolutionary groups were backing a political system that was dying throughout the world. However, they could still be useful because they were extremists willing to take actions they believed would hurt the governments of the countries they'd been forced to flee or the political ideology they hated with fanatical zeal.

"We'll remain in Yemen as long as possible," Hawran announced. "Long enough to organize our forces and prepare to move to a new base of operations. I already have a site for relocation in mind."

"A place where we can set up training bases and a command headquarters?" Kaborya inquired. "That might not be easy to find. Our plan will require several months for training, preparations, establishing necessary connections in other countries and much more.''

''I estimate it will take more than a year for us to be ready to begin the actual mission,'' Hawran declared. ''However, when the time comes for action, we'll be prepared for every facet of the operation. The enemy won't suspect anything until it's too late. Any interest the Intelligence networks of the West might have in the vessels transporting my Iranian forces will have dissipated long before the time we carry out our attacks. They'll never connect us with the sabotage assaults or guess where our base is located.''

''So many things can go wrong,'' Kaborya said solemnly. The Palestinian had been stationed in Yemen for more than a decade and seldom ventured from the training camps. He hadn't been involved in a major terrorist campaign since the 1980s and felt some ambivalence about Hawran's scheme.

''Maybe things will go wrong,'' the Iraqi major replied with a smile, ''but the plight will be with the United States and their infidel allies.''

CHAPTER ONE

Mack Bolan followed the blue Nissan Sentra XE through downtown Miami to Little Havana. The car seemed headed for the Palmetto Expressway, but it turned onto a side street and began making its way through the noisy maze of the Cuban district. The Nissan's irregular travel pattern suggested the driver was either lost or trying to shake a tail.

Bolan wasn't concerned that the two men in the Sentra had spotted his vehicle. The warrior, known as the Executioner, drove a black van specially designed for the field. The rig was equipped with state-of-the-art surveillance equipment that included a heat-sensor-detection system plugged into a computer in the rear of the vehicle. The sensor had been used to identify the Nissan when Bolan first began surveillance outside the Biltmore. The size of the car, heat distribution of the engine, muffler and tail pipe, and the body heat of the driver and passenger were registered and recorded by the computer. The different intensities of heat from machine and men combined to form a positive ID based on heat patterns composed by the computer. The sensor detector had a range of two miles.

Bolan glanced at the monitor under the dashboard. A multicolored blip on the screen revealed the exact location of the Nissan even when the car wasn't in view of his eyes. The men in the Sentra might be using an evasive tactic to try to lose police or federal agents they feared might be following them, but there was no way they'd be able to shake the Executioner and his high-tech van.

The vehicle had other special surveillance gear. A rifle microphone with a laser locking system allowed one to eavesdrop from a distance. A periscope with a telescopic lens could be used for spying from long range. Special fiber optics permitted clear night vision, and a long-range camera and video could acquire photographic evidence. A radio transceiver, a sophisticated fax machine and a second computer terminal linked Bolan to Stony Man headquarters while in the field.

In an emergency the van could be used for combat. The rig was armor plated, and the glass was bullet resistant. A steel-pipe battering ram was installed under the front and back fenders. John ''Cowboy'' Kissinger and Gadgets Schwarz had personally supervised the alterations to the vehicle. Schwarz had even included a unique ''remote control'' option. The van could be driven short distances by using a pocket-size control unit. To operate it, one simply used two buttons and a dial. The former worked the accelerator and brake while the dial controlled the steering wheel. This device allowed the user to operate the van from the back of the rig, using the periscope and avoiding being a target behind the windshield. One could also use the remote unit to drive the van from outside the vehicle.

The rig was equipped with more gizmos than Bolan had used with his old ''war wagon'' when he was conducting campaigns against organized crime in the bad old days.

The Executioner had been asked to go to Miami after Hal Brognola, director of the Sensitive Operations Group, learned the identity of a man who'd arrived at the international airport less than twenty-four hours earlier. Airport security cameras had filmed a group of passengers that deplaned from an Athens flight, and a number of visitors from the Middle East were among them. Subtle screening of guests from this troubled part of the world was being conducted by the National Security Agency due to concerns about terrorism.

More than a thousand acts of terrorism had been committed in the United States within the past two decades, and combating terrorism was a primary concern of the honchos at Stony Man Farm. When Hal Brognola and his team learned about the airport surveillance through computer links to the NSA, they also tapped into information about the individuals who'd received their special interest.

One passenger on the Athens flight had arrived with an Egyptian passport, claimed he had nothing to declare and brought only a single carryon. However, a computer check revealed that his physical description fit that of Rashid al-Khemit, a former member of the infamous Black September terrorist group and last reported to be a member of the Palestine Rejection Front. If the man was Khemit, it was unlikely he'd come to Miami for a quiet vacation.

THE GARISH NEON SIGNS of nightclubs and taverns bathed the streets with multicolored hues as Bolan continued to pursue his quarry through Little Havana. The pulsating rhythm of Spanish music rose from every street corner, but Bolan paid scant attention to the colorful and lively atmosphere as he tracked the Nissan.

Khemit's car headed south to the Dixie Highway, then on past the Miami city limits. The vehicle eventually headed onto a side road toward a deserted area.

An abundance of cypress and sycamore trees replaced the mammoth resort hotels and towering skyscrapers. Bolan switched off his headlights when the lack of traffic and streetlights made them a liability in the darkness. A pair of infrared night-vision goggles allowed him to safely drive without the headlights.

The blip on the screen came to a halt. Bolan reduced speed when he noticed he was only a mile from the parked Nissan. As the van climbed a hill, the warrior spotted a house below, with the blue Nissan parked in front.

The Executioner stopped the van in the shadows of the cypress trees at the shoulder of the road, good concealment for the big black rig. He moved to the periscope and adjusted the telescopic lens. An ornate iron fence surrounded the property. Modern and practical, the split-level ranch house wasn't typical of the area. It certainly didn't resemble the Old South dwellings that offered quaint charm in contrast to the fast-paced and garish setting of Miami.

Three other cars were parked alongside the Nissan. Expensive automobiles, Bolan noted. Two large men, built like NFL linebackers, stood on the porch. The warrior had met enough hardguys to recognize one even from a mile away.

The warrior read the address on a sign above the front gate, then slipped into the back of the rig to feed the information into the computer link to Stony Man Farm. He keyed in the code for identification and switched on the rifle mike. The long-range microphone rose from the roof of the van, and the laser beam began to scan the area. Bolan used the periscope to aim the laser as he punched the buttons of the tape recorder. If he could locate Khemit conversing with someone in the house, they might not be speaking English. A recording of the conversation could be translated later.

The computer terminal screen and fax machine began producing data. The laser beam found a window and detected the vibrations of voices against the glass pane. The beam bounced back to the laser mike and transmitted the conversation.

The voices spoke English, but Bolan let the tape recorder run nonetheless. Any evidence obtained in this manner wouldn't be admissible in a court of law, but Stony Man didn't always use standard or even strictly legal methods. A record of the conversation might prove useful later for voice-print identification.

"I'm not too thrilled about having you here at my crib, Khemit," a voice complained. The accent suggested English wasn't the man's native tongue, but he'd clearly developed considerable fluency. "The cops sniff around me like this was a fuckin' doughnut shop. They don't have anything on me, but the Feds will start poking their snouts into my business if they find out who you are."

"Interpol doesn't have me on any lists concerning recent fugitives of justice, Mr. Garcia," a voice re-

plied. The slightly guttural accent and British pro-
nunciation of Khemit's words was distinctly different
from Garcia's. "Perhaps the Israelis are still interested in my whereabouts, but Mossad has enough
problems at home. They won't have much time to
worry about an Arab or two traveling to the United
States."

Bolan was satisfied Khemit's identity was confirmed, but he turned his attention to the computer
and fax to see what the Farm had given him concerning "Mr. Garcia." He wasn't surprised by how rapidly the Stony Man base had responded to his call for
information. Aaron Kurtzman commanded the data
banks and ran his section of the operations in a swift,
efficient manner.

The Executioner glanced at the material. The house
belonged to Miguel Garcia. The son of respectable
Cuban immigrants, Garcia's criminal record began at
twelve, when he'd started running drugs for a gang.
However, as an adult he'd avoided conviction for any
felony offenses. Garcia had been arrested several
times, but charges were either dropped or expensive
lawyers had managed to get him off on some techni-
cality.

Garcia stood trial only once, charged with illegal
sale of automatic weapons to local Miami gangs.
Witnesses mysteriously disappeared or changed their
testimony. Jury members became suddenly reluctant
to convict the career criminal. The judge changed his
attitude halfway through the trial and appeared to find
fault with the district attorney's case while accepting
virtually everything the defense had to say about the
"harassment" of the accused. Needless to say, Garcia

was found not guilty. Shortly after the trail, the judge took a vacation in the Cayman Islands and seemed to be able to afford an increased number of expensive luxuries.

The Miami police, FBI and DEA all suspected Garcia was an illegal arms dealer, selling guns to youth gangs and cocaine syndicates. He handled everything from stolen handguns to serious military hardware. He'd become wealthy and influential as a gunrunner, but so far even the IRS had failed to nail him.

A fax printout of Garcia's mug shot revealed the full face and profile of a man with dark, broad features set against a round head, framed by long black hair. The gunrunner's eyes were dark and hard, and a smug smile pulled at his lips. He looked as if he'd known that the authorities wouldn't be able to hold him for long.

So far Garcia had been invulnerable to the law. But the Executioner had a different brand of justice, and it didn't rely on a courtroom or judges. Mack Bolan had vowed long ago that the savages wouldn't inherit the earth, and he'd do anything and everything to stop them.

"You're here now," Garcia said. "Let's do business. I understand you want some heavy-duty firepower, Khemit. I can supply you with some MAC-10s and M-16 assault rifles tonight—if you have the cash."

"We'll need more than a few guns," Khemit replied. "I was told you could supply me with anything short of ballistic missiles. We need various types of small arms—submachine guns, assault rifles and side arms, to be sure—but we also want some light machine guns, grenades and no less than two hundred kilos of plastic explosives.''

''Two hundred kilos?'' Garcia responded with astonishment. ''That's a lot. What we talking about, man? C-4? Tetryl?''

''Please, Mr. Garcia—'' Khemit's voice carried a sigh as he spoke ''—I assume that you know your business. Give me some credit that I also know my trade. Tetryl is not a plastic explosive. It's a hard-cast explosive similar to TNT.''

''But it's more powerful than TNT,'' Garcia stated. ''I'm not trying to put anything over on you, Khemit. I can get you some tetryl, but two hundred kilos of C-4 is going to be difficult to come up with.''

''Another RDX compound may be an acceptable substitute,'' Khemit assured him, ''but we need the pliable and easily concealed qualities of a plastic explosive. We would also like to purchase a number of rocket launchers and ammunition. Perhaps some grenade launchers, as well.''

''When you said firepower you weren't kidding. You're also talking about getting enough military hardware to land my ass in a federal prison for the next fifty years if I get caught with all this shit.''

''Isn't that an occupational hazard in your profession?''

''Yeah,'' Garcia admitted, ''but I charge more when I have to take on extra risks that are that serious. This is going to be a hell of an expensive order.''

''You'll get your money,'' Khemit assured him. ''Just be certain we get our weaponry.''

BOLAN GLIMPSED MOVEMENT outside a window of the van. Two or more figures approached from the knoll where the vehicle was parked.

The warrior drew his Beretta 93-R from shoulder leather, the sleek black pistol a comfortable weight in his hand. The Executioner had planned for a soft probe, but he was armed in case the mission turned hard. He carried extra magazines for the Beretta, as well as a customized silencer for the muzzle of the weapon. A wire garrote was curled in a pocket like a sleeping snake, and a K-bar combat knife was sheathed at the small of his back.

Bolan slipped the van's remote unit into a pocket and headed for the door at the opposite side from the approaching enemy. The dark-tinted glass of the vehicle would prevent the men from peering inside the rig. With stealth and a little luck, Bolan could emerge from the vehicle on the blind side without being noticed.

He moved silently to the cypress near the van, hid behind the trunk and watched three men advance. All three carried pistols. One gunner stepped to the rear of the vehicle while the other two sneaked along both sides of the rig. One guy shuffled toward the driver's side, his buddy approaching the opposite flank, unaware Bolan was concealed by the tree.

The Executioner slipped from cover and crept up behind his unsuspecting opponent, the handles of the garrote in his fists. As the gunner tried to peer through a window, Bolan looped the wire over the guy's head. With lethal expertise, the warrior pulled the handles and snapped the wire noose tight. He held on to the garrote and continued to pull as he kicked a booted foot into his enemy's forearm, the blow jarring the pistol from the guy's numbed hand.

The wire cut deep into the gunner's neck and throat, and his body went limp. The warrior hauled the corpse to the cypress.

The man at the rear of the van had heard the shuffle of feet and glanced around the edge of the rig. He saw a figure by the trunk of the tree and pointed his Smith & Wesson pistol, holding his fire when he recognized his comrade. In the shadows, he couldn't see the garrote wrapped around the corpse's neck.

"Hector!" the gunner at the rear of the vehicle whispered harshly. "¿Qué haces tú?"

He walked forward slowly, puzzled by Hector's behavior. The third hardman appeared from the front of the van and also stared at the figure of Hector leaning against the tree trunk. He suddenly noticed that his friend didn't move, although his knees were slightly bent and his arms dangled lifeless and limp.

Bolan held the handles of the garrote in one fist and propped the corpse against the tree. The Beretta filled his other hand, silencer attached to the muzzle. He suddenly released the body and aimed the 93-R at the remaining pair. The silenced pistol coughed a 3-round burst, 9 mm parabellum slugs piercing the heart and lungs of Bolan's closer opponent. The man collapsed to the ground, dead.

The surviving gunner swung his Smith & Wesson toward Bolan's position. The Executioner crouched low as the revolver boomed. A bullet chipped bark from the trunk above his head. The Beretta spit flame, and another trio of muffled rounds split the gunman's face. Dead before he hit the ground, the third hardman wilted against the side of the van.

Voices shouted in both English and Spanish. Lights burst into life in the house, and the security gates parted to allow the departure of gun-toting guards who bolted from Garcia's property to investigate the trouble on the knoll.

"When it rains," Bolan muttered philosophically as he took the remote unit from his pocket.

He pressed the buttons rapidly. The van's engine growled to life, and headlights came on to bathe the approaching gunmen with harsh white light. The closest guards skidded to a halt and tried to aim their weapons while half-blind from the unexpected glare.

Bolan snap-aimed the 93-R and opened fire. Two short bursts brought down a pair of hardmen, parabellums buried in vital organs. The silencer reduced muzzle-flash, as well as reducing the noise of the pistol shots. The rest of the Garcia's security force was unable to determine where the shots had come from. However, the van appeared to be an obvious source. They opened fire with a variety of handguns, machine pistols and at least one semiauto shotgun.

Bullets and buckshot pelted the armor-plated vehicle, the projectiles ricocheting off the reinforced steel and the thick windows. One headlight burst apart when bullets shattered lens and bulb. Bolan keyed the remote to release the brake and activate the accelerator. The unoccupied van rolled forward.

The guards continued to fire at the vehicle, concentrating on the windshield in an effort to take out the "driver," while Bolan jogged behind the moving van. He saw the muzzle-flash of the gunner armed with a

subgun and recognized the guy's heat as a Heckler &
Koch MP-5, a high-quality firearm in the hands of a
bottom-of-the-barrel hood. The Executioner aimed his
93-R and took out the guy with a 3-round burst.

Bolan thumbed the remote button for the brake,
and the van came to an abrupt halt. The enemy fire
ebbed slightly as the guards were surprised when the
vehicle stopped. The warrior quickly dropped to the
ground, lay on his back and wiggled under the rear
fender.

He crawled beneath the belly of the van and located a trapdoor near the muffler, which he un-
latched and pushed open. Two seconds later he was
inside the van.

The warrior stayed low as he moved along the floor
to a storage compartment. The shooting outside the
rig ceased, and Bolan knew this meant the gunners had
decided whoever was in the van had probably been
wounded or killed in the battle. They'd certainly approach the vehicle, with caution and weapons held
ready.

There was little time, Bolan realized as he opened
the compartment and reached inside for the assortment of weapons stored there. The Executioner extracted an Uzi submachine gun and several grenades.

The Executioner rammed a clip into the Uzi's pistol grip and chambered a round, then hooked four
M-26 fragmentation grenades to his web belt. Bolan
returned to the trapdoor, paused to grab magazines for
the Beretta, then slipped through the opening.

Underneath the van once again, he saw the legs of
the gunners who surrounded the vehicle. The men
were confused. The van had stopped, but there were

no bullet holes in the shatter-resistant glass or armored body of the rig.

Bolan keyed the accelerator button on the remote unit, and the van suddenly lurched forward. The hardmen cried out in surprise and jumped away from the big rig. The warrior remained on his back and didn't move as the van rolled above him. The vehicle passed over, and he rolled into a kneeling stance, Uzi pointed at a pair of gunmen who were still staring at the van.

The Executioner triggered the Uzi, a quick burst chopping the life from two luckless guards. A third man swung around the front of the van, a Browning shotgun filling his fists. Bolan's Uzi took the guy out of play before he could get off a round, the impact of the parabellum swarm punching the gunner to the ground in a bleeding heap.

Bolan ran alongside the rig and thumbed the remote dial. The unit activated the steering wheel, and the van turned suddenly. Two gunmen yelled in alarm and pain as the vehicle slammed into them. The Executioner darted to the rear of the van and found three more Garcia soldiers. Only one man remained on his feet and fired a Colt pistol at the windows of the vehicle. The other guards had been knocked down by the rig and were busy trying to crawl away from the wheels.

The Uzi spit fire and death. The *pistolero* had started to turn to face Bolan. He stopped a trio of slugs with his chest, and the force threw him back into the side of the still-moving van.

Bolan used the remote unit to alter the direction of the van. He pointed it at the iron gates of the fence and increased pressure on the accelerator button. The vehicle charged toward the barrier as more gunmen opened fire from between the bars of the fence. The warrior jogged behind the van, using the armored rig for cover.

He pulled the pin from a grenade as man and machine closed the distance to the gates. Bolan lobbed the deadly orb high, and it sailed over the roof of the van and above the spear-point peaks at the top of the fence. The grenade landed among a group of enforcers and exploded with devastating effect. The screams of ravaged victims announced that the fragger had been on target.

The van hit the gates. The steel battering ram smashed Garcia's version of a portcullis and crashed through the iron doors. Surviving guards darted across the lawn to flee the charging vehicle. Bolan tracked their progress with the sights of his Uzi and emptied the clip. He discarded the spent magazine and shoved home a fresh mag.

The Executioner headed toward the rear of the house, mounted the steps and opened the back door. He sprayed the room with a sustained burst before entering. A quick look revealed an empty kitchen.

Bolan moved on to the next room, an ornate dining room, which was also empty.

Because the house was a split-level ranch model, Bolan didn't have to worry about attack from upstairs. However, he hadn't reached the part of the house where the rifle mike had tapped into Garcia's conversation with Khemit. There were more rooms in this wing of the house, and Bolan had no idea how many more enemies might be located in this area or what sort of weapons they might have at their disposal.

The numbers were falling in more than one direction. The gunshots and grenade explosion would certainly be reported. Garcia's ranch house was located in a fairly remote area, but the noise would be too great to go unnoticed and neighbors within four miles would hear the sounds of combat. The police would most likely already be on their way to investigate.

Bolan couldn't be there when the police arrived. He had to wrap up business quickly and haul out of there before the boys in blue came hurtling up the hill with sirens blaring.

The warrior moved through the hall and approached the first door. He stood clear of the portal and fired a short burst into the lock, and the door swung inward. There was no return fire. He swung around the archway, Uzi up and ready.

The room was an office, handsomely furnished with a large teakwood desk and rows of bookcases. A huge globe was located at the center of the room, mounted on walnut brackets, and a well-stocked bar with leather-bound stools and a large ornate mirror filled one wall.

The office was unoccupied aside from the lone motionless figure sprawled on the lush blue carpet. Bolan stepped closer and looked down at the lifeless face of Rashid al-Khemit.

The Executioner headed for the hall, stopping at the doorway when two shadows streaked across the marble mosaic flooring beyond the office. A pair of men walked from another room and headed for the front door. One appeared to be a generic strong-arm thug, burdened with a large aluminum suitcase and an M-16 assault rifle. The other man was shorter and not as muscular. Bolan recognized the flat features from the mug shots sent by fax from Stony Man. The gunrunner carried another metal case and a Glock pistol in his other hand.

They didn't see Bolan as they concentrated on the entrance to the building. The Executioner stepped from the office and pointed his Uzi at the backs of Garcia and his hardman.

"Freeze!" Bolan ordered. "Drop your weapons and raise your hands!"

The pair stopped and stood rigidly. The bodyguard's shoulders shifted slightly, as though he were considering making a move. But the M-16 clattered to the floor. The hardman also dropped the suitcase and raised his hands to shoulder level.

Garcia cursed under his breath and reluctantly let his pistol and case fall. Hands raised, he turned slowly to face the Executioner.

"What the fuck is this?" Garcia demanded. "You don't look like a cop. Who you working for? The Colombians? I do business with them, man. You're making a big mistake...."

"Grab the wall," Bolan ordered. "Spread-eagle. You're familiar with the position, so don't waste my time."

Garcia and the hardman obliged. They faced the wall, palms flat on the surface and feet apart. Bolan stepped closer and swiftly rapped the frame of his Uzi across the skull of the muscle boy, who slumped unconscious to the floor.

"Bastard," Garcia snarled, and whirled to thrust his right arm at Bolan.

A diminutive over-under derringer appeared in Garcia's hand, popping from beneath his sleeve cuff like a magician performing a deadly trick. Bolan's battle-honed reflexes saved his life. His hand shot out like a striking cobra to deflect the derringer, the blow forcing Garcia's arm upward as the tiny gun barked. A .38 Special round plowed into the ceiling as Bolan grabbed the arms dealer's wrist and held the derringer at bay.

The Executioner's other fist held the Uzi's pistol grip. He pointed the muzzle low and squeezed the trigger. A trio of slugs slashed the terrazzo floor, ricocheting near Garcia's legs. One round punched through the gangster's instep.

The gunrunner screamed and hopped backward on one foot. Bolan stepped forward and silenced Garcia with a fist to the chin. The Cuban gangster collapsed at the Executioner's feet.

"Come on, Garcia," Bolan remarked as he leaned over and grabbed the groggy man by the lapels of his jacket. "You're going for a ride."

CHAPTER TWO

Aaron "the Bear" Kurtzman gazed at the computer screen, chin on his fists, elbows braced along the armrests of his wheelchair. Although confined to the chair since a terrorist's bullet to his spine had left him partially paralyzed, Kurtzman still resembled his great shaggy namesake. He still seemed big and powerful even in the chair.

In many ways Kurtzman remained a giant. His courage and determination had allowed him to adjust to his disability rapidly, and he was still the best computer jockey in the business. Because Kurtzman was the best, he controlled the artificial-intelligence data bank center of the Stony Man operation.

"Anything useful?" Mack Bolan inquired.

"Garcia has started to talk to the Feds," Kurtzman answered. "He tried to pretend he didn't know who Khemit was, but they played your tape recording of their conversation. Of course, they refer to each other by name."

"So he admitted he knew who Khemit was. What did he have to say about the hardware the Palestinian wanted?"

"Claims he only knew Khemit was a big buyer from out of town and figured he was going to take the weapons back to the Middle East to fight the Israelis." The Bear shrugged. "I guess Garcia figures that'll make him sound like a patriot American who wouldn't give military hardware to somebody he thought would conduct terrorism in the States.''

''Upstanding citizen,'' the Executioner commented dryly. ''Why did he kill Khemit?''

''He thought he wasn't for real,'' Kurtzman answered as he wheeled the chair toward the coffeemaker. ''When you hit the place, Garcia figured it was a raid by the police or the Feds. That made him jump to the conclusion that Khemit must have been an undercover cop of some sort involved in setting him up for the bust. So he offed Khemit and tried to run out with as much money as he could carry.''

''Garcia had a lot of guns on duty,'' Bolan remarked.

''Want some?'' Kurtzman asked as he raised the coffeepot in one hand and a cup in the other.

Bolan shook his head.

''Suit yourself,'' the Bear replied, and poured himself a cup. ''The information I sent you was based on previous surveillance of Garcia's house by the Miami police, DEA and FBI. Garcia had extra guns on loan from some of his friends. Apparently he was worried about Khemit. Terrorists are unpredictable. He might have been afraid Khemit would have a gang of fanatics hit the house and take it apart to steal the weapons instead of buying them.''

''Garcia didn't have the kind of firepower on hand that Khemit was looking for,'' Bolan stated. ''Any idea what Khemit planned to do with enough explosives, machine guns and assorted firearms to slaughter half the population of Boston?''

SOAR WITH THE EAGLE!

And in 1992, the Eagle flies even higher with more gripping adventure reading.

Introducing four new exciting miniseries that deliver action and adventure at a fast pace....

HATCHET

In the air and on the ground, behind the desks and in the jungles . . . Gold Eagle's action-packed series of the Vietnam War will arrive in February with Book #1: BLACK MISSION. Books #2 and #3 of this hard-hitting miniseries about a Special Forces Hatchet team will be available in June and October. (224 pp., $3.50 each)

CODE ZERO

It's a license to track and terminate for agents of Centac, an elite unit within the DEA, and it's your license to experience an exciting new miniseries from Gold Eagle. In each thrilling volume of CODE ZERO, agents of Centac fight the high-stakes and high-risk battle against drugs. Look for Book #1: SPEEDBALL in March. Books #2 and #3 will follow in July and November. (224 pp., $3.50 each)

TIMERAIDER

This new miniseries from Gold Eagle is the ultimate in action adventure fiction with a time-travel twist. In TIME RAIDER, you'll follow the adventures of an eternal warrior who travels through time to fight battles of the past. Look for Book #1: WARTIDE in April. Books #2 and #3 will appear in August and December. (224 pp., $3.50 each)

CADE is a fascinating new miniseries from Gold Eagle about near-future law enforcement. In crime-torn New York City, a new breed of cop brings home the law— Justice Marshal Cade and his cyborg partner, Janek—a steel and badge team that makes the rules—and breaks them. Look for Book #1: DARKSIDERS in May. Books #2 and #3 will appear in September and January 1993. (224 pp., $3.50 each)

When you fly with Gold Eagle, you'll soar to new heights of adventure.

GOLD EAGLE ®

Available at your favorite retail outlet.

GES92
Printed in Canada

"Well," Kurtzman began with a sigh, "Khemit was a bad boy. He was directly involved with several acts of terrorism and sabotage in the Middle East, according to Mossad and the CIA. When he was with Black September, Khemit is believed to have worked in Europe with Carlos the Jackal in the midseventies."

"That's when Carlos was connected with the Popular Front for the Liberation of Palestine?" Bolan inquired, mentally leafing through his memory concerning recent terrorist history. "Before he had a falling-out with George Habbash and Wadi Haddad?"

"Falling-out?" Kurtzman said with a chuckle. "Carlos was on the PFLP's hit list after he screwed up in Paris and killed Michel Moukarbal. As you know, Carlos was never as clever or efficient as his legend made him out to be. He tended to be trigger-happy, and he panicked when he killed Moukarbal. The guy was one of the PFLP's top operatives in Europe. Habbash and Haddad were pretty upset when Carlos blew away one of their most valuable team players."

"Carlos has been out of the terrorist picture for a long time," Bolan remarked. "What was Khemit doing after his European tour with Black September?"

"Moved on to the Palestine Rejection Front," Kurtzman answered as he returned to his terminal with a cup of thick black coffee. "Apparently he was in a cell commanded by Kaborya. You've heard of him?"

"Sounds familiar," the Executioner replied, "but it's hard to keep track of all the celebrities in the world of international terrorism. What's Kaborya's claim to fame?"

"He was minor league until he denounced Arafat for being a wimp. Yasir might want the PLO to be accepted as a moderate political movement for a Palestinian homeland, but Kaborya wants the revolutionary fires to remain hot and violent. His cell is believed to be responsible for the mortar shelling of an Israeli school bus in 1980, the assassination of an Egyptian diplomat in Greece in 1981 and a bomb attack in a beer garden in West Germany that killed three American servicemen in 1983."

"Kaborya and his followers haven't been up to much for the last eight or nine years?"

"Last reliable source I have on the guy claims he was with one of those terrorist camps in Yemen," Kurtzman stated. "That's probably where Khemit was hanging out for the past few years."

"Training terrorists?" Bolan asked.

"That seems the most likely theory, based on limited information," the computer wiz confirmed. "Those Yemen camps hosted a real mixed bag of international terrormongers."

"Your memory is pretty good, Aaron," Bolan remarked. "Sure you need all these computers when you recall so many facts just using the gray matter inside your head?"

"This stuff is still fresh in my mind because I've been doing research ever since Khemit was identified in Miami," the Bear said modestly. "Trust me, I need the computers, Mack."

The Stony Man computer room was Kurtzman's domain, and his kingdom was filled with machines. Bolan was not even sure what some of the contraptions were called. The Bear's data banks were great monoliths of metal and plastic. Even micronized information had to be stored in large devices because the volume was so great. Kurtzman's computers could communicate throughout the world. He could tap into other Intelligence agencies' networks and prevent them from doing likewise to Stony Man.

Aisles between machines were barely wide enough to allow the Bear to pass through with his chair, yet he handled the equipment with more efficiency than most could operate a pocket calculator. Kurtzman sipped his atrocious coffee and surveyed his private world with satisfaction.

"Let's move away from Kaborya and terrorist bases in Yemen," Bolan suggested. "Khemit is the only terrorist we know about for sure. I doubt he came all the way to Miami to buy military arms. There are huge gunrunning operations throughout the Middle East, the Orient and the Pacific he could have turned to. I think he planned to conduct a terrorist operation here in the States, and he didn't intend to use all those weapons himself."

"I know," Kurtzman agreed. "I've been trying to get together information on Garcia, Khemit and Kaborya to come up with a connection. I'll keep burning the midnight oil. Too bad you had to turn over Garcia to the NSA. Maybe our people could have got more answers out of him."

"I doubt Garcia knows anything of any real value. He was aware Khemit was a terrorist and guessed the guy planned to conduct business here and not in the Middle East, but that's about it."

"You're probably right," Kurtzman admitted. "By the way, since most of the evidence against Garcia isn't admissible in court, the NSA is going to kick the son of a bitch out of the country. Garcia gets to keep most of his ill-gotten financial gains and move to a country of his choice. He'll probably set up business again in the Cayman Islands or Brazil.''

"That figures. Thanks for the information, Aaron.''

"Let you know when I come up with some more,'' the big man promised, and turned his attention once more to his computer.

THE EXPLOSION OCCURRED without warning. Brognola watched the smiling, middle-aged couple on the TV screen. The man wrapped an arm around his wife's shoulders and held her close as they posed by the open gate of the building in the background. The blast tore apart the archway to the structure and shattered at least one window, the couple vanishing from view as the scene suddenly became a blur of swirling images.

"This videotape was shot less than an hour ago,'' the President of the United States told his guest. "The video cam belonged to the couple on the screen. They were killed by the explosion, as were four people inside the British embassy. At least five others were hospitalized.''

"They were British tourists?'' the big Fed inquired, and reached into a jacket pocket for a cigar.

The President nodded. "They were visiting the United States to celebrate their twenty-fifth wedding anniversary. Since they were in Washington, they decided to pose in front of their country's embassy. It was the last thing they ever did. By the way, their son shot the footage. Both his hands were torn off by shrapnel from the blast.''

Brognola had met with the President many times in the past, but it had been a while since he'd seen him looking so worried. The sabotage of a British embassy in America's capital was certainly serious and more than adequate to call in Stony Man to deal with the act of terrorism. Yet, as terrible as this atrocity was, the big Fed had a gut feeling there was more.

"At the same time this terrorist bombing occurred here in Washington," the President went on, "similar incidents happened in France and England. The U.S. embassy in Paris and the French embassy in London were attacked. The bombs went off within minutes of each other."

Brognola sucked in a tense breath. Obviously someone was striking out at all three countries simultaneously, a warning, perhaps, of things to come.

"Has any group taken credit for the bombings?" Brognola asked, studying the President's face.

"No," the President stated as he sank into a chair by the table. "Of course, we expect a flood of crackpots claiming they're responsible."

"This has to be the work of an international terrorist network," Brognola told him. "Probably a large organization, obviously well-coordinated and ruthless."

"Obviously," the President echoed grimly. "I don't need to tell you how serious this is, Hal. The United States, Great Britain and France have something in common that might very well be the reason these three countries have been targeted by the terrorists."

"I can think of several things America has in common with England and France," Brognola commented, "but the one that seems most obvious, and most likely to be connected with these terrorist attacks, is that they were all members of the coalition forces in the war against Iraq."

"The war was to liberate Kuwait," the President corrected.

"We liberated it from Iraq," Brognola said with a shrug. "Anyway, we both know what we're talking about."

"I need your team for this one, Hal. Including Striker."

"We'll need cooperation for a mission that'll cover three countries and could extend even farther. You'll arrange liaisons with the Intelligence networks in England and France?"

"I've been in touch with the British prime minister and the president of France. You'll have complete co-operation from the highest levels of government in both countries."

"Okay," Brognola commented. "This is going to be tough enough without having to fight through tons of red tape."

"That won't be a problem," the President assured him. "I want you to know how important this mission is."

"They all are."

"Yes," the President agreed with a nod, "but this time we're facing a situation that could lead to war. I'm sure you're aware that many people were angered by our involvement in the Gulf War. Although Saudi Arabia welcomed our troops and we went there to rescue Kuwait, some Arab nations accused the U.S. and other Western countries of 'Arab bashing,' as the press might say."

"And you think the recent acts of terrorism might be state-sponsored actions directly ordered by a Middle East country still upset about the Gulf War?" Brognola guessed.

"I think it's very possible. Iraq could be involved. You might recall Saddam threatened to send terrorists to attack the United States and our European allies."

"He said a lot of stuff that never happened," Brognola reminded. "You have any proof Iraq is guilty of state-sponsored terrorism in this case?"

"Not really, but some of my advisers are already convinced. Others suspect it might be combined forces of the governments of two or more countries. You know Saddam tried to mend fences with Iran and woo it as an ally. The Iranians aren't exactly our best friends in the Middle East. We can't ignore the list of possible governments, which include Jordan as well as Iraq, Iran, Libya, Yemen and even Syria. We have to know if these terrorist attacks are the work of independent forces or if we have cause for going to war once again."

"Then I'd better get the hell out of here and get my people to work," Brognola stated as he rose from his chair.

CHAPTER THREE

Bolan joined Leo Turrin and Jack Grimaldi in the den of the farmhouse, and after the usual greetings, he got right to the point.

"Do you have any inside Intel on Justice Department investigations in Florida, Leo?"

"I know some people there," the little Fed replied. "What sort of info you need?"

"Anything you can get on a gunrunner named Garcia. He had a mishap last night, and his business has gone down the tubes."

"I'll see what I can come up with," Turrin promised.

Brognola marched into the room, accompanied by Barbara Price. The ash-blond beauty wore a loose-fitting jumpsuit and carried a clipboard under her arm. The lady was the primary mission-controller and overseer of Stony Man Farm.

"We've got a big problem, gentlemen," Brognola announced. "That is to say, the President has a big problem and he wants us to handle it. Let's adjourn to the War Room. Katz and Lyons are already there."

"Gadgets and Manning took off with Kissinger," Turrin stated. "They're testing some new hardware."

"Brief them when they get back," Brognola said. "We have to get on this pronto."

YAKOV KATZENELENBOGEN and Carl Lyons waited in the War Room. Physically the two men had little in common. Katz was middle-aged, with iron-gray hair and was slightly overweight. An artificial limb was attached to the stump of Katz's right arm, and the steel hooks of the prosthesis jutted from the sleeve cuff of the Israeli's tweed jacket.

Lyons was tall, blond and muscular. The bulge of his ever-present Colt Python was conspicuously visible under his left arm. A former cop, Lyons still favored the big .357 revolver to autoloading pistols. He was a big, tough guy who never gave up and had earned his nickname "Ironman" over and over again.

Both men were unit commanders of elite fighting men. Katz was the group leader of Phoenix Force, and Lyons captained Able Team. The Israeli was an intellectual, a master linguist fluent in six languages and possessed a working vocabulary in a dozen others. He was a scholarly combat veteran, and his career extended across nearly five decades. Lyons had gained most of his education on the streets and in the proverbial school of hard knocks.

Despite their different backgrounds, Katz and Lyons were alike in many ways and shared a mutual respect for each other's ability. Their special commando units seldom worked together, but apparently the next mission was big enough to demand the combined forces of Phoenix and Able. That meant it had to be very big indeed.

Brognola arrived with the retinue of Stony Man personnel from the den. Bolan and the others took their seats around the massive conference table, while the big Fed moved to his chair and armed himself with a stack of file folders before he began the briefing.

The Stony Man director related the details of his meeting with the President, informing them of the terrorist attacks on the embassies in Washington, London and Paris. The others listened intently, aware of the gravity of the situation. A terrorist network that could strike at three different embassies in as many countries was extremely well organized and well trained.

"And the President figures Iraq is responsible for this mess?" Lyons asked, frowning.

"Well, I'd say it's the top suspect," Brognola replied. "And with good reason."

"A great number of terrorist organizations operate without direct state support," Katz reminded the Stony Man chief. "Iraq is hardly the only country that sponsors terrorism. Libya, Iran, Syria and Cuba are all veterans peddling terror abroad. Let's not forget that the KGB once had its finger in that pie, too. Could still have."

"Khaddafi hasn't been involved with terrorism much since Tripoli was bombed a few years ago," Grimaldi commented. "I wouldn't count him out as being behind something like this, though."

"Maybe," Turrin said as he sat back and steepled his fingers on his chest, "but I think Cuba and Syria are unlikely under the circumstances. Castro doesn't have anything to gain by sponsoring something like this."

"The Cuban government still regards itself to be a revolutionary Marxist-Leninist regime," Barbara Price stated. "That means they still have an interest in exporting so-called liberators and supporting alleged revolutionaries in other countries. Don't forget thousands of Cuban troops are still stationed abroad in Africa, parts of the Middle East and Central America.''

"Syria is still sponsoring terrorism," Katz said. "Assad might be opposed to Saddam's actions in the Gulf, but he has expansionist goals that are similar to Iraq's present government. Syrian troops might be on the same side as the U.S. and other Western democracies, but that doesn't mean there aren't any terrorist training camps in Syria or that Assad isn't still anti-American."

"This is all conjecture," Bolan declared. "We need facts. What have we got so far about the bombings?"

"A bunch of dead and wounded," Brognola answered. "That's just about it."

"We won't learn anything sitting around here," Lyons said. "Let's hit the bricks."

"Able Team is experienced with domestic terrorism," Price announced with a nod. "Carl, you and your men should immediately head for D.C. We'll arrange full cooperation with the police, FBI and whoever else is involved in the investigation of the attack on the British embassy."

"Carl and Rafael are in the Gulf of Mexico taking part in an undersea training operation," Katz said. "As soon as they arrive, we'll head for Europe." He referred to Calvin James and Rafael Encizo, two members of Phoenix Force.

Brognola nodded his agreement, but Price had another suggestion.

"McCarter is already in London. We'll arrange co-operation from the prime minister so that McCarter can start working with the teams handling the embassy sabotage investigation. The rest of Phoenix can go directly to France and start looking into the attack on the U.S. Embassy in Paris."

"David is a good man," Katz said, "but he isn't the most tactful individual, and his temper gets the better of him from time to time. McCarter shouldn't be left on his own too long. Not with this sort of mission."

"Good point," Brognola acknowledged. "McCarter can start immediately, but we'll send the rest of Phoenix as soon as we assemble the whole unit. You guys figure out if you want to handle London or Paris or split up and cover both simultaneously."

"What about Striker?" Turrin inquired. He looked at Bolan. "Guess you get to pick which incident you want to handle."

"I want to follow up on the incident involving Garcia and Khemit in Miami. Maybe it's too soon to think there's a connection with that incident and the D.C. bombing, but I think it's a hell of a coincidence that an international terrorist veteran like Khemit was trying to purchase a ton of military hardware less than twenty-four hours before a terrorist attack in the nation's capital."

"All right," Brognola told the warrior. "You'll go back to Florida double-quick."

"Encizo used to investigate maritime claims when he was in Miami," Katz reminded the Stony Man boss. "He and James can be in Florida within an hour."

"I can use their help," Bolan stated. "We'll try to wrap up business in Miami as fast as possible and move on to the next site depending on what we find there.''

''Okay,'' Brognola said as he began to leaf through the folders. ''Here's what we've got for you guys concerning the information acquired so far. The Bear is hard at work collecting more data even as we speak. Like I said, we don't have much so far.''

''I take it everything else takes a back burner until this is cleared up?'' Turrin inquired.

''Damn right. And the rest of us will be busting our asses while Striker, Able and Phoenix are in the field.''

''What about me?'' Grimaldi asked.

''With that broken arm? You can't fly combat missions,'' the big Fed countered. ''Sorry, Jack. You can help with transport.''

''Shit,'' Grimaldi complained. ''I guess you're right.''

''Trust me, Jack,'' Brognola began, ''we're all going to have our hands full. We've got a hell of a lot to do, and we can only guess how long we have to get it done before the terrorists strike again.''

No one in the room doubted that the terrorists would indeed strike again.

CHAPTER FOUR

"I'm very pleased to announce that the first phase of our operation has been accomplished," Major Hawran announced. "The American, British and French embassies were attacked on schedule. The strikes were carried out without incident."

The Iraqi officer addressed his terrorist comrades from a platform, a map of the world stretched across the wall behind him. He wore a green-and-brown desert camouflage uniform with a side arm holstered on a hip. It was important that he always appeared to be a confident and efficient battlefield commander.

Sharif Mohandra and other Iranians rose from their chairs and began chanting "Allah! Allah!" as they raised clenched fists above their heads. Hawran smiled, pleased by the enthusiasm of his Persian alumni.

Kaborya and others present were uncomfortable with the emotional outburst of the Iranians. Although Kaborya had worked with Hawran and his "reeducated" followers for more than a year, he still didn't fully trust them. The Palestinian considered the Iranians to be unstable religious fanatics, too emotional and unpredictable to be truly reliable.

Of course, Kaborya was accustomed to dealing with extremists. He'd been born in a refugee camp in Jordan. His parents told how they'd been driven from their homeland of Palestine by the Jews. He was taught that the country called Israel was their rightful land, and one day they'd return to reclaim it.

Kaborya learned to hate the Israelis and long for a "homeland" he'd never seen, a country that existed only in the hearts and minds of the Palestinian people. He believed the Islamic leaders who claimed the Jews were devils and enemies of God. Kaborya believed because he wanted to believe. This justified his hatred and prejudice against the Jews and other non-Muslims. If he was on the side of God against His enemies, this sanctioned violence and killing.

As a youth, he'd joined the PLO and participated in numerous guerrilla raids into Israel, eventually becoming a member of the militant and ultraviolent Black September. Fluent in English and French, Kaborya had been a valuable operative in Western Europe and had carried out several terrorist attacks on U.S. military bases, as well as Israeli embassies.

He'd joined the Palestine Rejection Front after Black September was officially disbanded. However, his terrorist activities placed him on the most-wanted lists of Mossad and Interpol and a dozen other Intelligence and law-enforcement agencies. This had caused him to eventually flee to the safety of the terrorist training camps in South Yemen.

During his time at these camps, Kaborya had met dozens of terrorists of many different nationalities. Russian and Cuban advisers had ruled the camps when he'd first arrived. Lessons in small arms and sabotage were always accompanied with propaganda sessions filled with Communist rhetoric. The recruits were constantly reminded of their "duty" to the "liberation'' of the masses enslaved by the capitalist imperialists.

Kaborya gradually realized the Soviets and Cubans were using them for their own political ambitions. The KGB wanted the terrorists to cause unrest and domestic problems in the countries of the USSR's opponents. He came to recognize the foolishness of his comrades and members of other extremist outfits from Europe, Japan and Central America. Because they were fanatics, they embraced violence and eagerly used it as their primary method of expression against governments they opposed. Small groups of radicals couldn't hope to overthrow powerful governments and establish themselves as the new regime, but the religious fanatics believed God would somehow grant them victory, and the political zealots thought the people of the world would one day embrace their simpleminded notions and herald them as heroes who paved the way to utopia.

However, the illusions of his youth vanished too late for Kaborya. He recognized his former folly, but he'd already chosen what side he'd fight for. He still opposed Israel and its Western allies, especially the United States. He resented the Soviets for taking advantage of the Palestinian resistance movement. The Communists weren't interested in the Palestinians regaining their homeland—unless Moscow could control it as a satellite country.

Hawran's scheme was crazy, but the madness had been well plotted and the players organized for precision performance in the field. Kaborya didn't think they could crush the United States, England or France, but they could hurt these countries. They could deliver terror and devastation to the prosperous nations of the West, which would be payback for the British occupation of Palestine prior to 1947 and the support of Israel by the United States.

Eventually Kaborya hoped to strike out at Israel and the Soviet Union to achieve some revenge for other wrongs he felt he'd suffered at their hands. For now he'd work with Hawran and enjoy what victories they could claim together. Future retribution would wait for a better time. If nothing else, Kaborya had learned the value of patience.

Other veteran terrorists from the Yemen camps had also grown accustomed to waiting. Klauss Zeigler had fled West Germany in 1982 after an effort to revive the old Baader-Meinhof gang failed to achieve the desired results. The original leaders, whom the terrorist outfit was named for, had been dead for years before Zeigler had joined up. A twenty-year-old zealot, Zeigler was seduced by the appeal of so-called revolutionaries trying to tear down the establishment and erect a new socialist egalitarian order.

The angry young man was ten years older, but not much wiser, in Kaborya's opinion. The Baader-Meinhof gang had been manipulated by the KGB but Zeigler still pretended the terrorist group had fought to liberate the people of West Germany, to throw off the yoke of capitalism. The fact East Germany quickly abandoned communism and embraced democracy within a year after the wall came down only served to make Zeigler more bitter. He claimed the German people and the Soviets had sold out to the Americans. They were all traitors except Zeigler and the few fellow German radicals who remained faithful to the "truth."

Arnoldo Lipari's background was somewhat different than Zeigler's. He was a slum kid, born to a poverty-ridden neighborhood in Rome, the sort of place overlooked by tourists and largely ignored by the city government. Zeigler had come from a Bavarian middle-class family, and hadn't learned to hate capitalism until he'd fallen in with leftist intellectuals. Lipari got most of his education in the streets and soon associated poverty with Italy's egregious inflation.

He wasn't impressed by the magniloquence of Communist spokesmen, but Lipari realized the Communists were opposed to the system he blamed for all his personal woes. Communism couldn't be any worse than what Italy suffered under the current government, he reasoned. Since Italy had the largest Communist Party in Western Europe, Lipari's views weren't regarded as particularly exceptional or alarming.

However, the Partito Comunista Italiano wasn't radical enough for Lipari. He wanted change and he wanted it quickly. The youth had found a group that was taking drastic action against the establishment. Best of all, it offered him a violent outlet for his anger and frustration.

He became a member of the Italian Red Brigades. Lipari willingly participated in arson and assaults against alleged rich capitalists. Most of the victims were just store owners, travel agents and teachers with political views contrary to the faction's extremist beliefs. Lipari didn't hesitate when his cell leader ordered him to "kneecap" a minor-league diplomat

with the American Embassy. The youth and two
comrades had caught the American in front of a restaurant and sprayed the man's legs with a volley of
7.65 mm rounds from a Skorpion subgun. Bullets destroyed both kneecaps and crippled the diplomat for
life. Lipari had pulled the trigger and he enjoyed it.

He and other terrorists were forced to flee Italy,
eventually finding sanctuary in South Yemen. Lipari,
Zeigler and other terrorist expatriates spent their time
training for future violence and fueling one another's
hatred. They were pumped up for something special
that would once again allow them to strike out at the
capitalists they loathed. Hawran's scheme was the
stuff of dreams to the terrorists.

Kaborya noticed that the Italian and German terrorists were uneasy with the frenzied attitude of the
Iranians. The two men had denounced religion in the
name of Marxism and regarded the Muslim zealots as
superstitious lunatics. Worse, the European atheists
qualified as the worse kind of infidels to the Islamic
fanatics, and they realized the Iranians would gladly
cut them to pieces without Hawran's restraining control.

The Iraqi major appreciated this, as well, but he
knew politics and terrorism often had strange bedfel-
lows. Iraq and Iran had been enemies for centuries,
and their eight-year war had been bitter, ferocious and
costly for both sides. Yet Saddam Hussein and the
Iranian leader were willing to kiss and make up when
it came to fighting the U.S. and Israel. Syria was vio-
lently anti-American and even more opposed to the
Jewish state of Israel, yet that didn't stop America

and Syria from forming an inchoate, if shaky, alliance to stand against Iraq.

Hawran waited for the shouting to subside before he continued to address the group.

"We have claimed our first victories," Hawran announced in a loud, clear voice. He spoke Farsi but switched to English, a language understood by the majority of the non-Iranians in the room. "But the next phase of our mission is already in progress. Our comrades in the lands of our enemies have brought the battle to the infidels. The enemy knows he's a target. Soon he'll know the terror has just begun."

Hawran smoothly continued the speech, speaking swiftly to prevent a lapse long enough for the Iranians to start chanting again. He pointed at the map. Small flags of different colors were pinned at points where terrorists were located and strikes planned against targets in the United States, Great Britain and France.

"While our comrades prepare the next attack," he declared, "we must all do our part, as well. We must train and be ready for action in the field. We must plan, prepare and pray for God to grant us success."

Another round of chants erupted. Hawran decided to omit his conclusion to the speech and allowed the cheering Iranians to provide the finish with their fierce cries of dedication to the holy war. He joined in the chants and soon led the congregation in the Islamic hallelujahs.

Zeigler and Lipari were simply annoyed by this display, bored with what they regarded as Hawran's inflated ego. The chanting and excited behavior of the Muslim extremists was monotonous. The Europeans had witnessed dozens of such demonstrations with Hawran acting as head cheerleader and considered this another ordeal of ennui so the Iraqi could show off once more.

Kaborya knew better. He realized Hawran was maintaining control of the Iranians because it was necessary to constantly reinforce his influence. Hawran never stopped scheming and manipulating others. Kaborya wondered how trustworthy such a cunning and deceitful ally could be.

CAPTAIN GEDKA STOOD at the archway to the hall, watching Mohandra and several other Iranians as they performed a series of exercises. Dressed in baggy gray sweat suits, the men chanted verses from the Koran as they stretched their limbs and spines.

The athletes gathered up large Indian clubs that resembled huge bowling pins. They continued to chant as they wielded the clubs in circular patterns.

"They call this *zohahn*," Major Hawran explained. The Iraqi stood beside Gedka at the mouth of the hall. "It's a unique form of meditation through physical exercise. The practice is part of certain Shiite sects. These religious athletes develop their bodies to honor God by seeking to improve the temples of their bodies."

Gedka nodded because he didn't know what other response to make. An officer in Somali military Intelligence, Gedka was not familiar with Iranian or Shiite practices and didn't care to learn about them. He knew Hawran, the Iranians and the others at the base were terrorists. That was enough to make him uncomfortable with his current assignment.

Not that Gedka was accustomed to the company of gentle scholars and pacifists. The Somali government and military had a history of using harsh tactics. Maintaining a socialist dictatorship, the leaders ruled with an iron hand. Government controls were used to repress the masses. Human rights violations, including torture, were common practices. Captain Gedka had personally participated in the brutal interrogations of alleged dissidents.

Nonetheless, Gedka believed Somalia's extreme methods were justified for the sake of national security. He didn't feel Hawran and his terrorist followers has such a "noble" reason for their actions. Yet several members of the people's assembly had authorized Hawran and his people to set up their base on an island off the coast of Somalia. Gedka wasn't certain of the origin of the authorization. Perhaps President Barre knew nothing about this affair. Perhaps he had ordered it himself.

Gedka has been assigned the unenviable task of acting as liaison officer between factions of the Somali government and the terrorists. However, he once again justified this in the name of national security and the best interests for the future of Somalia. The terrorists paid a fortune in gold to "rent" the island after they had been forced to leave Yemen. Hawran had also made a promise to help Somalia take control of the Ogaden region of Ethiopia.

Somalia wasn't regarded as a good neighbor by Kenya and Ethiopia. Heavily armed and extremely ruthless Somali poachers frequently crossed the border into Kenya to slaughter elephants for ivory. The poachers had no qualms about killing anyone who tried to stop them, and furious gun battles occurred between the ivory hunters and park rangers in charge of protecting Kenyan wildlife.

When Somali guerrillas had invaded the Ogaden region in the mid-1970s, Ethiopia became even less happy with its neighbor. Ethiopia had problems of its own, coping with a fierce civil war that didn't appear any closer to a conclusion than when it had started. The Somalis had thought Ethiopia was too busy with the internal conflict to stop their takeover of Ogaden. They were wrong. With the help of Soviet and Cuban troops, the Ethiopians had driven the Somali forces back across the border.

Guerrilla fighting continued over the region, but Somalia officially denied any direct involvement in these actions. Of course, Somalia still wanted to claim Ogaden. Hawran assured them Iraq would help capture this territory after the U.S. and other western forces withdrew from the Persian Gulf.

Captain Gedka had his doubts. He didn't believe Hawran was acting on direct orders from the Iraqi government. Baghdad might know what Hawran was doing and wasn't trying to stop him, but it was unlikely even Saddam Hussein would officially sanction a terrorist conspiracy as ambitious as what Hawran was planning. Gedka also doubted Iraq would back Somalia in an effort to take Ogaden.

Of course, there was a lot of talk about the jihad and how the Islamic holy war would crush the infidels and Muslims would unite to take over the world. Gedka knew better. Like ninety-nine percent of Somalis, Gedka was a Sunni Muslim. He also arrested, tortured and killed other Sunni Muslims when ordered to do so by his government. Sunni and Shiite sects fought each other with burning hatred unless they joined forces to fight a mutual enemy. When the infidel threat subsided, the ancient rivalry between the two Islamic sects would revert to normal.

Gedka had no faith in the jihad or the promises of Iraqis in general, and Hawran in particular. He'd never noticed Arabs were interested in Africans unless the Arabs wanted to exploit them one way or the other. Somalia would probably do well to avoid making deals with Iraq.

"I trust you've learned of the attacks on embassies in the United States, France and England," Gedka remarked in Arabic, a common language in Somalia. "Were your people involved in these incidents, Major?"

Hawran continued to watch the athletes as he spoke. "If I did know anything about those incidents, I'd be unwise to speak of it," he answered. "And the less you know about such things, the better."

"I don't mind being ignorant of your activities unless they threaten the safety and best interests of Somalia."

"We're soldiers for God," Hawran stated. "We're not terrorists. Are you afraid the United States will invade Somalia? That fear became reality for my homeland, you know. I can certainly relate to your concern."

"An invasion doesn't worry me as much as the loss of economic and military support from the Americans," Gedka confessed. "You promise we'll receive Iraqi support in the future, but the Americans have made good their promises for more than a decade."

"Only after Somalia broke off relations with the Soviets and the Cubans."

"You're not offering us something for nothing, either," Gedka reminded him. "In return for their aid, the Americans were allowed to use military bases in Somalia since 1980. You might remember those bases are still here. They might take an interest in your little island if they have any reason to suspect you're involved in the terrorist . . . I mean the jihad warrior attacks on the embassies."

"They have no reason to suspect us," Hawran replied. He studied the strong features of the Somali officer and added, "Unless someone leaks information. I can trust my people, Captain. Can I trust you?"

"If your plans succeed, Somalia will be in an excellent position to become one of the most powerful and important nations in Africa. Some high-ranking persons in my government and the military believe your jihad will succeed. I simply follow orders and do my job, Major."

Hawran realized Gedka's remark was elliptical. The African didn't have to state that he doubted the jihad would work or that he thought his superiors had made a mistake by agreeing to Hawran's terms. Yet Gedka wouldn't leak information to the Americans or anyone else. He was a trained dog of the state and accustomed to acquiescing to orders even if he considered them to be wrong or foolish.

"Do your job well, Captain," the Iraqi warned. "We can't allow any mistakes. You don't want to become our enemy. None of our enemies will be safe from our retribution."

CHAPTER FIVE

The big black Oldsmobile Ninety-Eight cruised the streets of Little Havana like a steel shark, Mack Bolan at the wheel. Unlike his previous visit to the Florida city, the Executioner didn't have the Stony Man battle van. He had something more valuable and reliable in a fight.

Rafael Encizo and Calvin James had met Bolan at the airport when he arrived. The muscular Cuban and the tall, lean, black warrior from Chicago were members of Phoenix Force. Tough, smart and professional, they were good men in any kind of emergency. Both men were fluent in Spanish, and Encizo knew Little Havana like the back of his hand.

The Olds wasn't equipped with high-tech gear and remote-control gadgets, but the Ninety-Eight was a well-made car. The four-door luxury auto was sturdy, as well as handsome. The 3800 V-6 engine would allow the Olds to maneuver better than the "wonder van," and it would generate a lot of speed.

The Justice Department had outfitted the Ninety-Eight with several modifications. The reinforced glass was shatter resistant, and some armor plating had been installed in the doors and hood. The original design of the car included extended front and rear fenders, which made it fairly easy to fix steel-pipe battering rams underneath each end of the vehicle.

James and Encizo had also picked up some weapons when they got the Olds. Stony Man provided them with two Walther P-88, double-action 9 mm pistols and a pair of mini-Uzi machine pistols, standard hardware for Phoenix Force. They'd also received one Beretta 93-R, a Desert Eagle .44 Magnum and a full-size Uzi subgun. Since Bolan had to take a commercial flight to Miami, the Phoenix duo had his chosen weaponry waiting when he arrived.

The Executioner checked the hardware as he sat in the backseat and explained the mission to his companions. Encizo handled the wheel while James examined the file folders containing what little information Stony Man had been able to assemble concerning the embassy attacks and the Khemit-Garcia incident.

"We heard about the embassy sabotage on the radio," James said, shaking his head slightly. "Kind of figured this was why we were called in."

"Everybody was called in for this one," Bolan replied.

"I looked through the list of guys stationed at Garcia's house when you hit the place," Encizo remarked, his gaze still fixed on the road. "Several were associated with Ernesto Marti. He's been a major player for two decades in Miami. Marti's expertise is smuggling, and he specializes in moving people into or out of the country."

"People?" Bolan inquired with interest. The warrior screwed a silencer to the threaded muzzle of his Beretta as he spoke, satisfied with the equipment.

"Yeah," Encizo confirmed. "Marti helps individuals who need to get out of the United States because the law's breathing down their necks. He quietly smuggles them to the Bahamas or the Caribbean without having to travel by conventional methods that might include encounters with the police or the Coast Guard. His service also brings into the U.S. people who want to do illegal business here without the authorities knowing they're in the country. Marti has been successful for a long time because he doesn't directly move drugs or weapons, although his clients are usually involved in those trades."

"How were the hardguys at Garcia's place connected with Marti?" Bolan asked. "They were strong-arm goons. Not the sort to be involved with a smart guy's operation."

"Marti has connections in other lines of criminal activity other than smuggling," Encizo explained. "The gunmen you tangled with weren't on Marti's payroll. They were free-lance contract workers. The only thing we could find they had in common was that they all did work for Marti and he arranged for them to work for local syndicates in and around the city. Mostly protection rackets and loan sharks who needed some experienced leg-breakers while their regular employees were out of action."

"You know where we can find him, Rafael?" Bolan asked as he slipped the 93-R into shoulder leather under his jacket.

"That's not exactly a state secret in Little Havana. Marti runs some legitimate businesses here. He has a men's clothing store, a couple pawnshops and a tavern or two. Marti owns them, but he has other people manage them. His favorite is a restaurant called the Plato de Langosta, which he personally operates as owner and manager. It's the most respectable of his businesses, so it's the one he most wishes to be associated with.''

"And that's where he usually hangs out," James commented. "I hope Marti is there today. It'll save us time trying to hunt down the sucker."

They traveled the streets at a good pace, considering the traffic. The sleek black Olds received an occasional stare of admiration, but luxury cars weren't uncommon in the area. The rich tended to drive vehicles more expensive than the Ninety-Eight. A Mercedes or a limousine in Little Havana usually meant a big dope dealer was showing off his ill-gotten wealth.

The Olds approached the Plato de Langosta. The restaurant was designed in a Spanish hacienda style, with a sign bearing a bright red lobster set against a white plate as an iconographic advertisement. A few cars were in the parking lot, but Encizo had no trouble finding a space.

"We don't want to jump to any conclusions," Bolan reminded the Phoenix pair. "Marti is dirty, but that doesn't mean he knows any details about Garcia's business with Khemit or whether the incident is connected with the terrorist strike in Washington. This is a public establishment. We don't want to have a gun battle with a bunch of civilians in the line of fire."

"Gotcha," James assured the Executioner as he patted the bulge of the Walther pistol under his jacket. "But I'm glad I got my good-luck piece just in case."

"Marti isn't the sort to resort to violence in his own restaurant," Encizo commented. "Still, he's not a gentleman and he hasn't lasted this long in the criminal trade by being a pushover. If he feels cornered, he'll bite just like any other rat."

They walked to the restaurant and were greeted by a slim woman with a lovely face. Her red lips offered an intriguing smile, and the neckline of her bright scarlet dress plunged low enough to reveal an eye-arresting display of cleavage.

"*Buenos días, señores,*" she said. "How may I help you?"

"*¿Dónde está el señor Martí?*" Encizo asked bluntly.

"He isn't here," the woman replied in English. She looked away from the three men and cast a nervous glance at the dining room. "I don't know where he is...."

"Then we'll just leave a note for him," Bolan said as he brushed past her and headed for the dining room.

James and Encizo followed, ignoring the woman's protests as they marched between the rows of tables. Diners barely noticed the trio, preoccupied with their meals and conversation.

The decor was elegant but somewhat gaudy, and the waiters were dressed in white-and-red uniforms that resembled a demented fashion designer's idea of an updated version of Napoleonic naval officers at a military ball. Despite the ridiculous outfits, the waiters were burly young men with faces as hard as granite. They glared at the three intruders and watched them make their way across the dining room.

Bolan and his companions located a corridor at the rear of the restaurant. Two large men flanked a door.

They turned to stare at the commandos with looks calculated to instill fear in the most hardened heart.

"What the hell do you guys want?" one of the hardguys demanded.

"The lady at the front must've called ahead," James remarked. "This is Marti's office, huh?"

"And they're the doormen," Encizo added with a thin smile.

"This is a restaurant," the man who appeared to have mastered speech growled, "not a goddamn comedy club. You guys aren't cops or you'd be waving badges and warrants. That means you'd better get out of here before they carry you out in body bags." The guy nodded in the direction past Bolan's shoulders.

Three waiters stepped behind Bolan and the Phoenix pros. One guy slipped a set of brass knuckles over his fingers and clenched his fist, another had drawn a blackjack from a pocket and the third held a length of steel chain. No guns or knives, Bolan noticed. The muscle boys didn't want to kill anyone on Marti's property.

"Wait a second," Bolan said, holding his hands up, palms raised in an innocent gesture. "There seems to be a misunderstanding here."

He suddenly swung a left hook to the jaw of the nearer doorman. The man was caught off guard by the blow and fell sideways into his companion. The second guy was startled but not hurt. Bolan changed that when he snap-kicked the guy in the groin.

The Executioner didn't give his opponents time to recover. He closed in and slammed an elbow stroke to the battered chin of the first hardguy. Then an uppercut to the man's face knocked him back into the door.

The big warrior's hands shot out and grabbed the throats of both guards. His grip like steel talons, he held the stunned opponents firmly and rapped their heads together. The men collapsed to the floor in limp heaps.

The waiter with the chain raised his weapon to attempt to flog Bolan with the steel links. Calvin James suddenly unleashed a high tae kwon do kick, the edge of his boot slamming under the attacker's raised arm. The man gasped in pain from the powerful blow to the nerve center at his armpit. James quickly grabbed his opponent's wrist and drove a knee kick under the man's ribs.

James shoved the dazed hardguy into the waiter sporting the knuckle-dusters. The remaining man wasn't certain whom to use his blackjack against. He saw Encizo reach inside his jacket and immediately decided the Cuban was his target.

Encizo moved forward and lashed out with the Cold Steel Tanto knife clenched in his fist. The Cuban kept his body low and put his entire body behind the motion of the thrust. The thick, seven-inch blade sliced the waiter's forearm before the guy could swing his sap. Encizo stamped a boot heel into his opponent's kneecap and delivered a heel-of-the-palm stroke to the guy's wounded arm. The blackjack fell from numb fingers.

Bolan turned and drew the Beretta 93-R from leather. James had taken the chain from his opponent, then moved behind him and wrapped the metal links around the guy's neck. The waiter with the brass knuckles wasn't able to throw a punch at James because the Phoenix fighter used his captive enemy as a shield. Mr. Knuckles saw the pistol in Bolan's fist and lost interest in James. He raised his hands in surrender.

Encizo rapped his opponent behind the ear with the Tanto's handle to knock him unconscious, while James choked off the second waiter's wind to get the same result. The remaining waiter continued to stare at Bolan's gun.

"Tell your boss everything is okay," the Executioner demanded. "Better sound convincing."

"Your life depends on it," Encizo added, and pointed the slanted tip of the knife blade at the hoodlum.

The waiter knocked on the office door. "Mr. Marti!" he called out in Spanish, trying to keep his voice steady and confident. "This is Luis. Everything is all right, sir."

"What happened?" a voice responded from the opposite side of the door. "I heard a fight out there."

"Well, sir..." Luis began. He was uncertain how to address Marti's remark.

Bolan jammed the Beretta at the base of the guy's skull to encourage creativity. Luis swallowed hard and spoke.

"We had a little trouble from a couple of drunks," he lied smoothly. "One of them claimed to know you."

"Is Manuel or Julio with you?"

"They took the troublemakers down to the basement to get some information out of them, sir."

The door latch turned with a metal click, and Marti opened the door wide enough to peer outside. Bolan slammed a boot into the door, and it smashed back into Marti. The Executioner entered the office as the man staggered from the unexpected blow. Marti held a hand to his eyebrow, freezing in place when he saw Bolan's gun.

"No one has died here today," the warrior stated. "Let's keep it that way."

Marti slowly raised his hands. He was a short, portly man, gray hair dominating what remained on his balding pate. He didn't look very dangerous, but Bolan knew better than to judge a man by his appearance.

"If you want money..." Marti began.

"Information."

Bolan heard the sound of a hard object striking flesh, followed by a soft moan. He didn't even glance over his shoulder, confident that what he heard was Luis being knocked unconscious. Marti's eyes expanded with alarm as he watched James and Encizo drag the senseless man into the office. The Phoenix fighters hauled in the rest of the hardmen.

Bolan glanced about the room. The office was furnished with a leather sofa and armchairs, a neatly kept Plexiglas desk and a well-stocked bar. Several suitcases were on the floor by the bar.

"Going on a trip?" Bolan asked.

"That's not against the law," Marti answered. "But you're not a policeman, are you?"

"I'm the man with the gun. That's all you need to know. You're not going to leave this room until you tell us what you know about a gunrunner named Garcia."

"You recently supplied him with some gun-toting hired help," James added as he closed the office door. "So don't tell us you don't know the guy."

"He needed extra security," Marti explained, shrugging.

"And he just happened to contact you," Bolan remarked. "Curious that you're taking a trip now. Seems like you're afraid of something. That heavy-handed behavior by your men reinforces that."

"I'm not afraid of anything or anyone," Marti insisted, "except for crazy men like you who threaten me at gunpoint."

"Then you must be very worried about some of your recent customers," Bolan said. "I hear you specialize in smuggling people into the country. My guess is that's how you got involved with Garcia in the first place."

"Khemit entered the U.S. with a fake passport on a commercial flight from the Middle East," Encizo reminded the Executioner.

"But we're dealing with a major international terrorist operation," Bolan insisted. "Khemit was trying to buy enough weapons and explosives to arm dozens of men. All of them wouldn't enter the U.S. through conventional transportation. They'd also need American money, forged papers, connections with men like Garcia and other things that only someone with your underworld contacts could help them with."

"You guys Feds?" Marti asked with a sigh. "Let's work something out. I need to get out of the country for a while. You don't know what these people are like. They're crazy and they'll blame me when they find out Garcia and Khemit were taken out. They'll think I leaked information to the FBI or CIA or whatever."

"You'd better tell us now," James warned. "Who did you help sneak into the U.S.?"

"I don't know their names. I don't need names. They didn't tell me where they were from, but I think they were Arabs or Iranians. I've met some of them before, and these people's language sounded the same."

"But you don't know the language they spoke?" Encizo asked.

"Look, I don't know who these people are. They wanted me to get them from Mexico and the Caribbean to the U.S. I was paid well and I didn't ask questions."

"And they also wanted weapons, so you hooked them up with Garcia," James remarked.

"Not exactly," Marti answered. "I put them in touch with other arms dealers, but the gunrunners couldn't get them the sort of military hardware they wanted. When Khemit arrived, a deal was already arranged with Garcia. I helped Garcia get extra security because he was worried about doing business with a person with a reputation like Khemit's."

"Reputation?" James snorted with disgust. "The guy was a terrorist. What the hell did you think he was doing in America? Didn't it bother you to help somebody who was here to carry out sabotage and murder innocent people?"

"I'm just a businessman," Marti replied. "If I hadn't helped him, someone else would have."

"Yeah," Bolan muttered, "I've heard that rationalization before. Now you're not so happy with that arrangement. You figure some of your clients might come after you and you don't want to be here when they come calling."

"I cooperated with you," Marti insisted. "Let me leave. If you take me in, I'll deny everything and I have a very good lawyer. None of this can be used in a court of law."

"Where can we find these other clients?" Bolan asked. "The ones you're afraid of."

"I wish I knew. I'd gladly tell you so you could go after the bastards before they can come for me. All I know is they needed forged passports and other ID—drivers' licenses and stuff like that. I don't even know if they're still in Florida."

"Not all of them," Bolan commented. "We want to know who the people were who supplied forged papers, guns and other items to the men you smuggled in. We also want detailed descriptions of any of the so-called immigrants you were directly involved with."

"I want my lawyer," Marti replied sternly.

"Let me have ten minutes with this guy," Encizo announced as he pushed back his jacket to reveal the Tanto in a belt sheath in a cross-draw position. "I'll make him talk."

"Will that be necessary, Marti?" the Executioner asked.

"No," the man replied with a sigh. "I'll make a list of names."

CHAPTER SIX

"Can't you do something about this McCarter character?" Hudson Connors asked as he paced the conference room at New Scotland Yard.

Ian Bandon glanced up at Connors. The lanky American seemed on the verge of a nervous breakdown. Connors's shoulders twitched, and he plucked at his clothing as if trying to rid himself of invisible parasites. Bandon was a veteran of the British Security Intelligence Service. He'd participated in many dangerous assignments before the Cold War started to thaw. However, Connors's career in the CIA had consisted of rather prosaic and safe duty with the U.S. Embassy in London. The man wasn't prepared for a serious mission that involved violence.

"McCarter doesn't work for the SIS," Bandon replied. "In fact, we thought he was attached to the CIA as a cut-out operative."

"Hell, Bandon," the American scoffed, "McCarter's a British citizen and not the type the Company would hire to get involved in a situation like this. Maybe some yahoos might use him as a mercenary."

"I don't think Mr. McCarter is a mercenary," Bandon commented as he scanned the data on his computer screen. "He has a colorful and rather mysterious career. McCarter joined the army as soon as he was old enough to enlist and soon became a member of the Special Air Service.''

''That's the elite paratrooper outfit,'' Connors inquired, ''that's sort of like the Green Berets?''

''Something like that. McCarter saw a lot of action in the SAS. He was a 'special observer' in Vietnam and participated in covert operations there. He was later stationed in Oman during the conflicts in the 1970s and spent some time in Hong Kong and Northern Ireland. He was also among the commandos in Operation Nimrod.''

''What?'' Connors asked with a frown.

''You don't remember Operation Nimrod?'' Bandon asked, surprised. ''On May 1, 1980, the Iranian embassy in London was seized by a gang of Iraqi terrorists. A number of British citizens were among the hostages. The SAS sent in a special CRW team. That's Counter Revolutionary Warfare team, which essentially means an antiterrorist unit. The raid was a great success. No hostages were killed during the action. The SAS took one terrorist captive and killed the rest. The entire raid took place in less than twelve minutes.''

''And McCarter was part of that?'' Connors asked. ''Okay. I guess that makes him some kind of hero. What's he been doing since?''

''I haven't been able to find anything on file about his activities in the past few years. Apparently he's made a lot of trips to and from the United States. He appears to be involved in some sort of supersecret organization that SIS hasn't been able to tap into.''

''CIA hasn't been able to get anything on the guy, either,'' Connors admitted. ''Somehow the son of a bitch managed to get authority straight from the White House and your prime minister."

"Hopefully they knew what they were doing when they granted McCarter this status," Bandon said, and shook his head slightly.

"I have less faith in the wisdom of politicians than you seem to."

The door opened, and both men turned to see Inspector Stephen White storm into the room. The burly Scotland Yard police officer was clearly aggravated. His busy eyebrows knitted, and his mouth was twisted into a scowl. Connors and Bandon guessed McCarter was responsible for the inspector's consternation.

"That bloody idiot is having my people run checks on stolen automobiles," White declared. "He also wants us to stock up on Coca-Cola soft drinks. Got a bit miffed when all we had was ginger ale and grape soda in the damn vending machine."

"Great," Connors moaned, and rolled his eyes toward the ceiling. "McCarter's using his authority to have Scotland Yard run down a bunch of unrelated bullshit. Probably personal stuff."

"And he's trying to make us his damn errand boys," White complained. The inspector folded his arms on his thick chest and glared at Bandon. "If you ask me, there are too many agencies getting involved in this embassy-bombing affair. Your people, the CIA, the French Sûreté and God knows who else. None of you even know who this McCarter chap works for."

"We've already discussed that, Inspector," Bandon assured him. The SIS officer took a pack of cigarettes from his pocket and shook one loose. "Just try to humor McCarter for now. The PM and the American President seem to think he's something special for some reason.''

"No offense to Mr. Connors here,'' White began, "but this is none of the Americans' bloody business. A French embassy was attacked, so I guess we have to give the frogs their due and put up with Sûreté. Still, this happened in London, and that makes it my jurisdiction. This isn't even a concern for the Yanks.''

"Like hell,'' Connors replied. "Maybe you don't follow the news, Inspector. A British embassy was bombed in Washington, D.C. And an American embassy was attacked in Paris at the same time the French embassy was hit here. Whoever's gunning after us is hitting all three countries, and that means Americans in England could be next.''

He stared at White and added, "By the way, my mother happens to be of French descent. I'll thank you not to use ethnic slurs like 'frogs' when you're around me, Inspector.''

"I beg your pardon,'' White said with a curt nod. He resisted the urge to tell Connors what he really thought of the American's objection to his remark about the French. White considered Americans to be a collection of mongrels without any real sense of national identity and a confused hodgepodge culture that seemed incapable of producing anything worthwhile.

Connors was a typical example of an American, in White's opinion. The Yank's mother was French and his father was Irish, two ethnic groups White regarded as inferior. His own heritage was Anglo-Saxon, and he was glad. He wouldn't want any French or Irish or some other "undesirable" genes mixed into his DNA. America was only good at spending money, and they mucked up whenever they tried to do anything else. White didn't want Connors or the CIA anywhere in the United Kingdom, let alone messing around in a criminal investigation he considered his responsibility.

"So here's where you all wound up," a voice announced as the door opened once more. "Thought you blokes might have taken off to look for some birds for a shag."

The three men recognized the Cockney accent and blunt commentary. Reluctantly they turned to watch David McCarter stroll into the conference room.

"We're right here, Mr. McCarter," Bandon said, forcing his tone to remain polite.

"Probably bitchin' about having to work with me, eh?" McCarter asked with a grin. "Why not? Everybody else does."

"I can't imagine why," Connors muttered, and cast a suspicious glance at the folder in McCarter's hand. "What's that? Your shopping list? Want to have some constables pick up your groceries?"

"No," McCarter replied, "this is some information I got from the chaps in the auto-theft section."

"Mr. McCarter," Bandon began, frustrated by the encounter, "I fail to see what connection there could be between the embassy bombing and stolen automobiles."

"That's why you're lucky I'm here," McCarter explained. "You see, there were witnesses to the bombing who reported seeing a car speed away at the time of the explosion. Naturally people don't interpret what they see the same way in a stressful situation. Descriptions of the vehicle varied a bit, but enough people said it was a dark blue car and 'looked foreign' to make those pretty likely features. Two even pinned it down as a Volkswagen Rabbit.''

"I read the reports," White said with a sigh. "The eyewitnesses couldn't even agree which direction the damn car went."

"They don't have to," McCarter replied. "Some of your bobbies found a dark blue Rabbit over at Regent's Park. It was abandoned right along Park Road."

"That's a few blocks from Grosvenor Square," Bandon remarked, "but it's a straight line up Baker Street from the embassy to Regent's. You might be right that this could be the car."

"It might have just been in the area and fled when the bomb went off," White complained. "Even if it is the terrorists' car, I doubt they left fingerprints or any other clues that will be much help. Still, that's Scotland Yard's area of expertise. We've got the best forensic people in the world."

"I think they're already playing about with microscopes and chemistry sets," McCarter said, fishing a pack of cigarettes from his jacket. "I had them check something a bit more direct. Turns out the license plates are phony. Serial number on the body of the car matches that of a stolen yellow VW. Sure enough, they found some of the original paint color along the inside door."

"So the car was stolen," Connors said with a flutter of nervous hand gestures. "Not surprising the terrorists didn't buy or rent a car for something like this."

"Yes," McCarter agreed, and fired up a cigarette, "but this VW had been stolen six months ago. The blue paint job had been done about the same time.

Also, the serial numbers on the engine weren't the same as the body of the car. These numbers do match another stolen VW that was found about five months ago with many of its parts missing. Including the bleedin' engine.''

"What's your point, McCarter?" Bandon wanted to know.

"Sounds to me like this car spent some time in a chop shop. Thieves steal the cars, take them to a chop shop where the vehicles get different parts and a new look so they can be resold without the new owner getting arrested five minutes after he drives onto the street.''

"I'll be damned," Connors remarked in a surprised voice.

"Hopefully not," McCarter replied with a shrug, "but that's between you and the Almighty, mate. Now, I had the auto-theft gents come up with a list of the biggest chop shop outfits in London. You know how the law works. Sometimes coppers know everything some villains are up to, but they can't prove a bleedin' thing.''

"I think Mr. McCarter might be on to something here," Bandon said as he turned to White. "Perhaps Scotland Yard should look into this.''

"Yes, sir," the inspector admitted reluctantly. "We'll check into these auto-theft shops immediately.''

"I'll go along with your blokes, if you don't mind," McCarter offered. "Hanging about here isn't my style. This looks to be the closest thing to being in the field we'll have for the time being. This Sherlock Holmes business isn't my forte.''

White did mind, but he nodded his agreement.

A LAYER OF FOG FLOATED from the Thames to drift across central London, but the police cars made good progress in spite of the poor driving conditions. David McCarter and Inspector White sat in the back seat of the lead vehicle. The Scotland Yard officer frowned as he watched McCarter draw a blue-black pistol from under his wrinkled jacket.

The gun was a Browning Hi-Power. A superb pistol marksman, McCarter had been a member of the British Olympic shooting team in the 1970s. He liked the Browning and trusted his skill with the weapon.

"You have a permit for that thing?" White inquired, unhappy that McCarter was packing heat.

"Somewhere or other," the commando answered with a shrug. He jacked a round into the chamber, set the safety and slid the Browning into shoulder leather.

"You won't need that gun, McCarter. These are auto thieves, not IRA terrorists."

"They might be connected to terrorists, and that means they might be dangerous. I know you London bobbies like to think you handle any type of criminal without a gun. I also know more and more police here are carrying guns because the real world isn't as proper and polite as you blokes wish it was."

"I have a service revolver," White assured him. "I've been ordered to carry it at all times until this case is closed. That doesn't mean I want any shooting."

"Better to shoot than be shot," the Phoenix fighter replied.

The cars arrived at the Wells's Garage. Sounds of hammers on metal and hissing blowtorches penetrated the metal bay doors. McCarter and White walked to the side door while other cops circled around the building to cover the back doors. The inspector pounded a fist on the door until a voice responded from inside.

"What the hell's your problem?" a man demanded. "We're closed for the day. Come back tomorrow."

"Open the door!" White commanded. "This is official police business, and I've got a warrant. We'll break the door down if we must."

There was a long pause before the voice behind the door spoke again.

"Just a moment, Officer. I'll get my supervisor."

"Make it quick," White ordered. "We don't have all night."

The inspector turned to McCarter, who glanced up at the windows and roof of the building, wondering if a skylight or trapdoor to the roof might allow the people who operated the chop shop to escape.

"They're not going to fly away, McCarter," White assured him. "Don't worry. We've got them boxed in and they know it."

A bay door began to slide open, metal clattering as the door rolled up from the threshold. Two constables waited beside the police car parked in front of the building, watching the bay door open as calmly as one might observe a herd of grazing cows. They obviously assumed the car thieves would surrender to the will of Scotland Yard.

Headlights appeared at the open door, the hulking form of a two-ton truck surrounding the two great white orbs. The engine growled to life, and the vehicle bolted through the opening, the startled constables leaping out of the way of the charging truck.

The vehicle crashed into the parked police car and sent it skidding across the street to slam sideways into a lamppost. White and the other London lawmen were stunned by this unexpected violence, but McCarter was ready.

He raced toward the truck, drawing his weapon on the run. The vehicle had backed away from the police cruiser and was headed for Kennington Park. As McCarter sprinted to the cab section, the twin muzzles of a sawed-off shotgun poked through the open window of the passenger's side.

The Phoenix fighter raised the Browning and triggered two rounds, relying on instinct and years of combat shooting. Orange flame streaked from the muzzle of the Hi-Power, and the cracks of the high-velocity 9 mm slugs echoed in the fog-laced night. The shotgunner's head recoiled as the 9 mm destroyers connected. A death twitch pulled a trigger, and a burst of buckshot exploded from one of the barrels to send a bellowing yet harmless message into the sky.

The Phoenix commando didn't change direction. He continued to race after the truck and leaped to the cab before the driver could stomp the gas pedal. McCarter's feet found the running board, and he grabbed the door handle with one hand. His other arm thrust through the open window and pointed the Browning at the horrified face of the truck driver. The guy was already pale and terrified, his coveralls splashed with the brains and blood of his dead companion.

"Stop the truck or you get the same!" McCarter ordered.

The driver hit the brake, and the rig came to an abrupt halt. McCarter braced his elbow inside the door frame to keep his arm from bouncing and waving the Browning away from the driver's head. The man behind the wheel glanced down at the shotgun in the lap of his dead passenger.

"Grab for it, and they'll have to clean your brains off the dashboard," McCarter warned. "Get out and put your hands up. Keep them high and in clear view. If I get a hint you're even thinking of reaching for a weapon or making a run for it, you're dead."

The driver opened the door and obeyed McCarter's instructions. White and his men approached, slightly embarrassed, yet relieved the danger appeared to be over.

"Get your guns out!" McCarter shouted at the trio, aware that more opponents might be inside the rear of the vehicle.

His concern proved valid when a shotgun roared from behind the canvas tarp. One of the constables went down, his torso ripped and bloodied by a burst of buckshot. The other policeman dived for cover behind a newsstand. Armed only with a truncheon, there was little he could do.

Inspector White dropped to a kneeling stance and reached inside his coat for his revolver. Unaccustomed to carrying a gun, he was slow and clumsy. White found the grips of the Smith & Wesson .38 and pulled. The draw was awkward, and the hammer caught on his coat as he tried to clear the holster. He looked up and saw the muzzles of a shotgun swing toward him.

"Bloody hell!" McCarter rasped as he ran back to the driver.

The wheelman's attention had turned to the gun battle, and he didn't see McCarter until the commando had closed in. The Browning frame slapped into the side of the man's skull hard enough to knock him to the ground.

The Phoenix fighter fired three rounds into the rear of the truck gambling there were no explosives or flammable substances sequestered there. The immediate threat to the lives of the police and himself made this calculated risk acceptable in McCarter's judgment.

Canvas burst apart as a shotgun returned fire blindly. The gunman at the mouth of the tarp was distracted and forgot about Inspector White. The cop had finally drawn his revolver, but McCarter had already moved into position at the back of the rig. His Browning barked twice, and the gunman toppled from the tailgate. The cut-down shotgun clattered on the pavement beside him.

"Stop shooting!" a voice called from the rear of the truck. "I've had enough, dammit!"

Yet another sawed-off scattergun was tossed to the ground, its barrels broken open to show the weapon was empty. McCarter still suspected a trick and remained alert even as a lone figure climbed from the tailgate. White ordered the man to assume the position and stepped forward to frisk him.

McCarter held the Browning ready and yanked back the tarp to peer inside. Other than some boxes and a couple of cloth bags, the vehicle was empty. Mc-

Carter noticed the constable had stepped from cover and examined the fallen uniformed cop.

"Officer Wilkins is dead," the man said in a stunned voice.

"Go check on the driver," McCarter told him. There'd be time to mourn the death of the policeman after the danger was over. "Cuff the son of a bitch before he decides to take a walk."

The constable nodded and headed to the front of the rig.

McCarter watched White frisk the other surviving hood. The guy was a burly brute with a mop of blond hair and a face that appeared to have stopped a lot of punches. His accent suggested he was a Cockney, probably born in a neighborhood near McCarter's old block. Another poor kid from the East End, the Phoenix warrior realized. He'd been one himself and understood the temptation to adopt a life-style of crime as an escape from poverty.

But there were other ways to get out of the slums. McCarter had done it, and he didn't have a great deal of sympathy for those who choose a crooked path.

The commando approached White and his prisoner, noticing White had once again put away his revolver while he frisked the man.

"He's clean," White announced as he reached for his handcuffs.

The brute suddenly whirled and drove an elbow to White's chest. The inspector staggered from the blow and lashed out a fist in retaliation. The hardguy blocked the punch with a forearm and grabbed White's other arm with his free hand. The guy's head snapped forward to butt White in the face, and the inspector sagged to the ground.

McCarter stepped forward, unleashed a kick and drove the toe of his boot under the prisoner's ribs. The man groaned and started to fold from the kick. The Phoenix fighter swung his Browning, attempting to hit the man, but the guy blocked the blow and grabbed McCarter's arm. He pulled hard and sent McCarter hurtling into the side of the truck.

The commando grunted from the impact. The hardguy held on to McCarter's arm and tried to wrench the Browning from his grasp. But the Phoenix warrior didn't intend to allow the opponent to claim his pistol. He dropped the weapon and thrust a back kick to the guy's abdomen, then followed through with a solid left hook to the big man's jaw.

The punch barely rocked the guy. McCarter then clipped him with a backfist, which didn't have much effect, either. A hand snared McCarter's wrist, then a fist lashed out at the commando's face. McCarter ducked the punch, but his opponent closed in for a head butt.

McCarter reared back to avoid the other man's skull, grabbed the front of the guy's coveralls and shoved his fist under the guy's chin to prevent another head butt attempt. Then he rammed a knee to the man's unprotected groin.

The hardguy wheezed in pain from the blow to his manhood. McCarter bent an elbow and hooked the front of the joint to the side of his opponent's head. The man staggered, and his eyes finally became glazed from the punishment. The Phoenix fighter snapped his skull in a head butt of his own and scored a powerful blow to the other guy's nose. A right cross sent the brute to the pavement in a dazed heap.

Inspector White slowly got to his feet as sirens wailed and flashing lights filled the street. Police cars converged on the garage and soon surrounded the area. McCarter located his Browning and returned the pistol to shoulder leather. White dabbed blood from his nostrils and split upper lip.

"What the hell did that bastard hit me with?" the cop wondered aloud.

"You're not from the East End, are you, Inspector?" McCarter inquired with a shrug. "Not a lot of attention to Queensberry Rules there. By the way, you'd better learn how to use that gun if you intend to carry it."

White glared at the commando, but there was little he could say because he knew McCarter had saved his life, as well as prevented the criminals from escaping.

Uniformed figures emerged from the cars and rushed to the scene of the confrontation. Two other men stepped from a car driven by CIA agent Connors. McCarter immediately recognized the big Canadian and the one-armed Israeli.

"Well, you chaps missed a bit of excitement," he declared with a grin. "Glad to see you made it to London. Maybe now we can get this mess straightened out."

"I'm curious to hear what progress you've made so far," Yakov Katzenelenbogen remarked. He glanced down at the dead and unconscious figures on the ground. "Some I can see for myself."

"They started it," McCarter insisted.

"Are you two his friends?" Inspector White asked without enthusiasm.

"Don't hold that against us," Gary Manning replied with a sigh.

CHAPTER SEVEN

Harold Carey didn't like to be bothered during his lunch break. He was a creature of habit and was annoyed when anything interrupted his regular routine. He intended to have his lunch whether the federal investigator liked it or not.

The boss informed Carey that morning that a special investigator from the Department of Justice would visit the office to talk with him about some recent passengers who used the travel agency to book their flights out of Miami. He was supposed to remember every customer who came into the place? Granted, Barnway's Travel Limited was a small company, and people weren't beating down the door to fight their way to his desk to ask him to handle their travel plans. Nonetheless, Carey saw at least two hundred customers a week, and most of them were quite forgettable. He was usually too busy checking available seats on airline flights to pay much attention to what a client looked like.

Carey had been a travel agent for nine years. The business ran in peaks and valleys that varied with the changes in the economy and certain times of year when people made more trips out of the city. Barnway's Travel was a long way from number one in the business, but Carey encountered enough customers on a daily basis to be sick of listening to them by the end of the week.

The Fed probably figured he could stroll in, wave a badge and browbeat Carey into coming up with some obscure details about whomever the hell they were looking for. Ten to one the person they wanted was a fugitive of some sort, a drug dealer or an embezzler, perhaps. More likely someone guilty of income tax evasion. That was the goddamn crime of the century to the Feds.

Well, he wasn't going to jump through hoops for this special investigator, regardless of how important the guy thought he was. Determined to follow his personal regimen as much as possible, Carey loosened his necktie and sat at his desk, about to enjoy his lunch.

"Mr. Carey?" a feminine voice inquired. "I believe you're expecting me."

He looked up and saw that a lovely blond lady had quietly entered the office. A blue jacket with matching skirt displayed the alluring curves of her fine figure, and she smiled as she opened a handbag to take out a leather ID folder. Barbara Price showed Carey a card with her photo next to Special Investigator in bold print.

"I'm Barbara Richards with the Department of Justice," Price explained, using the cover name on the card.

"You...?" Carey began with surprise. He quickly rose from his chair and nearly knocked over the coffee cup in his haste. "Uh, yes. I was expecting you, ma'am. Please have a seat, Ms. Richards... I mean, Inspector Richards."

"Barbara is okay," she assured him. "This is an informal meeting. We just need to ask you a few questions about some recent clients who booked flights out of Miami through this agency."

"I'll be happy to help any way I can."

Price sat in the chair facing Carey's desk. She crossed her legs, and the skirt hem rose high enough to draw Carey's attention. Price removed a notepad from her purse and placed it on her knee. Carey directed his gaze to the visitor's face.

"For reasons I can't go into at this time," Price began, "the Justice Department needs to know any details you might recall about these individuals."

She handed Carey a list of names that had been compiled from Aaron Kurtzman's computers after Mack Bolan had returned from Miami with information extracted from Marti. The Bear had run a computer check on the names of airline, bus and train passengers who had departed Miami in the past week. He discovered several passenger tickets had been bought in Miami by persons using Indian or Pakistani names. All had booked flights on the same airline and all had headed for Washington, D.C. Although the dates varied, all used the Barnsway's Travel agency.

"We get a lot of people in here...Barbara," Carey began. He looked at the list and noticed the unusual names next to dates, flight numbers and passenger seats. "Wait a minute. I do remember these guys."

"You handled their tickets personally?" Price inquired. She already knew the answer. She wouldn't be meeting with Carey otherwise.

"I sure did," he confirmed. "You see the dates here? These guys came into the office in three separate groups on three separate days. They weren't supposed to be connected with one another, but I was suspicious of that from the beginning. They were too much alike for it to be just coincidence."

"How were they alike?"

"Well, for one thing, they all dressed alike," Carey answered. "Cheap black suits, white shirts and skinny ties. They looked like they were headed for a cut-rate funeral. Acted like it, too. They were solemn, tight-lipped and surly. Only one guy from each group talked. I don't know if this man was the only one who spoke English in each group or whether he was just elected as a spokesman."

"Can you describe any of the spokesmen?"

"They were alike, too," Carey replied, shaking his head. "They were polite in a cold sort of way. They spoke English fairly well, but with a heavy accent. Of course, they said they were from India and Pakistan. Looked like they were. Dark complexions, black hair. Of course, a lot of Hispanics can be described that way, but I know lots of Cubans and Puerto Ricans. These guys were different."

"These men weren't clones from a genetic laboratory," Price insisted. "They couldn't all look and act exactly alike. Think carefully Mr. Carey. Were any of the spokesmen particularly tall or short? Thin or fat? Did they have long hair or short? Mustaches or beards? Any visible scars or birthmarks?"

Carey noticed how appealing Price's lips were when they pursed slightly while pronouncing words with *B* or *P.* He was also paying attention to what she said and thought for a moment before he replied.

"One guy had a long scar along the side of his face." He traced a finger across his left cheek to demonstrate. "Looked like a knife wound. See a lot of those around here, and it sure looked like somebody carved his face pretty good."

"What else did you notice about his face?"

"It was lean and he had a trimmed beard with no mustache," Carey replied, surprised that he remembered this detail. "Sort of like those old pictures of Abe Lincoln. This same guy had real dark eyes. They looked almost black, and he nodded his head a lot, little short bobbing gestures when he talked."

"This was one of the spokesmen?" Price asked. She jotted down information on the notepad as Carey spoke.

"Yeah," he confirmed. "The others didn't make much of an impression. One guy was sort of short and had a moon face that didn't fit the rest of his body. He also looked down at the floor a lot. You know the way some people do when they're lying and they don't want to look at you? I hadn't thought of it before, but that was how he acted."

"That's good, Mr. Carey. Anything else?"

"No..." His eyes widened when a memory struck home. "Wait. I remember several of them were missing some fingers."

"In which group?"

"At least one or two in each group was shy a finger or two. I thought at the time it was kind of weird. Didn't think they'd have that many industrial accidents in India and Pakistan to be chopping off fingers that often. Of course, I don't know what the medical treatment is like over there. Maybe crocodiles or snakes bit them off. I don't know."

"How did they pay for the tickets?" Price asked.

"In cash," Carey recalled. "That was unusual, too. Every group paid in cash. They didn't look like they had much money, but the leader of each group pulled out a wad of bills and paid for the tickets, with plenty of dough left when he finished."

Carey's eyes moved to Price's legs again. Her skirt had ridden about two more inches. She had great legs. In fact, everything about the woman was gorgeous. Why the hell was she working for the Justice Department? She was too beautiful to be a Fed.

"Is there anything else you can add?" Price asked.

"Sorry," he said sincerely. "I can't think of anything else."

"Okay." She smiled as she returned the notepad to her purse. "We appreciate your help, Mr. Carey."

"You can just call me Harold...uh, Harry," he urged.

Price rose from the chair, gripping the hem of her skirt and tugging it down. Carey looked at her face and once again held her captivating smile.

"If there's anything else I can do..." he began.

"We'll let you know," Price assured him. "Thank you very much, Harry."

He watched her leave the office and knew he'd never see her again.

HAL BROGNOLA MET PRICE at the entrance to the main house at the Farm. The big Fed looked tired. His shirt was open at the throat, and he hadn't shaved for at least twenty-four hours. As he ushered Price inside, she asked what had happened while she was in Miami.

"Able Team is in D.C. looking into the bombing of the British embassy," the Stony Man chief replied. "Striker is going to join them. Encizo and James are headed for Europe to meet up with the rest of Phoenix Force. Katz sent us a coded message from London. You know how careful he is."

"He doesn't make many mistakes," Price commented.

"He can't afford to. Anyway, it seems McCarter may have come up with a lead worth looking into. Nothing definite so far."

"What about the FBI, CIA, NSA and the other Intel outfits?" Price asked. "Any useful information?"

"Don't even mention them to me right now," Brognola muttered. "I had to spend two hours with the deputy director of the Company today. He wants to know who the hell we are and what right we have overseeing his case officers in the United Kingdom. Seems the CIA man in London has had his feathers ruffled and he's bitching about it."

"Well, he was dealing with McCarter," Price said with a sigh. "Katz and Gary will help smooth things out. They're both more tactful than David."

"That doesn't take a hell of a lot. FBI arrested Ernesto Marti when he tried to flee the country. They found four million dollars stashed in his luggage. Some of it was marked bills from a Dade County bank job a few months ago. Marti claims he doesn't know anything about the bank holdup, which may be the truth. He's also complaining that some federal 'killers' leaned on him for information and forced him to talk under extreme stress and fear for his life. He claims this is the reason he decided to flee the country. Says he was afraid of being railroaded."

"Didn't mention the terrorists?"

"Hell no," Brognola replied. "The FBI has been playing you-scratch-my-butt-I'll-scratch-yours with NSA lately. They got wind of an edited version of what happened with Garcia. Now they want to know if our people were involved in Marti's decision to get out of town."

"So you're getting headaches from the Bureau, too?" Price asked.

"Doesn't stop there. You know how many outfits are involved in the British embassy bombing? The FBI, NSA, Justice Department, the Washington, D.C. Police Department, the BATF, the Secret Service and British Intelligence are all scrambling over this one. Since the American branch of Interpol is out of the Justice Department, the British might decide to send some people from their own branch associated with Scotland Yard. It's a circus, and everybody wants to be ringmaster."

"And we sent in Able Team with White House authority." Price guessed what the problem was.

"You got it," Brognola said with a nod. "Everybody wants to know who these mysterious guys are and why they rank so high. These people are crying about who has jurisdiction so hard they must not have much time left to hunt for the damn terrorists."

Aaron Kurtzman wheeled his chair into the entrance hall, greeted Price with a wave and asked if she had a chance to work on her tan while she was in Florida.

"I tried to use the reading lamp over my seat on the plane," Price answered, "but I couldn't get it hot enough."

"Pity," the Bear said as he unfolded a computer printout sheet. "I came up with some more stuff on the alleged Indian and Pakistani tourists from Miami. None of them checked any luggage into the baggage compartments of the planes they boarded. That means all they had was carryons that would have to go through security and X rays."

"So they didn't smuggle any weapons on board," Brognola commented.

"Exactly," the computer wiz confirmed. "None of them had arranged hotel reservations or car rentals. That means they must have already had somebody waiting to pick them up at the airport and some place to stay after they arrived. So far, I don't have any leads as to who that might be or where they might be holed up."

"Well, it all supports Striker's theory about a connection with Khemit," Brognola said. "Too bad that's not a hell of a lot of help at this point. How'd you do with the travel agency, Barb?"

"A couple of decent descriptions of two of the suspects," she answered. "The rest is pretty vague, aside from an observation that some of the men were missing fingers."

"I seem to recall in some Arab countries they still cut off a finger or even a whole hand for stealing," Kurtzman remarked. "I think they do that in Iran, too. Probably doesn't have anything to do with this mess."

"I wish all we had to worry about were a bunch of visiting thieves from the Middle East," Brognola replied. "Instead, we're after international terrorists and we don't know where or when they'll strike next."

CHAPTER EIGHT

The terrorists did strike again. At six-thirty in the evening, an explosion erupted on the property of the Virginia State Capitol in Richmond. Able Team learned of the sabotage from an FBI agent named Paul Beaumont. The Stony Man warriors left for Richmond within minutes after the report of the explosion.

The helicopter spotlight illuminated the twelve acres of the State Capitol property. The beautiful, manicured lawns had been violated by the blast, a ragged crater revealing the site of the explosion. Police cars had congregated at the scene of the attack. An ambulance was parked among the vehicles, but two figures on the ground already lay still, faces covered by white sheets. A tree had been uprooted by the explosion, but the blast hadn't reached the magnificent white marble Capitol building.

The pilot found a clearing on the lawn and touched down. Carl Lyons pulled back the sliding door and stepped from the aircraft, followed by Gadgets Schwarz and Rosario "Pol" Blancanales. As the Able Team commandos approached the scene of the terrorist attack, they were stopped by a Richmond police captain. Lyons showed the cop an ID with the cover name Kenneth Carlson next to his photo.

"You're with the D.C. investigation?" the captain asked.

"Yeah. How bad is the damage? I see two bodies, and one tree didn't make it."

"The dead men are security personnel on duty on the Capitol grounds," the policeman answered. "They were hit by the blast. Could have been a lot worse if the bastards had set off the bomb closer to the mansion."

"A beautiful building," Blancanales remarked as he eyed the handsome classical portico that ringed the marble structure.

"It's been the seat of Virginia's state government since 1788," the captain stated. "It's a historical treasure, Mister...?"

"Just call me Raoul," Blancanales replied with a slight smile.

"Anybody see this happen?" Lyons asked.

"Witnesses' statements have been taken, but I don't know that they'll be much help," the police captain answered. "Some witnesses even claimed they saw somebody out here firing a rifle from the back of a truck. Of course, no one heard any gunshots, and a bomb was used, not a rifle."

"Your witnesses weren't that far wrong," Schwarz announced as he examined the crater with the aid of a flashlight.

"What's that?" Lyons asked, stepping closer to the hole.

"There are bits of metal shell around the edge of the crater," Schwarz replied. "Some more are embedded in the bottom of the hole. It's shrapnel. From the depth of the shrapnel penetration, I'd say somebody fired a grenade launcher and the projectile landed right here."

"So the person who reported seeing a rifle wasn't just imagining things?" the cop asked with surprise.

"From a distance it would be easy to mistake a rifle for a grenade launcher," Schwarz confirmed. "Especially if a person didn't know much about small arms. Hell, there are even grenade launchers that fit under the barrels of rifles. The M-203 for example. Some rifles and even shotguns can be converted to be used as a grenade launcher."

"Must have decided it would be too risky to get any closer to the governor's house," Lyons speculated. "The security people probably spotted them approaching, and the terrorists opened fire with the launcher. Too bad for the security men, but it saved the lives of people in the building."

"Who did it?" the captain demanded. "The same crazies who set off that bomb in D.C.?"

"I wouldn't be surprised," Blancanales replied. "Unfortunately we don't have a definite lead as to who the terrorists are or where to find them."

"Great," the Richmond cop commented sourly. "So you fancy Feds aren't doing any better than we lowly local city police."

"If you guys can solve this mess, go ahead," Lyons invited. "I didn't think we were in competition. Since we're all on the same side, we'd do better to cooperate and work together."

"Fair enough," the captain said. "So tell me what you know so far about the bombing of that British embassy in D.C."

"We don't know shit," Lyons said bluntly. "Just don't tell anybody else I said that. Officially the FBI and the D.C. cops are supposed to be making encouraging progress on the case."

"I appreciate your honesty," the cop replied, "but it's not going to help me sleep too well tonight."

"None of us are going to get much sleep until this is over, Captain," Schwarz told him.

SOME OFFICES along Constitution Avenue have views of the Capitol Building, the Washington Monument, the Jefferson Memorial or the White House. Others overlook the Mall, where five of the most famous museums in America are located.

Eric Deckker didn't have such a view. He looked out the window of his office at the Department of Justice to see a sleazy bar, a Chinese restaurant and a parking lot.

Deckker had been disappointed with the office, but it had been part of a promotion to section chief. He soon discovered he was too busy to spend much time staring out the window, admiring the view. The job had more than a few headaches. Since he had been assigned to the embassy bombing case, those headaches had doubled, and he felt as if a mean little bastard with a hammer was living inside his skull.

The three mystery men with White House authority had just returned from Richmond. Special Agent Theodore Anderson of the FBI was also present, as well as another hotshot from the President's supersecret unit. The big man who looked as if he could stop bullets with a hard stare had entered Deckker's office and introduced himself as "Pollock."

"Maybe the terrorists didn't buy any major military hardware in Miami," Lyons remarked as he poured himself a cup of coffee, "but they got their hands on some somewhere."

"FBI forensics has identified the weapon used in Richmond as a 40 mm grenade," Anderson said wearily. "Cartridge-style projectile fired from an M-79 launcher."

"We used them in Korea," Deckker said, aware this told the others he was over fifty and easily the oldest guy in the room. "I thought those bloopers were obsolete."

"They are by modern military standards," Mack Bolan confirmed, leafing through some witness reports as he spoke. "But the M-79 is still a serious piece of hardware. The terrorists may have purchased some guns in Miami, but it's unlikely they got the M-79s there."

"Well, it seems we've been looking in the wrong place for the terrorists," Anderson remarked. The FBI man was a slender black guy who looked more like a clerk than a special agent. He adjusted his metal-frame glasses and added, "They've left D.C. and moved to Virginia."

"They hit in Virginia," Blancanales stated. "That doesn't mean they've moved operations to that state."

"If they hit in Arlington, I'd agree with you," Anderson replied. "That's just across the Potomac. Richmond is in the heart of Virginia. More than a hundred miles from D.C. These terrorists are functioning like serial killers. They strike in one state and move to another."

"That's a pretty big assumption," Schwarz commented. "Figure tomorrow they'll hit West Virginia or North Carolina?"

"It's possible," Anderson replied. "They might be carrying out hit-and-run operations. There's no solid link with the British embassy and the Richmond State Capitol grounds. That suggests their targets are uncertain and not necessarily connected."

"Joyriding and blowing stuff up for the hell of it?" Lyons scoffed, and shook his head. "I don't buy it, Anderson. I don't know why they hit the Richmond target, but I wouldn't count on them shuffling from state to state playing Ted Bundy with explosives."

"Maybe they moved to Virginia because we made it too hot for them to stay here in D.C.," Deckker suggested. "After all, they must realize half a dozen federal, police and Intelligence agencies are stalking them since they bombed the embassy."

"They figure they'll get less heat by moving to another state and carrying out another terrorist attack so we know where they went?" Lyons replied incredulously. "If they were that dumb, we'd have caught them by now."

"The Richmond assault is probably a distraction," Bolan announced. "Evidence strongly indicates at least some of the terrorists are Arabs. They're professionals, not just a gang of lunatics. They'll have specific targets and they'll plan the attacks in advance."

"Okay," Deckker said in a weary tone, "let's say you're right. That still doesn't help us find the sons of bitches. Any bright ideas about that?"

"The terrorists probably didn't purchase grenade launchers in Miami," Lyons began. "They could have done business with black-market gunrunners along the way, but my guess is they bought the military arms right here in Washington."

"Why here?" Deckker asked. "Why not Georgia or South Carolina?"

"Because D.C. could stand for 'Death City,'" Lyons replied bluntly. "This isn't only the nation's capital, but the murder capital of America, as well. There are street gangs running around Washington with automatic weapons the troops with Operation Desert Storm would have envied."

Anderson considered Lyons's corollary and realized the guy might be right. The FBI agent cleared his throat and said, "Okay, fella. How do we locate these gunrunners? The D.C. police haven't been able to. What makes you think we'll have any more luck than they have?"

"We'll find somebody who knows where to find the illegal arms dealers," Lyons explained. "We need to locate the leader of the biggest, most vicious gang in the city."

Deckker stared at the Able Team captain as if Lyons had suggested they go skinny-dipping in a piranha tank. The Justice man noticed Anderson roll his eyes toward the ceiling, but Bolan and the Able Team members didn't seem to regard the idea as being absurd.

"Do you know what these gangs are like?" Anderson asked. "Some of those kids with the D.C. dope trade are mad dogs on two legs. They're as dangerous as the terrorists. Maybe they haven't had formal training at some terrorist camp in the Middle East, but they'll start shooting if you look at them sideways."

"Then we'll look them straight in the face when we ask where we can find the gunrunners," the Executioner replied.

CHAPTER NINE

The Stechkin recoiled in Major Hawran's grasp. A wooden shoulder stock was attached to the butt of the Russian-made machine pistol, and he felt the impact at his shoulder as he aimed carefully and squeezed off three more shots. A silhouette target went down when the slugs scored another hit.

Kaborya grunted with grudging admiration at the Iraqi officer's marksmanship. Hawran nailed targets at a distance of one hundred meters with the Stechkin. Of course, the shoulder stock contributed to the weapon's stability. Nonetheless, a weapon was just a chunk of metal without the skill to use it efficiently.

Hawran ejected a spent magazine from the butt of the Stechkin and loaded a full 20-round replacement. He chambered a shell, pressed the selector catch from semi- to full-auto and moved to a new position along the firing line. The Iraqi pointed downrange and opened fire on two targets twenty meters from the shooter's table. The Stechkin chattered bursts of bullets at full-automatic mode. The silhouettes dropped from view after taking three rounds each.

Kaborya waited for Hawran to lower the pistol to the table before he approached. The major removed a set of ear protectors and turned to face the Palestinian. He recognized the disgruntled expression and knew Kaborya was worried about something.

"Bad news from one of our units in the field?" Hawran asked with concern.

"No," Kaborya assured him. "Good news from the unit in America. The attack on the State Capitol of Virginia was successful. They had to fire on some security guards, so the damage wasn't as great as we hoped."

"That's a slight disappointment," Hawran replied with a sigh of relief. "It's not a major target anyway. None of our people were captured or killed?"

"No. We seem to be doing well so far in the enemy countries. I'm concerned about our status here."

"Captain Gedka complaining again?" Hawran guessed.

"He wants to know what we're doing with the chemical-processing operations here. The captain and his superiors are afraid we're making poison gas."

"You didn't tell them we are making gas?" Hawran asked.

"Give me a little credit for some intelligence," Kaborya replied, offended by the Iraqi's remark. "You'd better give Gedka a little credit, as well. The man isn't stupid, and he knows we've got a chemical-processing operation here. The whole world is aware Iraq used chemical warfare against Iran, and Kurds living in Iraq. Gedka and the other Somalis don't need towering IQs to realize what we're doing here."

"The Somalis have too much to gain if we succeed," Hawran stated, shrugging off Kaborya's concern. "They won't turn against us."

"If there's an accident here, the Somalis will almost certainly be victims of the gases that would drift with the winds across their country," Kaborya insisted. "They certainly have reason to object to our activities here if these threaten their safety."

"The officials who know about us won't dare betray us because they'd put their own heads on the chopping block if they did so," Hawran insisted. "If they expose us, they'll expose themselves. They'd pay with their lives for the fact we wouldn't be able to conduct our operation here without their knowledge. Their duplicity would condemn them, and such men value their own lives and positions of power above all else."

"We should transport the gas canisters as soon as possible," Kaborya suggested. "The sooner we get the poison gas out of here, the better."

"The chemical compounds will be contained in warheads before being sent to the United States, England and France," Hawran reminded the Palestinian. "The artillery needed to deliver the poison payloads has to be constructed in those countries. It would be too risky to try to transport such cannons. They'd be too large to be smuggled into the enemies' countries. An American arms dealer tried to do so when he constructed a giant cannon for Iraq in 1989. The U.S. and British Intelligence discovered the parts of the cannon being transported to Iraq, and someone assassinated the arms dealer."

"I'm aware of that," Kaborya assured him. "I also recall how Erik Hellson tried to sell nuclear cannons two years ago. He'd discovered uranium deposits in Antarctica and used them for nuclear warheads developed at his metallurgy plant in New Zealand. Not sure what went wrong, but his operation was destroyed."

"We can learn from their mistakes," Hawran stated. "The cannons needed will be howitzer-style weapons, not enormous devices or bulky reinforced nuclear cannons. By having the cannons built in the enemy countries, we reduce the risk of transporting weaponry and being discovered while smuggling the devices into their territory."

"We don't know how effective these poisons will be," Kaborya reminded his superior. "Tests done here with animals have been successful, and I know you Iraqis used such devices effectively in the past. Still, the chemicals weren't processed in the primitive conditions we're forced to use here."

"A definitive test will soon prove how effective our poisons are in the field," Hawran said with a smile. "Meantime, you should find something constructive to occupy your time."

He patted the Stechkin on the table and added, "Perhaps you should do a bit more training and spend some time here at the firing range."

"I've spent the past ten years going through repeated training exercises," the Palestinian replied.

"Are you familiar with the Stechkin?" Hawran inquired. "It's a true machine pistol. We got some of these from the Russians when the Soviet Union was still supplying Iraq with a cornucopia of military arms. The Stechkin is an excellent weapon. The only drawback is it chambers the Russian 9 mm round instead of the 9 mm parabellum, which is more widely available throughout the world. Of course, I have the shells reloaded here so I have ample ammunition for my own personal use."

"I thought you and I wouldn't be fighting the enemy in the field," Kaborya replied dryly.

"Combat skills need to be honed constantly, my friend," Hawran insisted. "One never knows when it will be necessary to kill."

ROGER HAMLIN LOOKED AWAY from the glare of the lamp pointed at his face. The London car thief had been the ringleader of the chop-shop operation at Wells's Garage. The police had caught him trying to escape from a back door while his friends panicked and charged into the streets to take on the police with shotguns blazing. Hamlin was furious with them for that act of blind stupidity. A police officer had been killed in the encounter, and Hamlin faced charges of accessory to the murder.

"You're really in it this time, Roger," Inspector White declared as he stepped behind the lamp and towered next to the thief. "They'll put you away for the rest of your life for this—murder, resisting arrest, attempting homicide against police officers in the act of doing their duty, possession of unlawful firearms and assisting enemies of the United Kingdom and France in an act of sabotage that cost the lives of several other people."

"I didn't kill anybody!" Hamlin exclaimed. "Those shit heads what charged you blokes did that! As for sabotage, I don't know anything about that, and you can't pin that rap on me. Where the hell is my lawyer? I got a right to one...."

"You'd better talk to us first, Hamlin," Yakov Katzenelenbogen said as he leaned close to the thief and allowed Hamlin to get a good look at the three hooks of his prosthesis.

Experience had taught Katz that the sight of the steel hooks unnerved many people. That was especially true when a person was locked in an interrogation room in a police station and already scared out of his wits. Hamlin looked away from the Israeli and shut his eyes to avoid the full glare of the light.

"We know you didn't kill anyone," Katz assured him. "We might even believe your story that you didn't know your friends would start shooting when the police arrived. But something made them panic. Was it because you'd recently done business with someone who used your cars for the attack on the embassy?"

"I wouldn't do business with terrorists," Hamlin insisted.

"Maybe you didn't know they were terrorists until after the French embassy was attacked," Katz suggested. "If you cooperate with us, we can drop those murder and sabotage charges. You were just an accessory. We don't want you, Hamlin. Tell us who you sold that VW Rabbit to, and we'll make a deal."

"Sold it to some Pakistanis," Hamlin replied. "Sold them some other autos and a truck, as well."

"Pakistanis?" White asked with a frown. "Where do we find these Pakistanis? You sure that's what they were?"

"I don't know where they are," Hamlin replied. "And how do I know if they were Pakis or not? Bleedin' wogs they were. Said they were Pakis."

"Had you ever done business with these men before?" Katz asked as he took out a pack of cigarettes and offered one to the prisoner.

"Thanks, guv," Hamlin said, and accepted a cigarette. "I never saw them before. The Turk brought them to me. I did business with the Turk before. Since September or October of 1990, I reckon."

"Okay," Katz began and fired up his lighter for Hamlin, "where do we find this Turk?"

"Not sure. I know he doesn't live in London. Has some sort of farm or something like that. Reckon he's into something illegal, but I don't know what. Mind my own business, I do. Clients got a right to their business, and I don't ask too many questions."

"A man of professional ethics," White said sourly. "Don't mess about with us, Roger. You're in no position to hold back information. We don't have to make any deals, and you can still go off to prison for a very long time."

"I'm not holding back anything," Hamlin insisted. "I don't know any more than what I told you. The fucking Turk never used his name. We just knew him as 'the Turk.' Don't need more than that to do business with a man who pays in cash."

"We'll be talking to you later, Hamlin," White told him. "You can go back to your cell and rest for a while. Maybe that'll improve your memory."

An officer escorted the man from the room. Katz lighted a cigarette and strolled into the corridor, followed by White. The inspector gingerly touched the bandage taped across the bridge of his broken nose. He'd interrogate the brute who'd nailed him with the head butt. White was looking forward to that session.

"Well, do you believe him?" the inspector asked.

"I think he was telling the truth," the Israeli answered. "The terrorists wouldn't share any details with bottom-of-the-barrel hoods. It's unlikely the people he was in contact with were really Pakistanis or Turks, but I doubt Hamlin would know the difference if they were Arabs, Iranians or Indonesians."

"If they're pretending to be Pakistanis, we can start looking in the Pakistani neighborhoods here in London," White suggested. "Find out if there's anything suspicious about any of the new residents there."

"I doubt you'll find them in a Pakistani neighborhood," Katz told him. "Imposters might be able to fool some white auto thieves who never set foot outside London, but they'd never be able to convince Pakistanis they were Pakistanis themselves even if they spoke fluent Urdu or Punjabi."

"So where do we look for them?" White inquired, frustrated that even more outsiders seemed to be taking over what he considered his jurisdiction.

"We might do better to look for the Turk that Hamlin mentioned," Katz replied.

Calvin James appeared at the end of the corridor. The black Phoenix warrior and Rafael Encizo had arrived in London less than an hour after the gun battle at Wells's Garage. All five members of Phoenix Force were now in England.

"I hoped I'd find you here," James announced. "We just got some bad news. Something happened at a luxury hotel in Nice. French authorities aren't sure what caused it, but they've found dozens of people in the building dead from some sort of asphyxiation. Sounds like it's probably poison gas."

"How many were killed?" White asked with alarm.

"They're still hauling bodies out of the hotel," James answered. "The body count is already more than seventy."

"My God," the inspector said, shaking his head. "What are these butchers doing? What do they hope to accomplish by this senseless slaughter of innocent people?"

"Terrorists are in the business of creating terror," Katz answered. "I'd say they're accomplishing that goal."

CHAPTER TEN

The death toll at the Hôtel Suprême was eighty-three
by the time Katz, James and Manning arrived in Nice.
The resort city along the Riviera was a favorite spot for
tourists, usually associated with sunny beaches, colorful nightclubs and other playgrounds for those able
to afford them. It wasn't a place one expected to find
mass murder.

Pierre Bertin frowned when the trio approached him
as he stood near an ambulance parked outside the police cordon that surrounded the hotel. Lights flashed
and rotated atop police cars, and television crews from
half a dozen countries struggled to film the tragedy.
Police and firemen emerged from the hotel, carrying
prone figures on stretchers. The rescuers wore heavy
coveralls, gloves and gas masks for protection from
whatever invisible substance had invaded the building.

Some of the figures on the stretchers were draped in
blankets, with oxygen masks strapped to their faces.
Others lay motionless, their faces covered by blankets. TV cameras pointed at the grisly burdens, then
scanned the area to record the horrified faces of the
spectators that ringed the cordoned-off area.

Bertin was sickened and frustrated. The slaughter at
the hotel and the press preying on the disaster like a
flock of voyeur vultures was enough to enrage him.

Seeing the three mysterious commandos from the United States didn't improve his disposition. The Sûreté officer recognized the members of Phoenix Force. They'd been in Paris during a mission in 1988, and Bertin had worked with them. He couldn't deny they were very good at their business, highly skilled and as brave as lions in combat. However, they were also a pain in the rear.

"Welcome to Nice, gentlemen," Bertin said. "I'm sorry the circumstances of your visit aren't more pleasant."

"*Quoi?*" Calvin James replied with a puzzled expression.

"*Je ne comprends pas,*" Katz added in a flustered manner. "*Parlez-vous français, monsieur?*"

"*Oui,*" Bertin stated, and switched from English to French. "Of course I speak my native language."

"Let's try to avoid attracting attention," Katz urged in a quiet tone. "Speaking in a language other than French in this crowd might draw the American and British news crews this way."

"The less I see of them the better," Bertin remarked. "There's nothing to see here except what you have already witnessed. Come with me. We can talk privately. That is best."

The predawn sky was beginning to display the first streaks of morning light. Dark gray clouds dominated the sky and contributed to the lugubrious atmosphere of the solemn and gruesome scene. Bertin escorted the Phoenix commandos to a moving van parked by a curb. A man inside the vehicle rolled up the door to the back of the rig, and the Sûreté officer and the three commandos entered.

The interior was lined with surveillance equipment—tape recorders were mounted to the walls; closed-circuit television monitors showed different angles of the streets as a camera revolved from its hiding place on the roof. Bertin's assistant was even smaller, thinner and more bald than his superior.

"I take it that if you men are on this case there must be a connection with the hotel incident and the recent embassy sabotage," Bertin remarked. "By the way, I notice your two friends aren't here. The Briton and the Latin American."

"They're still in England," Gary Manning answered. "Our Hispanic amigo doesn't speak French, so we figured it was best he stayed with our other friend. He's more familiar with London so it made sense for him to stay there."

"Good," Bertin stated. He didn't like the British in general, and he particularly disliked the sharp-tongued Cockney. "As you've seen with your own eyes, the sabotage at the hotel is even worse than the embassy bombing. At least, if we judge such actions by the number of victims. Some survivors were taken to hospitals, but the doctors believe many won't live more than a few hours."

"What happened to them?" James inquired as he leaned against a wall and glanced down at a printout sheet.

"Chlorine gas. It was released into the air-conditioning system. The gas flowed through the air ducts and drifted from vents into the rooms throughout the building. Canisters of the gas were found with hoses linked to the air-conditioner system."

"Bastards," Manning muttered, and shook his head. "Why'd they pick an obscure place like the Hôtel Suprême? I'm glad they didn't use the gas in a larger resort because more people would have died, but I was wondering if any of the guests might have been specific targets of terrorists."

"Probably picked it because the air-conditioning system was easy to sabotage using the chlorine gas," James answered. "Most of the larger resorts probably have better filters and more-complicated air ducts. The gas would be dissipated and ineffective."

"That's what our experts in such matters think, too," Bertin stated, surprised by James's deduction. "Unfortunately no one has any idea who might be responsible. There are theories that the Iraqis might be behind this because the attacks on French, American and British embassies occurred simultaneously. You're aware another terrorist bombing took place in the United States?"

"In Virginia," Katz said with a nod. "We received word of the incident just before we left London. That hit doesn't appear to have been as well planned as the one here. Perhaps that means the terrorists have been in Nice for some time or one of their agents is familiar with the city and the resort hotels here."

"They'd have to know the hotel pretty well to be aware of the construction and weaknesses in the air-conditioning system," James insisted. "My guess is it had to be an inside job. Could be somebody on the hotel staff or someone who would have worked on the air conditioner. Maybe even the people who installed it."

"Sounds like a good place to start," Bertin agreed. He wondered if the Afro-American had been a cop at one time. The suggestion was a simple police procedure that might well be accurate. "We'll start checking on the hotel personnel and individuals involved in the maintenance and installation of the air conditioner. Any other ideas?"

"We're checking some leads in England," Katz replied. "Other members of our organization are involved in the investigations of terrorism in the United States. Any success in one area should help us find the terrorists responsible for all the terrorist activity because these are all clearly related."

"I hope you're right," Bertin commented glumly. "There's a possibility the mass murder here was the act of some copycat lunatics."

"Nothing is impossible," Manning remarked, "but I'd say that's extremely unlikely. The carnage at the hotel seems to have been planned some time in advance. It doesn't look like some sick whim. It can be a danger to postulate based on limited evidence, but I think we'll find all these incidents are connected."

"Probably," Bertin said with a massive shrug. "So where do we go from here?"

"We need to see inside the hotel for ourselves," James answered. "See if you can get us gas masks and protective gear so we can go in. We'll also need detailed information about the embassy bombing. Anything and everything Sûreté and CIA have."

"Are you in contact with the CIA case officer assigned to the U.S. Embassy in Paris?" Bertin inquired.

"Not yet," Katz replied, "but we'll have to meet with him and the others involved in the investigation. Are you connected with the Paris case?"

"Yes. Almost everyone in Sûreté was called in for the incident. However, I was sent here because other officers with more-senior ranking are in charge."

"We want you for our liaison officer," Katz said. "We've worked with you before, and we need someone we can trust. Sûreté will give you all the authority you'll need to get results for us. If any of your superiors don't like that, we'll take care of them. If we can't convince them to cooperate, I'm sure the presidents of the United States and France can."

Bertin only shrugged, but the gesture belied the satisfaction he felt that the Phoenix pros held him in enough esteem to want him as their main source with Sûreté. He also knew that the mysterious warriors could wield the influence they claimed through their connections with the White House and whatever supersecret organization they belonged to.

"Well, gentlemen," Bertin began, "let's get to work."

MACK BOLAN WASN'T SURE what time it was. He awoke aboard the C-130 transport as it began to descend for a landing. He glanced at his wristwatch, but realized it was still set to Washington time. The Executioner glanced out a port window and saw the harsh glare of sunlight. He saw little else and turned his attention to the gear he carried for the mission.

Stony Man had learned about the hotel terrorism in Nice and immediately contacted Bolan and Able Team in D.C. The Executioner was called back to the Farm for a briefing about the newest incident in France. Because Phoenix Force would divide their personnel to cover France and England simultaneously, Brognola and Price decided Bolan was needed in Europe to back up Phoenix. The Stony Man boss and the mission controller extrapolated that the next terrorist strike was likely to occur in England, since attacks had already occurred in the U.S. and France. All three countries had been targeted by the enemy.

Bolan couldn't fault this logic, but he wasn't sure this was the best strategy. Able Team was pursuing a dangerous source of information in D.C. and the trio might need his help more than the Phoenix warriors. Also, trying to second-guess terrorists was often futile because they operated in a manner that didn't always follow a pattern. The salient nature of the hit-and-run attacks didn't mean their next attack would be in England. Unless Phoenix Force had some idea where the terrorists might strike, little would be gained if they simply had to examine another site of destruction instead of preventing it.

Able Team would receive direct support from the rest of Stony Man, as well as the combined Intel and police agencies involved in the D.C. and Richmond investigations. Bolan wished he had more faith in some of those outfits. All too often, local cops and Feds competed with one another instead of cooperating to reach a common goal. They could get bogged down trying to find out what one another knew and trying to keep the competition from learning evidence they discovered. They could foul up an operation with pettiness, ego and bureaucracy.

Phoenix Force and Bolan would face the same problems in Europe.

The warrior unbuckled his safety belt as the plane touched down and taxied to a halt. He gathered up the duffel bag and slung it over his shoulder. There were no other passengers aboard the big plane, no one to ask what he had inside the bag. Bolan opened the sliding door and climbed down to the runway.

David McCarter, Rafael Encizo and Hudson Connors waited for Bolan beside a Land Rover parked near the runway. The warrior climbed into the back of the rig and placed the bag by his feet. The Stony Man operatives exchanged brief but sincere greetings, and McCarter introduced Bolan to the CIA officer. Connors didn't seem thrilled with the meeting. It seemed to him that hotshots with White House authority seemed to be arriving every eight hours, and all of them acted as if the CIA was supposed to be their willing servant.

"Are the other three in Nice?" Bolan inquired as Encizo sat next to him.

"Yeah," the Cuban confirmed. "They'll be in France for a while. We got a message that they're looking into some possible evidence at the hotel killings and the U.S. Embassy bombing in Paris."

McCarter was behind the steering wheel, and as he started the engine and drove the Rover from the runway Connors told Bolan that they'd arranged for customs to be waived and they could leave Heathrow without delay or inspection of the new arrival's luggage. The Executioner nodded. He knew this had been arranged before he left Stony Man Farm.

"What progress have you made here so far?" Bolan asked.

The others told him about the chop-shop raid and the information squeezed from Roger Hamlin. The Executioner was interested by the story about "the Turk" and wanted to know if they'd discovered any evidence that supported the car thief's claim that he was introduced to the alleged Pakistanis by such a person.

"Bandon came up with something," McCarter answered. "He's the SIS bloke. Turns out there's a fellow named Mohammed Kemel who has a small farm thirty miles outside London. Kemel is registered as a Turkish national, but he's on a list to try to qualify for British citizenship in the future. Not surprising since he's been spending flippin' great wads of cash since he arrived back in 1990."

"What's he been spending it on?" Bolan asked.

"Rented the farm for two years up front," McCarter answered. "Kemel has also stocked up on large amounts of canned food, bottled water, tea—mostly Turkish blend—lots of mutton, lamb and some beef."

"Bandon found out where the guy does most of his grocery shopping and got the information from talkative clerks," Connors explained. "They also found out he's bought a lot of blankets, cots and other stuff that suggests he either has some guests staying at the farmhouse or expects company soon."

"Sounds like this could be a base of operations," Bolan remarked. "Have you run a recon on the place?"

"Not yet," Encizo replied. "We heard you were coming, so we wanted to be here to pick you up in person and brief you on the mission so far."

"Then let's check this farm out as soon as possible and find out what's going on. The sooner the better. Our HQ brain center suspects the next terrorist attack will be somewhere in England and they'll probably carry it out pretty soon. If you guys have uncovered a terrorist base, we need to hit it before the enemy can strike again."

"Bloody right," McCarter agreed. "About time these bastards were on the receiving end. So far all the points are on their side of the scoreboard."

"Wait a minute," Connors began. "You can't just charge in there like John Wayne or Rambo or who-ever you guys think you are. For one thing, it'll take time to assemble enough commandos from the SAS or the Royal Marines to handle something like this."

"Time is something we can't afford to waste," Bolan told him. "Too many lives are at stake. We'll put together whatever we can for an assault unit, but we have to do it quickly. Even if just the three of us have to do this without backup."

"Why not?" McCarter said with a grin. "We've faced bad odds in the past."

"But most people aren't that eager to do it again," Encizo said with a sigh.

CHAPTER ELEVEN

Mary Packer gave birth to a son on April 4, 1967, in a so-called clinic on Twelfth Street that wouldn't have made a fit kennel. Young, poor and single, Mary named her child Martin Luther in honor of the great civil rights leader because she wanted him to have a name to live up to. The following year, on her son's first birthday, Rev. Martin Luther King, Jr., was assassinated in Memphis. Mary feared this would be an ill omen for herself and her offspring.

And she was right.

Luther Packer grew up in the tough ghettoes of Washington, D.C., with crime and poverty his main influence. His mother adopted a life-style of despair and turned to prostitution for extra income. The money went to support her heroin habit, and it was never enough to satisfy the monkey on her back. She blamed her miserable existence on her son. Mary tried to convince herself she'd be doing just fine if she wasn't saddled with a "worthless bastard brat." The boy was a victim of her frustrations, as well as the harsh environment of the D.C. jungle.

His mother died from a heroin overdose when Luther was fourteen. He was shuffled to foster homes more concerned with picking up an extra check from the government than raising a child who'd been severely scarred emotionally and mentally. The lad fell in with gangs and soon landed in a juvenile reform school for criminal behavior. When he returned to the streets, he graduated to felony crimes and began selling drugs in the Georgetown area.

This proved to be Luther Packer's road to power. Cocaine had become the most valuable drug on the street, but it remained beyond the price range of many potential customers. The introduction of crack allowed the coke syndicates to reach such individuals. Packer was one of the first D.C. dealers to appreciate the possibility of this market. He had read how popular smoking coca paste had become in Peru and Brazil and guessed the same concept could be very lucrative in the States. Packer considered himself to be a man of vision.

By the end of the 1980s, Packer controlled a criminal syndicate with more than two hundred employees. These ranged from mules and pushers to accountants and lawyers. Twenty-four years old and he had the world by the ass.

Packer's Mafia was one of the most feared organizations in D.C., and "Don Luther" lived like a king. He made a fortune every week. Of course, he had expenses. He had to be certain his people were trustworthy, and loyalty could be expensive. Suppliers had to be paid, police and auditors had to be bribed, other costs bit into Packer's profits in order to stay in business. He paid these expenses because they were necessary. Don Luther knew there'd always be someone waiting to take his place, and if the people he did business with were dissatisfied, they wouldn't hesitate to take him out and proclaim a new don.

Packer still enjoyed opulence far greater than any-thing he could have imagined as a child. He sat in the back of the long white limousine as it headed along K Street for Washington Circle. He wore a black suit with thin blue pinstripes, and a houndstooth tie. No flashy colors that looked as if he was trying to resem-ble a rainbow trout or big hats with oversized brims for Don Luther. Dignity and class were the images he wished to convey.

Sandra Sheppard sat beside the don. A stunning blonde with an alabaster complexion, she wore a low-cut evening gown and an array of jewelry worth a for-tune. Packer's woman had to present a special image, as well. The limo driver and a bodyguard filled the front seat. They were big, muscle-bound men who carried pistols under their tailored jackets in case they encountered trouble they couldn't handle with their fists. More bodyguards rode in the cars that escorted the limo. Don Luther always traveled with heavy se-curity.

The caravan approached the restaurant where Luther had reservations, and he was annoyed to dis-cover two large delivery trucks parked at the curb in front of the restaurant.

"I can't believe they're using your parking space," Sandra complained, pouting. "Call the management on the car phone and tell them to move those awful trucks."

"Deliveries are made in the rear," Packer said, sensing danger. "Something's wrong. Might be a trap..."

One of the trucks pulled away from the curb and rolled up the street. Packer recognized the red dinner jacket, black trousers and ruffled white shirt as the uniform of the restaurant's waiters, but he wasn't familiar with the face of the guy who emerged from the door. The man gestured angrily and said something to a pair of men dressed in work clothes. The pair carried large boxes and headed for the remaining truck. The maître d' followed them to the curb.

"Want us to keep goin', Mr. Packer?" the limo driver asked, obviously disturbed by the presence of the truck.

"No, Eddie. It's okay. These white boys just screwed up. Pull up behind the truck. I want to see how much the maître d' will grovel when we get out. Does my heart good to have a honkie kiss my ass."

He looked at Sandra's lily-white face and blue eyes. Packer smiled and said, "No offense, baby."

"Sure, Luther," she answered with a shrug.

"There ain't gonna be room for Joe and Leon to park unless they pull into the lot," Eddie commented, worried about dividing the security forces.

"Hell, they can circle around the block and come back after the truck's gone," Packer replied. "Only take a couple of minutes."

The limo moved up to the curb behind the delivery truck. One car of bodyguards pulled in behind the long white vehicle, but the other car loaded with Luther's protectors had to keep going for lack of a parking space in front of the building.

Joe and Leon were probably cussing up a storm as they discovered they'd have to go around the block again. Packer was amused by this and thought the bodyguards would have little trouble finding their way back. After all, they don't call it Washington Circle for nothing.

Tommy Hambert emerged from the passenger's side at the front of the limo. More than six feet tall and weighing more than three hundred pounds, Tommy was one big mean mother. He stationed himself by the back door, but waited for Eddie to get out and actually open the door. The driver was nearly as big as Tommy, but he was a little smarter and less vicious than the behemoth bodyguard.

Don Luther and his woman stepped from the limo. He made a show of adjusting his necktie and looked at the maître d' with disdain. Packer was surprised when he saw the guy close up. The dude had gray hair and he wore the sissy waiter's uniform, but his face was hard. He didn't look like a man you wanted to piss off.

"Hello, Packer," Gadgets Schwarz announced as he folded his arms on his chest. "We've been expecting you."

"About time you got here," Carl Lyons complained, and tossed his box onto the hood of the limo. "We need to talk, guy."

It was clear the "workmen" were no more genuine than the guy in the waiter suit. Lyons approached Packer, and Tommy stepped forward. The blond-headed Able warrior was pretty big, but the bodyguard was easily the heavier of the two. He figured he could knock Lyons in the gutter with a single clothesline under the chin. It was Tommy's favorite move. He had once broken a man's neck with the clothesline blow when he was playing football in high school. The bodyguard would be glad to do the same for this snotty honkie bastard.

"You got a badge and a warrant?" Tommy demanded. "If you do, better show 'em now. Otherwise, fuck off while you still got your head between your shoulders."

"I wasn't talking to you," Lyons replied. "I don't have time to waste on idiots like you."

Tommy bellowed with rage and charged. He swung his forearm for Lyons's head with all his massive weight behind the stroke. His forearm slashed air as his intended target seemed to vanish before the clothesline could connect. The bodyguard stumbled, thrown off balance by his own momentum.

Lyons had simply ducked and sidestepped the attack. He moved behind the slow-witted thug and slammed a fist to the man's kidney. The Able Team commando stomped the back of Tommy's knee and hammered another fist between the brute's shoulder blades. The hardguy's leg buckled, and he fell face-first into the hood of the limo.

"Shit!" Eddie exclaimed, and reached inside his jacket for his piece.

"No way!" Schwarz warned as he swiftly drew his own Colt Python from shoulder leather and pointed it at the driver.

Eddie brought out his hand with nothing but fingers and thrust his arms overhead.

Sandra grabbed Packer's arm and squeezed hard. He was stunned. The blond guy continued to beat the hell out of Tommy. He had the man by the hair and slammed his head into the limo. The bogus waiter had the drop on Eddie, and Packer realized he'd never make it back inside the limo to try to get the gun hidden in the bar compartment.

Shouts of alarm announced that the other bodyguards were getting out of the car behind the limo. Three members of Don Luther's security force rushed forward, guns in hand. They saw Lyons and Schwarz, but failed to notice Rosario Blancanales. Pol had taken advantage of the distraction to move along the side of the limo opposite from the sidewalk where the conflict took place. He rose from cover, a Heckler & Koch MP-5 submachine gun in his fists. The trio glimpsed the movement and swung their weapons toward the new threat.

Blancanales opened fire, spraying the bodyguards with 9 mm parabellums. Two opponents went down, their chests chopped open by the high-velocity slugs. Vital organs destroyed, the gunners thrashed about on the sidewalk, blood leaking from the fatal wounds.

The third gunman had avoided the lethal volley by accident more than deliberate action. Startled, he'd been off balance when the shooting erupted and stumbled clear of the line of fire. He still held a Colt .45 pistol and started to point it at Blancanales.

Schwarz's Python roared. A 158-grain hollowpoint projectile smashed into the gunman's chest, left of center. His heart demolished, the bodyguard spun from the impact of the .357 Magnum round and collapsed beside the still forms of his slain comrades.

Gadgets returned the aim of his big revolver to cover Eddie and Don Luther. Neither man had a death wish. They didn't try to reach for a weapon, aware the three mysterious warriors were too skilled and quick to expect such a tactic to be successful.

Lyons pointed a finger at Packer. "Get your ass in the truck," he ordered, his expression suggesting he didn't intend to accept a refusal.

Luther pried Sandra from his arm and walked to the delivery vehicle. He glanced at the street, hoping the second team of bodyguards might arrive. Packer was surprised to notice there was virtually no traffic in front of the restaurant. He didn't see any pedestrians nearby, either. Several figures appeared from the restaurant. They wore dark jackets with FBI in bright yellow letters printed across the front.

Special Agent Anderson was among the group. He carried a two-way radio in one hand. The other rested on the grips of a SIG-Sauer automatic holstered on his hip. The FBI man looked at the bodies of the slain bodyguards and shook his head.

"You guys said there wouldn't be any shooting unless it was necessary."

"It sure seemed necessary to us," Blancanales replied as he canted the MP-5 across a shoulder. "Did your people pick up the rest of Packer's people?"

"The D.C. cops stopped them at one of the roadblocks," the agent confirmed. "That was a good idea to block off the street after the limo arrived. Reduced the risk to innocent bystanders."

"That's why we did it," Schwarz declared. "You guys look after Packer's girlfriend and henchmen. We need to talk to Don Luther in private."

"I hope you guys know what you're doing," Anderson remarked. "We're bending an awful lot of rules here."

"Yeah," Lyons agreed with a shrug. "Feels good, doesn't it?"

THERE WERE NO WINDOWS in the back of the box-shaped delivery truck. Luther didn't know where they were taking him as he sat on the floor with two of the hard-eyed men who kidnapped him. They ignored his demands to talk to his lawyers.

"You don't need your lawyers because you're not under arrest," Blancanales informed him. "We just want to ask you some questions."

"And you'd better answer them," Lyons added. "You're a low-life drug dealer, Packer. I won't have any qualms about breaking your neck. Killing you would be a public service."

"Take it easy," Blancanales urged. "Packer will be taken out some other time. Right now we have other matters to deal with."

Packer wasn't sure if they were playing "good cop, bad cop" with him. He'd seen both men take out his bodyguards with ruthless skill. Neither could pass as a good cop, in Don Luther's opinion. To him, the only good cop was one he could buy off.

"A man in your position within the crime world makes a lot of contacts," Pol began. "I'm sure you know all about black-market firearms."

"I don't deal in guns," Packer stated. "Washington, D.C., has one of the strictest gun-control laws in the country."

"Yeah," Lyons said with a sneer, "and the highest homicide rate. Gun control just keeps honest people from having weapons for self-defense while scum like you ignore the law and use guns to commit crimes. Don't bullshit us that you care about breaking gun-control laws. Selling crack to schoolkids is illegal, too, and that doesn't seem to bother you."

"We don't have time for debates," Blancanales stated. "Somebody sold military hardware to terrorists. We figure they got some or all of their weapons from arms dealers here in D.C. Now, we want to know what you've heard about it."

"I don't know what the hell you're talking about," Packer replied.

"I was hoping you'd say that," Lyons said. "That means we have to force the information out of you. We're taking you to a nice remote area where you can scream your lungs out and nobody will hear. Maybe a few broken bones will improve your memory."

"You can't use confessions you get that way," Packer insisted. "That's not admissible in court."

"You've got the legal jargon down pretty well for a piece of street trash who pretends he's something more than a common gutter hood," Lyons remarked. "Trouble is, we don't intend to take you to court. If you don't talk, we'll work you over and they'll never find your body. If we can't get the guys we're after, at least we can rid society of you. That's not a bad consolation prize, if you ask me."

Packer looked away from Lyons. The big guy's cold blue eyes sent a chill through the gangster's body. This sort of thing wasn't supposed to happen to him. He was Don Luther. He was king of the jungle in D.C. and nobody leaned on the don. But these hardasses were serious, and they didn't give a damn about Packer's status as self-proclaimed master of the city.

"I don't know shit about terrorists," Packer began, "but I heard some Hanafis have been stockpiling a lot of heavy weapons. Automatic rifles, explosives, military shit."

"Hanafis?" Pol inquired. "Muslim scholars recognize the Hanafi school of Islamic law as one of the five systems used by Muslims to cover laws not included in the Koran. The Hanafi school of law is used in several Islamic countries, but is not part of American law."

"What?" Don Luther replied, confused by Blancanales's remark and surprised that the tough-looking Hispanic was knowledgeable about Islam. "Look, the motherfuckers call themselves Hanafi Muslims. I don't know about schools of law or that stuff. They're sort of a splinter group of the Hanafi Muslims who took over those buildings back in 1976. Maybe it was 1977. I'm not sure."

"I know what you're talking about," Lyons assured him. "A gang of fanatics who called themselves Hanafi Muslims made headlines all across the country when they invaded three buildings and held dozens of people hostage for almost a week. Probably got the idea after a guy named Cory Moore held some people hostage with a shotgun in Youngstown, Ohio, a few days before the Hanafis made their move. Moore had some weird demands. First he wanted all the white people to vanish from the face of the earth."

"Did he have any idea where you folks were supposed to go?" Blancanales inquired with amusement.

"Not that I remember," Lyons said. "I recall he also wanted to speak to President Jimmy Carter. The President admitted it might not be a good idea to talk with the guy because it might encourage others to imitate him. Carter got on the phone and chatted with Moore anyway. Moore wanted Carter to get on TV and publicly apologize for whites oppressing blacks for three hundred years or something like that. Carter didn't go along with that demand. When the Hanafi Muslims pulled their hostage act, Carter refused to talk to them period."

"I remember that now," Blancanales declared. "Those were the guys who threatened to start chopping off heads with machetes if their demands weren't met. Pretty strange demands, too. They wanted some movie to be banned from theaters. A movie about Muhammad the Prophet they considered to be blasphemy?"

"Yeah," Lyons confirmed. "They also wanted Muhammad Ali brought to them so they could kill him. I'm not sure what they had against him. They wound up surrendering without getting any demands met."

He looked at Packer and said, "I don't recall hearing much about that outfit since." Lyons studied the gangster's face and asked, "So the Hanafi Muslims are stockpiling weapons?"

"A splinter group," the don explained. "Similar to the same gang of Hanafis who pulled the hostage stunt here in D.C. back in the late seventies. They've been buying guns and explosives from D.C. arms dealers who have access to military compounds and stuff like that. They call themselves the African Crusaders, but don't get them confused with the Black Muslims or any other Afro-American movement. These guys are too crazy for anybody to want to throw in with."

"Are they based here in D.C.?" Blancanales inquired.

"No. I think they're in Virginia or Maryland. If they were operating out of my city, I'd know more about them. Not that I'd want to do business with them.''

"Muslims are opposed to drugs," Lyons commented. "It's against their religion to drink alcohol, let alone get into the shit guys like you peddle. Aren't the Black Muslims in New York driving crack dealers out of their neighborhoods?"

"Hey, I wouldn't do business with those assholes anyway," Packer insisted. "Especially with the African Crusaders. Those guys are big supporters of the Islamic jihad. *Any* jihad. They used to praise Idi Amin and the Ayatollah. More recently they've been going on about how great Saddam Hussein is supposed to be."

"And you're a real patriot, huh," Lyons snorted. "Well, I hate to admit it, but you've given us a pretty good lead to follow up. Guess we have to let you go because you cooperated with us."

Don Luther's eyes widened with surprise. He figured they would either kill him or frame him for some crime if they didn't have enough proof to put him away.

"Don't think we condone what you do," Pol added. "We happen to be men of honor and we keep our word, even when we give it to a drug-dealing bastard like you."

"What about my people?" Packer asked.

"They'll probably walk, too," Lyons answered. "Unless the Feds found them packing heat without a permit or they were carrying crack in their pockets or in the vehicle. The official story on the guys we killed will be they got shot down in a gunfight with a rival gang. I trust you're not stupid enough to argue with that version."

"No way," Packer assured him. "I just want to walk away from this mess and let you guys go after whoever it is you really want."

"You'll walk today," Lyons stated in a hard voice, "but I'm not going to forget you, Packer. If somebody else doesn't take you down—either the cops, the Feds or another gang—we'll catch up with you in the future. Next time you won't walk, guy. That's a promise."

He pounded on the door and told Schwarz to stop the truck. The vehicle came to a halt, and Lyons opened the door. Don Luther climbed from the rig. He looked up at a street sign that revealed he was on M Street, not that far from Washington Circle. The sons of bitches had been driving around D.C. all the time.

The truck moved on. Packer didn't turn to look until he was sure the rig was out of sight. He was relieved to be free and still in one piece, but he realized the three tough men who had abducted him for the Q-and-A session would keep their word about coming after him in the future just as they'd kept their word when they released him.

Don Luther no longer felt as if he was the king of the jungle. He'd met a trio of bigger, tougher lions who could come take his crown and bury his ass anytime they wanted. Packer's skin crawled with fear because he knew his days were numbered.

CHAPTER TWELVE

The farm was one of many along the quiet English countryside. From a distance it appeared to be a harmless little spread with a small flock of sheep grazing in the rich green fields. The house was two stories high, and the barn was approximately the same size. The buildings were a bit shabby and battered by the exposure to extremes of weather.

Mack Bolan observed the farm through a Night Observation Device. He was familiar with NODs, and the SAS model was smaller and better made than the bulky AN/TVS-4 he'd used for night recon in Vietnam. The Executioner examined the farm from a distance of about one thousand meters. The NOD could have been used at twice that distance, but Bolan had found a group of trees on a hill that provided good concealment, as well as an ideal vantage point to spy on the property of Mohammed Kemel.

The place wasn't as tranquil as it seemed. Two trucks and three automobiles were parked by the house and barn, and young men were posted by the vehicles. They were lean and tough looking, and were dressed in green work clothes that resembled fatigue uniforms. Despite the agreeable weather, every man carried a canteen on his belt along with magazine pouches and sheathed knives.

"I think we can safely assume we've found a nest of terrorists," Bolan announced. "Probably well trained in military or paramilitary camps somewhere in the Middle East."

David McCarter looked through the NOD while Bolan got to his feet and reached for an M-16 assault rifle propped against a tree trunk. An M-203 grenade launcher was attached to the underside of the barrel. Inspector White looked at the big warrior and frowned. The Executioner was dressed in a blacksuit, pistols in shoulder leather, and his harness and belt adorned with grenades, ammo pouches, knives and garrotes.

"What makes you think they've been trained in the Middle East?" the man from Scotland Yard demanded.

"Because they're carrying canteens. The farm has a good water supply with a well and indoor plumbing. Those guys are accustomed to carrying an individual water supply in case of emergencies and are probably used to needing water to compensate for loss of body moisture due to extreme heat. That probably means they're from a desert environment."

"Bloody Iraqis," Captain Fairton remarked as he canted a Sterling subgun across his shoulder. "Suspected they were behind this from the start."

Dressed in a dark uniform and flak vest, Fairton wore a sand-colored beret with the SAS insignia of a winged dagger. The Special Air Service had supplied Bolan and the Phoenix pair with a CRW assault group. The captain and his men were trained in counterterrorism and were more than willing to take on the opponents at the farm.

Bolan was pleased they'd gotten the SAS for assistance in the raid. It was one of the best antiterrorist outfits in the world. A soldier all of his adult life, Bolan had more faith in true military combat professionals than espionage agents or police officers. The others might be fine at their jobs, but when it came to war the best choice for the battlefield would always be a warrior.

McCarter was naturally happy to be working with his old regiment again, and his presence made the SAS more agreeable to taking orders from outsiders. They didn't know Bolan, Rafael Encizo or McCarter. Indeed, only McCarter was using his real name for the mission. However, the British commandos knew about Operation Nimrod, and McCarter had been part of it. That was good enough to convince them the mysterious Yanks had to know what they were doing, as well.

"Let's get our men into position," Bolan announced. "We went over this earlier today. Everybody knows what he's supposed to do. Any questions, better ask them now."

"You can't just charge in and start killing these people regardless of what they've done or what you suspect them of doing," White declared stiffly. "This is still a civilized country, and we're bound by laws and codes of proper conduct."

"We don't want to kill anyone," Encizo assured him. The Cuban commando was annoyed by White's attitude. The Scotland Yard inspector seemed to think they were deranged homicidal maniacs who found some emotional pleasure in the taking of human life.

"The problem is, the terrorists don't feel the same way."

"And you don't intend to even give them a chance to surrender?" White demanded. "I arrest people. I don't kill them."

"Then keep out of our way," McCarter growled, his temper beginning to boil.

"Inspector." Bolan didn't raise his voice, but an austere edge in the tone arrested White's attention. "We have a job to do. We don't know what sort of weapons the enemy has at the farm, but we know they used poison gas in Nice and explosives at four other locations. We can't afford to take any chances with these people."

"There are still laws..." White began.

"There's only one law in a situation like this," the Executioner said, cutting him off. "We have to stop them by whatever means possible. You can arrest anyone left when this is over."

Bolan drew his Beretta and attached a silencer. His shoulder holster was specially designed to accommodate the extra bulk, and he returned the 93-R to leather. Captain Fairton nodded, satisfied the debate was over and it was time to get to work.

"Let's do it," Bolan confirmed.

The Stony Man commandos and the SAS forces moved out in prearranged groups. The men were well armed. The SAS carried L1A1 assault rifles or Heckler & Koch MP-5 subguns. Encizo elected to use an H&K instead of an assault rifle or his Phoenix-standard micro-Uzi. McCarter tended to carry as much weaponry as possible into combat. He bor-

rowed an L1A1 in addition to his Uzi machine pistol.
Every man also had side arms, knives and grenades.

They surrounded the farm and assumed positions
based on individual expertise. The best rifle marks-
men remained at a distance to supply cover fire for the
others. Bolan, McCarter, Encizo and several CRW
troopers advanced while Captain Fairton commanded the backup forces. Stealth was paramount for
the Stony Man warriors and the SAS soldiers who accompanied them. They crept forward silently, using
the darkness and surrounding foliage to conceal their
movement.

The strike team had to crawl much of the way, using the unkempt grass and even the sheep for cover.
The docile animals bleated in alarm as the men crept
closer. Bolan froze in place, his body prone and the
M-16 pointed at the men near the vehicles. He knew
the others would assume the same ready stance, prepared for violence if the terrorists realized they were in
danger.

However, the men at the farm ignored the sheep.
The timid creatures bleated too often for the terrorists to pay heed to the warning. Mack Bolan continued to low-crawl to the barn. Then he got to his feet
and drew his Beretta.

McCarter and Encizo reached the farmhouse and
also prepared for action. The British ace had attached a silencer to the muzzle of his Browning Hi-
Power and held the pistol in a two-handed Weaver's
combat grip. McCarter pressed his back to the side of
the house and listened to the sound of footfalls. The
noise grew louder as someone approached the building.

Encizo raised a hand and signaled for McCarter to stay put. The Cuban warrior held the Cold Steel Tanto knife in his other fist. The Briton nodded and stayed in place while Encizo moved to the corner of the house. The footsteps came closer. The Cuban waited, knife held ready.

One of the men who had been stationed by the vehicles walked to the side of the house. He started to unbutton his trousers to relieve himself. The young terrorist had moved to the edge of the house to carry out this function in private, beyond the view of his comrades. He stepped around the corner and found Encizo waiting for him.

The Cuban plunged the slanted tip of the knife into the hollow of the man's throat. He grabbed the guy's shirtfront and slammed him against the wall as blood gushed from the terrible wound. Encizo saw the terror and pain in his opponent's eyes fade as life seeped away.

"A little messy," McCarter whispered.

Encizo responded with an erect middle finger and lowered the corpse to the ground. McCarter moved to the edge of the house and peered around the corner. Three men were still positioned by the vehicles. None of them seemed to be aware their friend had been dispatched from the realm of the living. The British commando judged the distance to be approximately thirty meters as he raised his Browning autoloader.

The muted reports of Bolan's silenced Beretta spoke first. One of the terrorists grunted and stumbled into the side of a four-door automobile, a trio of parabellum bullet holes in his chest. Another opponent grabbed his M-16 assault rifle. McCarter quickly sighted his weapon and squeezed the trigger. A 9 mm slug smashed into the gunman's forehead and blasted away his life before he could use his rifle.

The third terrorist dived for cover, his mouth open to cry for help and attempt to warn the others at the farm. Bolan followed the man's movement through the sights of his Beretta and fired another 3-round burst. The silenced 93-R coughed harshly, and two parabellums struck the guy in the side of the head and took him out of play.

The Executioner moved from the barn and padded silently to the collection of vehicles, M-16 in one hand and Beretta in the other. He adopted a cover position by the motor pool while several SAS troopers closed in. Some headed for the barn, others approached the house and the rest took up a defensive perimeter at strategic points around the property.

Without warning, a volley of automatic gunfire erupted from the hayloft at the second story of the barn. A sharp-eyed terrorist had spotted two SAS commandos and tried to blast the pair. He struck one man, but the other SAS soldier dived to the ground and rolled to cover by the brick well.

Bolan saw the muzzle-flash of the enemy weapon and heard the groan of the wounded trooper. There was no point in continued efforts at stealth, so the Executioner figured it was time to fight fire with greater firepower. He raised his M-16, adjusted the aim for the M-203 and triggered the grenade launcher. The recoil of the attachment rode through the rifle frame, and the kick jarred Bolan's hip. A 40 mm grenade hurtled from the big bore of the weapon and sailed in a high arc to the barn.

It descended into the opening of the hayloft like a vengeful meteorite. The shell exploded on impact, the blast tearing out one side of the barn and blowing a great hole in the roof. Hay, chunks of wood and various human body parts spewed from the ragged threshold of the loft. Flames appeared in what remained of the top portion of the barn.

"The gloves are definitely off now," the Executioner said as the battlefield blossomed all around him.

THE EXPLOSION TRIGGERED immediate reactions from both the terrorists and the assault unit. Windows shattered as rifle and submachine gun barrels smashed glass to open fire on anything that moved outside. The SAS forces had already targeted windows and doors. Their weapons responded as soon as a human shape appeared at an opening. Three terrorists were picked off before they could fire a single shot.

"I hope these guys are careful who they're shooting at," Encizo muttered as he ducked low along the side of the house.

"Don't worry, mate," McCarter assured him. "These blokes are SAS. It's my old regiment, you know."

"That's supposed to reassure me?" Encizo grunted, and took a grenade from his belt. "You ready?"

The Briton also selected a grenade, and both men pulled the pins in unison. They held the explosives for two seconds precisely, then lobbed them through windows on the first floor. Encizo and McCarter dropped flat on the ground and covered their ears, mouths open to help equalize the pressure in their skulls for further protection from the shattering force of the impending blast.

The grenades exploded in a combined fury that shook the farmhouse and sent debris streaming from the windows. The Cuban and British commandos shook fragments of glass, wood splinters and plaster from their heads and shoulders before taking gas masks from canvas cases on their belts.

SAS troops in the CRW unit at the inside perimeter of the defense line recognized the explosion as a signal. Four men opened fire with grenade launchers, gas canisters hurtling into already shattered windows on both stories of the farmhouse. Tear gas immediately ejected from the sputtering projectiles, the noxious green fumes flowing through the building.

McCarter and Encizo donned their gas masks and charged into the house. Dead and unconscious terrorists lay among the rubble they discovered. Victims of SAS sharpshooters and the concussion blasts, the majority were definitely out of the fight. Some were dead. Others had suffered ruptured eardrums and vicious battering from the explosions. One dazed opponent started to rise. Encizo stepped forward and stamped the metal stock of his weapon behind the guy's ear. The man moaned and slumped senseless to the floor.

Furniture had been tossed about the room as if a group of bulls had rampaged through the place. A number of mattresses were sprawled on the floor. The place had been used as an improvised barracks and housed far more people than it was originally designed to handle. Duffel bags loaded with gear were located near the beds.

The sound of violent coughing drew their attention to a trio of figures who stumbled, half-blind, from the adjacent room. McCarter and Encizo crouched low and remained still, partially concealed by the swirling green fog. The three terrorists could barely see, and they were almost overpowered by the fumes. The Phoenix pair didn't kill unless it was necessary, and they wanted to take as many opponents alive as possible for interrogation.

The debilitated terrorists staggered past the commandos, unaware of the hazard until the pair hit them from behind. McCarter took out one opponent. He grabbed the guy's hair with one hand and stomped the back of his knee to get the terrorist off balance. The Briton's other hand delivered a precise karate chop to the man's neck, knocking him out with no risk of serious injury.

Another terrorist started to turn when he heard his comrade gasp, followed by the sound of flesh striking flesh. Encizo slammed the frame of his MP-5 into the second man's skull. The blow propelled the terrorist to the floor in a stunned heap as the third man turned to see a bizarre sight. His eyes were blurred by the effects of the gas, and the masked heads of the Phoenix warriors reminded him of giant ants. The terrorist hissed and started to point a pistol at the bug-eye lens and plastic filter snout that concealed McCarter's face.

He was too slow. McCarter swung a roundhouse kick and booted the gun from his opponent's hand. The Briton followed with a hard hook to the guy's jaw, which sent the terrorist stumbling toward Encizo. The Cuban rammed the butt of his Heckler & Koch into his opponent's gut. The guy doubled up with a choked groan, and McCarter hit him with an uppercut that knocked the guy into a wall. They watched him slump unconscious to a mattress on the floor.

"Pleasant dreams," McCarter cracked, but the sound of footfalls on the stairs above them didn't amuse the Briton.

Three terrorists charged down the steps, carrying an assortment of firearms, and gas masks were strapped to their heads. At least some of the enemy had masks packed in their gear and had managed to don the protective devices. They glanced down at McCarter and Encizo. The Phoenix pair's faces were concealed by masks, and the terrorists weren't sure if they were friends or foes.

The two men didn't give them a chance to get a better look for identification. The Cuban raised his MP-5 and sprayed the stairs with a burst of 9 mm slugs. Bullets splintered the handrail and plowed into the torsos of two opponents. McCarter dived to the floor and shoulder-rolled to the foot of the stairs, landing in a kneeling stance, his micro-Uzi pointed at the raisers.

He squeezed the trigger and blasted the third terrorist with another dose of high-velocity death. The corpses tumbled down the stairs in a grotesque collage of arms, legs and bloodstained trunks. McCarter barely glanced at the twitching cluster of bodies. His attention was fixed on the living figure at the top of the stairs.

Another gas-mask-equipped adversary stared down at the Briton. He held a Sterling submachine gun, but he bolted from the edge of the stairs. This decision saved his life as the man narrowly avoided a burst of Uzi rounds from McCarter's compact weapon.

"Missed the bugger," the Phoenix ace growled with disgust, his voice muffled by the rubber and plastic filters of his mask.

"Stand clear," Encizo warned as he darted to the stairs, a grenade in his fist.

He hurled the metal egg up the staircase, and it landed in the corridor above. The Phoenix pair hurried away from the steps and moved to an archway for cover. The grenade exploded a shred of a second later. Encizo had lobbed an M-26 fragmentation model, and the blast sent more wreckage toppling down the stairs. Two badly mangled corpses were among the debris.

MACK BOLAN'S JOB WAS somewhat easier because the fire in the barn proved to have a portmanteau effect on the opponents hidden in the second building. The flames killed several terrorists and forced the others to flee the barn. However, the survivors were frenzied and desperate. They swung their weapons to and fro, spraying bullets in a wild and indiscriminate manner.

Strafing bullets hammered the vehicles Bolan used for cover. He ducked low and slid the barrel of his assault rifle around the rear fender of a sedan to return fire. The enemy was silhouetted against the brilliant background of the burning barn. The Executioner picked his targets and nailed them with controlled bursts of 5.56 mm slugs. It was like being at a very deadly arcade shooting gallery.

Some terrorists avoided Bolan's lethal marksmanship, but they were surrounded by SAS troops. There was nowhere to run. Rifle and subgun fire brought opponents down in every direction. One terrorist yanked a pin from a grenade, but stopped two bullets with his chest before he could hurl it. He collapsed, and the grenade exploded among his own comrades.

The entire battle lasted less than ten minutes—a lifetime for the majority of the terrorists. When it was over, Bolan and his allies rounded up a handful of survivors. It was impossible to make an accurate body count of the slain opponents. Many had been torn apart by explosions or consumed in the fire.

"All things considered," Captain Fairton remarked as he approached the Executioner, "I'd say things went pretty well. Unfortunately one of my men was killed and two were wounded. Lucky the pair was wearing their flak vests."

"I'm sorry about your men," Bolan told him. "It's tragic that the best of men are too often the ones that die too soon."

"None of us beats the clock forever," the SAS captain replied, trying to sound more cynical than he truly felt.

Bolan knew what clock Fairton referred to. The SAS Regiment memorial clock was located at Hereford. The names of the SAS soldiers killed in the line of duty were inscribed in the clock. One more name would be added to that list.

"I don't know how much information we can expect to get from some of the prisoners," Encizo commented in a weary voice. "Their eardrums were shattered, and they might even suffer from brain damage after the concussion grenades went off in their collective laps."

"Sort of figure most terrorists are a bit brain damaged in the first place," McCarter said gruffly. "Anybody contact White yet? He'll probably want to come see how badly we 'overreacted' so he can whine about how we handled the situation."

"He can wait," Bolan replied with a shrug. "We've finally won a round, but this mission is long way from being over."

CHAPTER THIRTEEN

Police Commissioner Daniel Lake wished the federal government would keep the hell out of his jurisdiction. The Feds never wanted to get involved when Baltimore needed help, but they were ready to tell him how to do his job when the figurative shoe was on the other foot. Lake had earned his position in the Baltimore police. He'd started out as a beat cop at a time when blacks had to be the very best just to keep their badge, let alone get a promotion.

Lake was proud of how far he'd risen from the ranks. He'd done it because he was a good cop. When the two Feds showed up at his office, Lake figured somebody had accused him of taking bribes or covering up information. Something shitty like that. He was surprised to learn one guy was with the FBI and the other claimed to be Special Agent Leonard Justice with the Justice Department.

"Bet you get a lot of kidding for having that last name," Lake remarked. "Justice with Justice?"

"It's not my real name," Leo Turrin replied honestly. "At least this way you won't forget which department I'm with. Actually I'm attached to the Interpol section."

"That handles crimes with international connections, right?" Lake asked. He was relieved that they weren't headhunters after his scalp, but he wondered.

"What about you, Anderson? You with the Maryland branch of the FBI or some other fancy section?"

"I'm with the D.C. branch," Anderson replied. "They shuffled me over here because I'm familiar with the investigation in the nation's capital."

Lake grunted. He didn't care much for the FBI or the Washington, D.C., law enforcement in general. They must be doing a shitty job because the city was a mess. Not that Baltimore didn't have its share of problems. But Lake suspected half Baltimore's crime would disappear if Maryland didn't have D.C. for a neighbor.

He wondered if they'd sent Anderson because the guy was really familiar with an important case or if the FBI man was just a token black to accompany Justice because they figured this would make Lake more obliging to whatever the Feds wanted. The police commissioner placed a wide buttock on the corner of his desk and stared at his visitor.

"Well, I'm awful impressed," Lake said dryly. "So what do you want?"

"What can you tell us about the African Crusaders?" Anderson inquired. "They're a splinter group of the Hanafi Muslims."

"I know who they are," Lake said, nodding his head. "We get complaints about them from time to time. Usually from white folks in the suburbs who are nervous about having a bunch of surly jungle bunnies in the neighborhood."

"How surly are the African Crusaders?" Turrin asked. "Have they been involved in violence or not?"

"A couple of them have been arrested for assault, and they've been accused of disturbing the peace, making threats and that sort of thing," Lake explained. "None of the charges held up in court. The Crusaders might have intimidated witnesses and got people to drop charges, but we can't prove that."

"You don't seem too bothered by that," Anderson remarked.

"Look, Mr. FBI," Lake began, "Baltimore has a high homicide rate, gangs running all over the city shooting at one another, drug dealers, armed robbery, muggers that don't mind bashing in old ladies' heads, pimps, prostitutes, arsonists, burglars and drunk drivers. Excuse me if I don't place a bunch of loudmouthed Muslim half-wits on a terribly high priority. The African Crusaders haven't killed anybody, robbed or raped anyone, and they're strongly opposed to drugs. That makes them angels compared to some of the scum we have to deal with."

"They might be a lot worse than you realize," Turrin told him. "A source in Washington claims the African Crusaders have been stockpiling military weapons. There's a strong possibility they might be connected with the terrorist attacks in D.C. and Richmond."

Lake frowned. It sounded as if the mighty Feds had been unable to find any real evidence so they were grasping at straws to try to justify their actions in the investigations instead of admitting they were barking up the wrong suspect tree.

"I realize the African Crusaders are critical of the U.S. government, and their political and religious views aren't popular," Lake remarked. He looked directly at Turrin and added, "Especially with white people. This is still America, and they have a constitutional right to freedom of speech even if what they say upsets people.''

"You think we're just picking on them because they're different?" Anderson demanded. "We ran a computer check on the members of the African Crusaders. Every one of them has a criminal record, and most of them have served some time for crimes of violence. You make it sound like we're trying to come down on a bunch of monks.''

"Okay," the commissioner said with a shrug. "You guys want to raid the Crusaders' house? If you don't have the address, I'll give it to you. A federal judge can give you the warrants you'll need. I'll even have my cops block off the streets for you. But you Feds can damn well handle the bust yourselves. Hitting the African Crusaders isn't going to be popular with a large segment of the Baltimore population, and I don't want my department to catch all the hell. In short, do your own dirty work."

"You're not the most cooperative cop I ever met," Turrin said bluntly. "You've got a gang of terrorists, or at least terrorist sympathizers, in your city, and you're concerned with public relations? Scared the mayor might want you to resign if something goes wrong?"

"You guys in D.C. elected a mayor who got busted smoking crack cocaine," Lake stated with disgust. "Don't talk to me about Baltimore's city administration. I'll tell you something else, gentlemen. This isn't Philadelphia and Mayor Goode isn't running this city. If you expect us to handle the African Crusaders the way they dealt with MOVE in Philly, you can get the hell out of my office."

"Don't worry," Turrin assured him. "We don't intend to blow up half a city block to take out the terrorists . . . unless it's really necessary."

The police commissioner wasn't sure if the little Fed was serious. The guy's face didn't suggest he was joking.

"We've been working with some people who have White House authority, and they don't play games, Commissioner," Anderson stated. "They don't mind stepping on toes, but they're also willing to put their asses on the line. They'll take bigger risks than they'll ask any of your people to take. They also get results."

"The situation we're facing is too serious to waste time with this petty crap," Turrin announced. "We've already got a judge to authorize wiretaps and other surveillance of the African Crusaders. We want your help. Okay?"

Lake nodded. "Okay. You fellas seem to think this is for real, and it sounds like you're going to handle the situation with some intelligence instead of charging in with hotheads or expecting my department to shoulder the burden."

"The burden is big enough for all of us," Turrin told him. "Let's just hope it won't be too big."

JACK GRIMALDI HANDLED the controls to the Bell helicopter with expert skill in spite of his broken arm. The Stony Man pilot was still miffed about being restricted to taxi service during such a critical mission, but he was glad he'd been given some sort of assignment. Just sitting around the Farm, wondering how the others were doing, would have driven him crazy.

The chopper hovered along the Blue Ridge Mountains. Grimaldi hardly needed to glance at his instrument panels. He'd flown the route so many times he only needed an occasional landmark below to find his way to the Farm. Leo Turrin sat in the co-pilot seat, but he didn't have to help the ace pilot. Grimaldi spotted the Farm, surrounded by forests. The four buildings and landing field didn't look very impressive from a distance. They weren't supposed to.

Grimaldi keyed his microphone and radioed the base. John Kissinger's voice responded and assured him that they'd already identified his aircraft. Grimaldi wasn't surprised. With all the state-of-the-art detection gear at the Farm, they ought to be able to identify a dragonfly and tell what sex the insect was.

The helicopter landed with ease. Turrin opened the door and stepped from the copter, ducking his head as the rotor blades continued to whirl. The strong current of the chopper propeller whipped at his clothes and raised a fog of dust as Turrin walked toward Hal Brognola, who waited at the edge of the landing strip.

"How'd it go in Baltimore?" the big Fed asked, raising his voice to be heard above the roar of the chopper.

"Not bad," Turrin replied. "We got cooperation from the police and the FBI. Hope this pans out. Able Team seems to be doing okay. They're eager to find out if this African Crusaders thing turns out to be for real. That dealer in D.C. could be full of it, you know."

"Able Team must think it's a good lead to put this much time into it," Brognola stated as they headed for the main house. "Want to hear some good news, Leo?"

"Let it fly."

"Bolan and Phoenix scored a win for our side in England. Took out a terrorist camp that housed thirty or more men. They had lots of weapons to keep them company."

"Good old Striker and the Phoenix Force boys," Turrin remarked with a grin. "Did they manage to take any of the terrorists alive? Calvin James is a real expert with scopolamine. Might be able to get some information out of the sons of bitches with some truth serum cocktails."

"James is still in France with Katz and Manning. I don't think he'll be able to help with the interrogation for a while. Hell, Striker just contacted me less than thirty minutes ago. Maybe James and the others have already joined him in London."

They reached the porch to the main house. Brognola punched in the coded access numbers on the steel door panel. The door opened, allowing the pair to enter. Grimaldi would follow after he refueled and checked over the chopper.

"Striker did say all the terrorists they captured needed medical assistance," Brognola continued as he and Turrin headed for the computer room. "The SAS and Scotland Yard are supposed to examine what's left of the terrorist base. SIS and CIA will probably get their lab people in on the investigation. I think Mack and Phoenix are probably getting some shut-eye. God knows they earned the right to some rest."

The door opened before the Fed could punch in the access code. Aaron Kurtzman sat in his chair at the threshold. He rolled back to make room for them to enter.

"Got some information from a computer tap on the CIA section at the Embassy in London," Kurtzman announced as he wheeled across the room to retrieve a printout sheet folded in a metal basket. "The Company, the Yard, British Intelligence, Sûreté and probably other outfits went a'hunting through the wreckage at the farm where the terrorists were based outside of London."

"Geez," Brognola muttered, "it'll be on the front pages of the London tabloids tomorrow. Just give me the condensed version of the data, Bear."

"Well," Kurtzman began, "they found the obligatory collection of automatic weapons, ammunition, explosives and that sort of stuff. There was an international transceiver radio, so they could have been in contact with comrades anywhere in the world."

"Figure they had time to get out a message to warn their buddies in France or the U.S. that they were getting slaughtered?" Turrin inquired.

"I doubt it," the Bear replied. "Apparently Bolan, McCarter, Encizo and the SAS hit them like a bolt of lightning. Fast and hard. The whole raid lasted just a few minutes after the first shot was fired. It wasn't likely that anybody was trying to make any long-distance calls under the circumstances."

"The enemy will eventually realize something went wrong anyway," Brognola predicted. "Not too hard to figure out. The terrorists were in touch with one another by radio, and when nobody answers calls or any get sent out, the others will guess something happened to the guys in England. Besides, we figured the terrorists were planning another hit in Britain. When it doesn't happen, the enemy will put one and one together and come up with minus one base of operations."

"The investigators think they found what that target was supposed to be," Kurtzman declared. "A wall map in one of the rooms at the farmhouse had circles drawn around the French embassy in London and a fancy hotel in Bristol. There were also several photographs of the resort and blueprints of the building."

"So the terrorists were stopped before they could carry out that hit," Turrin said with a sigh of relief. "Probably saved a lot of lives."

Cowboy Kissinger strolled out of the communications room adjacent to the computer center. The Stony Man arms expert nodded a greeting to Turrin. He'd heard most of the conversation and waited for an opportunity to contribute to it.

"They also found a number of Korans at the farmhouse," the Bear continued. "These were printed in both Arabic and Farsi."

"Oh, shit," Turrin said, and shook his head. "Farsi is spoken in Iran. Looks like the Iranians and the Iraqis have joined forces for terrorist actions against the West."

"Let's not jump to conclusions," Brognola urged. "Muslim scholars throughout the world read the Koran in Arabic. It was the language of the Prophet Muhammad. A lot of Iranians study the Koran in Arabic. There's also the possibility the Farsi copies of the Koran were brought as a way of throwing us off the track if the base was raided. They could be terrorists of a different nationality who'd like us to think they're Iranians.''

"Sort of unlikely," Kurtzman remarked. "But I guess we have to consider every possibility at this stage. Leo might be right. If he is, we've got one hell of a problem. Hell, the whole world will have an enormous problem. If Iran and Iraq are now partners and carrying out terrorism against the U.S., Great Britain and France, that can be considered justifiable cause for war for all three countries. That means we could go to war against both Iraq and Iran.''

"And they'll employ terrorism as a way of extending the battlefield to the countries of their enemies,'' Kissinger added in a grim tone. "And it could get a lot worse than what's happened so far. You tell them about the cannon yet, Aaron?''

"Cannon?'' Brognola asked with raised eyebrows.

"They found a disassembled cannon in the barn at the farm,'' Kurtzman explained. "It was among the charred rubble and hidden under the remains of the structure after it burned down.''

"From the description and length of the barrel,'' Kissinger began, "I'd say it's a howitzer-style cannon. Range would probably be about two to five miles, depending on what sort of projectiles are used.''

"But they didn't find any shells for the weapon,'' the Bear added. "Probably lucky for Striker and the others at the raid that the enemy didn't have any ammunition for the cannon, or they might have kept it assembled and loaded.''

"If they could get their hands on a cannon and all the other weapons,'' Turrin said, "why didn't they have shells for it? Doesn't seem to make much sense having a weapon like that without ammunition.''

"That might be because the shells were being specially built for the cannon,'' Kissinger replied. "If we're dealing with Iraq, Iran or—God help us—*both* countries, there's a good chance ammunition being prepared would be loaded with poison gas.''

"Iraq used such gas against Kurdish citizens in Halabjah,'' Kurtzman added. "They were also used in the Iran-Iraq war. Of course, it's against the Geneva Convention. Saddam and the Iraqi government don't seem too worried about that. For that matter, the UN didn't do much about it when Iraq used such outlawed weapons.''

"My God,'' Brognola said softly. "If the terrorists had a cannon in England, we'd better assume they have one in France and the U.S., as well.''

"You can bet they'll also try to get the poison-gas shells for the cannons as soon as possible and launch an attack at one or more well-populated areas,'' Kissinger added.

"Yeah,'' Brognola agreed with a solemn nod. "That means the mission is even more deadly than we thought it was. We might have very little time left before the terrorists strike with one of those poison-gas cannon shells.''

"Let's hope our guys in the field get lucky,'' Turrin said grimly.

"We need more than luck,'' the Stony Man chief insisted. "Leo, I want you to go back to Baltimore and personally see to it the surveillance teams on the African Crusaders are doing their job. I want the FBI, Justice, NSA or whoever to supply them with translators in Arabic and Farsi in case they get lucky and eavesdrop on the terrorists themselves.''

Brognola turned to Kissinger. "John, I want you to drive the wonder wagon to Washington, D.C., and give it to Able Team. Schwarz helped build that van with all its high-tech gizmos. I want them to have every possible advantage we can give them.''

"You got it," the Cowboy said with a nod.

"You plan to tell the President what we've got so far?" Kurtzman asked. "I don't know what the hell he can do about it.''

"He already did the best he could when he assigned us to the mission," Brognola replied. "This is our responsibility, gentlemen. We have to succeed. Stony Man has never had a mission more important than this one."

CHAPTER FOURTEEN

Calvin James gazed out an office window at the Eiffel Tower. Once again he saw it only from a distance. James had been in Paris twice before on previous missions, but he'd never been able to really see the sights. Phoenix Force operations were always hectic, and the commandos tended to be busy stalking the enemy or staying alive.

"Maybe next time," James said with a sigh as he turned away from the window.

"What did you say, Monsieur Johnson?" Pierre Bertin inquired.

"Nothing important," James assured him. "Any luck with those prints, Saunders?"

He addressed the question to Gary Manning. The Canadian studied photographs of footprints found at the U.S. Embassy in Paris and the hotel resort in Nice. He'd blown up copies of the photos to examine the prints in detail. Bertin thought the big Canadian was giving this matter much more time than it deserved.

"When did you first get this passion for footprints?" the Sûreté officer asked as he watched Manning place a magnifying glass to one of the photos.

"I learned the importance of tracks from reading signs when I was hunting deer with my uncle," Manning explained. "One can learn a lot from tracks.

They tell how large the animal is, approximate weight and how long the quarry was in the area."

"The abilities of Daniel Boone have always impressed me," Bertin said dryly, "but I fail to see how this will help."

"Luckily some other people in Sûreté and the CIA weren't so quick to dismiss this evidence," the Canadian remarked. "I wouldn't have these photographs without their help."

"Well, did you find anything useful or not?" James asked.

"Yeah," Manning replied. "Several boot prints were made by the same type of footgear. The boots had rubber soles with patterns designed in combinations of lug and broken bars."

"Lug and broken bars?" Bertin asked, confused by the description.

"Boot soles have different type patterns designed for traction and special use," Manning explained. "The lug-and-broken-bar pattern here suggests the terrorists wore a type of combat boot. Probably designed for desert combat."

"You're sure these were left by the terrorists and not by investigators or embassy guards?" Bertin inquired.

"None of them wore boots with these patterns," the Canadian answered. "Also, two distinct pairs of boots can be identified by the amount of wear on different parts of the tread. One of the terrorists wore the same pair of boots when he sabotaged the resort in Nice. The same distinct footprint was found there, as well as at the embassy."

"Fascinating," the Sûreté officer said without enthusiasm. "So it definitely connects the two incidents. We already assumed that."

"We know a little more than that," Manning insisted. "We now know one of the terrorists is about one meter and seventy-one centimeters tall and weighs roughly seventy kilos. The other guy is slightly taller and about five kilos heavier. The desert-style combat boots suggest there's a good chance they've spent a fair amount of time in an appropriate environment for such footgear. The boots weren't new, and they've seen a fair amount of use in rugged terrain."

"So you think the terrorists are from the Middle East?" Bertin asked with a frown. "That does seem the most likely possibility. Unfortunately there are thousands of foreigners from Middle Eastern countries living in France."

James picked up a data sheet and noticed an item of interest. "Maybe we can reduce the number of places we have to look for the terrorists," he announced. "It says here there were traces of a white powdered substance found in the boot tracks. A chemical analysis of the material revealed it to be natural chalk. Soil analysis suggests the chalk residue is from the vineyards of the wine country east of Paris."

"Some of the finest grape harvests are from that area," Bertin stated. He wrinkled his brow and added, "That does seem an unlikely place to find Arabs or Iranians or whatever these people are."

Yakov Katzenelenbogen entered the Sûreté office. "Pollock, Sanchez and Carver are flying out here later today," he announced, using the cover names for Bolan, Encizo and McCarter.

"Where'd you get this news flash?" James inquired.

"Gerard got the information from the Company case officer in London," Katz explained.

Bertin grunted. Andrew Gerard was a CIA operative in Paris. Sûreté wasn't happy that the American Intelligence network was involved in what the French considered to be their investigation, but they reluctantly admitted the Americans had some right to be concerned about the bombing of their embassy.

"We expected them to come after their successful raid on that terrorist base in England," Manning commented. "I'll be glad when they arrive. Like to know a few more details than what they were willing to risk telling us in that coded message."

"Security is a vital concern," Katz reminded him. "We don't know enough about the enemy to be sure they're not sophisticated enough to tap into communication sources and decode messages."

"It's not going to take them long to figure out something happened to their buddies in England," James declared. "I don't think that will convince the terrorists here in France they ought to surrender."

"They might decide to lay low for a while until they get orders from wherever the command headquarters is located," Katz stated as he took out a pack of cigarettes. "More likely they'll retaliate and try to hit another target to compensate for the destruction of their operation in England."

"Maybe we can nail them first," Manning said.

The others shared with Katz what they'd discovered. The Phoenix Force commander barely glanced at the enlarged photos of the boot prints. He acknowledged Manning's superior expertise in reading tracks and trusted the Canadian's opinion. Nor did Katz bother to examine the chemical analysis reports because he had equal faith in James as a chemist.

The men of Phoenix Force had worked together for almost a decade and they knew they could rely on one another. They respected the individual skills and expertise of each teammate. Phoenix Force trusted one another with their lives, and they knew the feeling was mutual with each man in the unit.

"Considering the abstemious nature of Islam, it is unlikely a group of Muslim terrorists would be employed by or residing at a vineyard," Katz commented. "Terrorists are usually fanatics, either political or religious. Politics and religion tend to blend together with Muslim fanatics."

"Well, they wouldn't have gotten that much chalk residue on their boots unless they hung around the area for some time," James insisted. "The soil analysis seems pretty accurate to me."

"Don't misunderstand me, Mr. Johnson," Katz explained, using James's cover name. "I'm sure the terrorists have been hiding at the vineyards. If we're lucky, they're still there. My point is that we should be able to locate them very easily if this is true."

"Do you have any idea how many Arabs, Turks and Iranians are living in France?" Bertin inquired. "Not to mention individuals who claim to be Indian or Pakistani."

"I know the majority of those people are living in Paris and other major cities," Katz replied. "I also know non-French citizens living in less populated areas attract a great deal of attention. The people we're looking for wouldn't go unnoticed in the wine country."

"You might be right," Bertin said with a shrug. "I'll contact the police at Reims. That's the capital of the Champagne region. We'll find out if the people we're looking for are there or not."

"I sure hope so," James commented. "Well, let's get ready to meet our friends at the airport. I always feel more confident about kickin' ass when we're at full strength."

MACK BOLAN FELT A SENSE of déjà vu when he arrived in Paris. Once more he emerged from a C-130 on a runway of an international airport of a European capital. He was accompanied by Rafael Encizo and David McCarter, but two other Phoenix commandos were there to meet him at the runway.

"Welcome to France, gentlemen," Bertin announced with a curt nod. He recognized Encizo and McCarter. The Frenchman was less than ecstatic to see the British commando again.

The Sûreté officer stood beside Calvin James and Gary Manning. He would have preferred to remain at his office instead of chauffeuring about the mysterious commandos, but he had no choice. Bertin had never before met the big man dressed in black. He certainly wouldn't have forgotten the warrior's hard, piercing eyes, which seemed to be able to see right through a man.

The Executioner carried his duffel bag from the plane and headed for the moving van parked near the runway. The others followed. Bertin gestured at the driver to be ready to leave after they got in the back.

The men climbed inside the rig and pulled down the sliding door.

"This isn't the most agreeable method of transportation," Bertin apologized with a shrug, "but it's a secure way to travel. We're safe from eavesdropping devices, and no one can read our lips from a telescope perched atop a building. I'm sorry there are no windows. You'll have to see Paris some other time."

The men exchanged information. The good news about the successful raid in England was juxtaposed with the revelations concerning the cannon found at the terrorist base. If the enemy had such a weapon at the farmhouse in England, it was to be assumed that the terrorists in France probably had a cannon, as well.

The Executioner and his Phoenix allies had already come to the same conclusion as Cowboy Kissinger at Stony Man HQ. The cannon wasn't assembled because the enemy didn't have ammunition, and they didn't have cannon shells because they planned to use special ammo. The most likely choice of such weaponry were warheads loaded with poison gas or some other chemical-warfare agent.

"What you suggest is a terrifying possibility," Bertin remarked with a troubled expression. "The enemy could fire these poison-gas shells into the center of Paris and kill hundreds, perhaps thousands, in the process."

"We already saw what they did in Nice," James said grimly. "The bastards have a supply of chemicals that can be used for lethal compounds. Any luck interrogating the terrorists taken prisoner back in England?"

"Not before we left," Encizo answered. "They haven't even been able to establish the nationalities of the men found at the farmhouse. The evidence supports the probability at least some of them are Iranians."

"Iran might have a motive for attacking the U.S. Embassy," Bertin began, "but they would have no reason to attack France or England unless Iran has become secret allies with Iraq. Saddam is the only enemy with a motive to attack all three countries."

"That's not necessarily true," Bolan stated. "There are still extremist groups and hostile governments opposed to any democratic or so-called capitalist system. When this thing started, we found a Palestinian terrorist in Florida who was connected with this business. There's no evidence he was ever associated with Saddam or Iraq."

"A great many Palestinians are supporting Saddam's jihad," Manning reminded the Executioner.

"Yeah," Bolan admitted, "but Khemit was believed to have wound up at a terrorist training camp in South Yemen along with his cell boss Kaborya. Most of the Palestinians who wanted to join the Iraqi army to fight against the Desert Shield forces were young zealots. So are most involved in the *intifada*. The old pros in the terrorist business are less apt to put their tails on the line unless they've got some reason to think they'll get some kind of personal gain in the process."

"Some might pay a man like Khemit quite well for his services as a go-between," Bertin said.

"Money isn't that important to extremists like Khemit," Bolan stated. "They're interested in other rewards. Power, prestige and influence mean more to men like that than money. They want to be feared and respected."

"Or revenge," Encizo added. "A lot of those old-school terrorists are hanging on to hatred and resentment like their lives depended on it."

"Well, they've devoted most of their lives to extremist attitudes," McCarter commented. "It's never easy for anyone to admit they backed a losing cause. Terrorists are nut cases to begin with. Naturally they'll continue to blame everything on whoever they regard as their enemies and figure somehow the nasty old ogres are responsible for all their problems."

"So they get bitter and resentful," James said. "All that's left is trying to get even with whoever they believe screwed up their lives. I guess that's easier for a lot of people than admitting they screwed up themselves."

"A fascinating insight," Bertin said without enthusiasm. "Nonetheless, there's still a very strong possibility Iran and Iraq have joined forces against the West. It's also feasible Libya or some other Arab country, hostile toward the West, might join them, as well."

"That could happen," Manning acknowledged. "Especially if they can goad Israel into responding to an attack. Saddam failed to do it, but somebody else might succeed. Most Arabs would be inclined to side with an enemy of Israel if the conflict appears to be Arab against Jew."

"It's not our job to declare war," Bolan stated. "We don't know what's going on. If this is state-sponsored terrorism, our governments will have to decide whether their actions justify war.''

''Yeah,'' James remarked. ''Of course, attacking a foreign embassy could be enough to convince the politicians to declare war. The Iraqis invaded the French embassy in Iraq in 1990, and Iranian rebel forces took over the U.S. Embassy in Tehran in 1979. Neither event resulted in France or Uncle Sam making a declaration of war.''

''The French got to settle that score when they took part in Desert Storm,'' Bolan said. ''Any luck trying to pinpoint the vineyard where the terrorists may be located?''

''We think we've found it,'' Bertin replied. ''A certain vineyard in the Champagne region went out of business two years ago. It was a bad year for the grapes, and some of the smaller outfits didn't make it through with enough crops to continue. Anyway, this vineyard was purchased by a man from Guadeloupe named Armand Gelee. Interpol is still checking into this man's background. So far, we know little about him except he purchased the vineyard, but hasn't been using it to produce grapes for wine.''

''That's odd,'' Manning added, ''but it isn't illegal or proof that the guy is associated with terrorism. However, people in the neighboring property have been watching Gelee's property. The neighbors are sort of curious because these people aren't French.''

''Which means they're not white,'' James said dryly. ''The neighbors described the 'suspicious characters' on the Gelee spread as being dark and swarthy. They figured these guys were probably Pakistani or Indian refugees trying to dodge immigration.''

"Let's hope this is the terrorist base," Encizo said. "I don't think it will take long before the enemy strikes again."

MAJOR KARIM HAWRAN frowned as Kaborya entered the room. The Palestinian's expression told the major that the man was once again upset about the mission's progression. Perhaps Captain Gedka was complaining about Somalia's being connected with their activities. Hawran didn't want to listen to his subordinate's verbal drudgery. He was tired of the Palestinian mulling over everything that could go wrong instead of concentrating on how well their conspiracy had unfolded thus far.

"Our operation in England is finished," Kaborya announced in a flat, hard voice. "The British Special Air Service located the base, launched a successful raid and killed or captured every one of our people stationed there."

The news stunned Hawran as if he'd been slapped across the face. Under different circumstances, Kaborya would have been pleased to see Hawran's annoyingly smug confidence shaken. The news of their first defeat was too serious for the Palestinian to feel any satisfaction with Hawran's dismay.

"How long ago did this happen?" the Iraqi asked, his face taut with stress.

"Less than twenty-four hours ago. We suspected something was wrong because no radio messages were coming from our people in England and efforts to signal them had also failed."

"I know," Hawran said grimly. "I had hoped they'd simply been forced to maintain radio silence or perhaps even leave the base to set up elsewhere."

"They're wiped out," Kaborya stated. "It's a major news story throughout the world now. The British are very pleased about it."

"We have to assume the bases in France and America are also in jeopardy. The only option we can take is to order the men in the field to take action immediately. Have the cannon shells been delivered to the remaining bases?"

"Yes," Kaborya assured him, "but even if our men strike another target before the authorities find them, they might not be able to relocate at a new base fast enough to avoid the fate of their comrades."

"I hope you're not being so pessimistic with the others. The Iranians believe this to be a religious war, and we must assure them that we believe God favors our cause."

"That won't reassure Zeigler, Lipari and the other Europeans," Kaborya declared. "Jiro won't be impressed, either. I've known these men for years. They don't believe in any god. Even their faith in Marxism has faded since they've been fugitives from their own countries for so long."

"They didn't have to leave South Yemen and come with us," Hawran remarked. "I thought they wanted to be part of a real revolutionary effort instead of simply sitting about the desert camps to discuss such things."

"None of them is eager to be a martyr for a cause that's going down the drain. You know as well as I the situation in Yemen had gotten worse and they were motivated to join us because they needed somewhere to go to avoid being tracked down by the various police and Intelligence organizations still pursuing them."

"They'll just have to stay here now," Hawran said, unconcerned about the disgruntled handful of non-Muslim terrorists at their base. "There isn't much they can do about this situation. They know too much for us to let them go, and they won't get anywhere trying to convince the Iranians to rise up against us."

"You sound very sure of yourself."

"I made the Iranians who they are today," Hawran said with unfettered pride. "I reshaped their minds and molded their personalities. They'll follow me because *I* am the holy war to them."

Kaborya couldn't deny the major was right. The Iranians were completely loyal to Hawran. The Iraqi's power over them was uncanny and frightening, but Kaborya was more worried about Hawran himself. The major clearly enjoyed the might he wielded, and his ambitions were growing. Ambition could be a dangerous trait in a man who commanded small yet fanatical forces.

"What about the next phase of our plan?" Kaborya asked as he glanced at the wall map. "The part that will require us to return to the Persian Gulf."

"We've been preparing for it," Hawran replied. "Our forces in America and France will carry out their missions. Whether they succeed or not, we shall proceed with our campaign against our enemies in the gulf."

Kaborya nodded. He realized they'd gone too far to pull back now. It had been too late for the Palestinian to choose another path for more than a decade. Kaborya had studied the history of the Middle East and the region he called his homeland. The Roman Empire had once ruled Palestine. Kaborya recalled a Latin phrase: *alea jacta est.*

Indeed, he thought solemnly, the die is cast.

CHAPTER FIFTEEN

Gadgets Schwarz sat inside the "wonder wagon," and monitored the high-tech surveillance gear he'd helped install in the rig. Rosario Blancanales was no stranger to such equipment. The Politician and Schwarz had once worked as private investigators after they'd served their time in Nam and left the service.

Blancanales kept himself busy at the periscope-camera, scanning the streets to be certain no one was surreptitiously approaching the big black van. The rig was parked a block from the two-story house used as a headquarters for the African Crusaders—far enough to avoid being too suspicious, yet close enough for Schwarz to use the laser microphone to eavesdrop on conversations inside the house.

Leo Turrin entered the van via the driver's side door. Blancanales had spotted the little Fed and was glad to see Turrin carried a bag of groceries.

"Got a big thermos of coffee, too," the Justice man announced. "Might consider putting in a coffee-maker and a microwave in the future."

"Just don't let the Bear be in charge of the coffee," Pol remarked as he opened the bag and selected a sandwich.

"Anything interesting?" Turrin asked.

"Conversations are pretty dull for the most part," Gadgets replied. "Oh, they've been talking a lot of crap about having a revolution and getting even with the Man for oppressing them. Mostly the sort of wet-dream stuff you hear from angry young men who don't intend to do anything but run their mouths.''

''They're supposed to have enough military weaponry to do more than talk big,'' Turrin commented. ''Don't tell me Don Luther gave us a bum steer.''

''They got guns, explosives, grenades and launchers,'' Schwarz assured him. ''I've heard them talking about all their hardware and even heard the metal click-clack of an occasional rifle bolt. BATF might have grounds to raid the place, but we haven't been able to establish a definite link between the Crusaders and the terrorists responsible for all the recent incidents that led to our presence here.''

''We haven't been carrying out surveillance for more than four or five hours,'' Blancanales reminded the other men. ''We can't expect them to discuss terrorism twenty-four hours a day.''

''Why not?'' Turrin muttered. ''I feel like that's what I've been doing since this mess started. Nothing happening on the FBI wiretap?''

''These guys don't use the phone much,'' Schwarz said. ''When they do, they watch what they say. Pretty suspicious characters in there. They seem to assume the cops or the Feds might have the line tapped.''

''Where'd they get a notion like that?'' Turrin said with a sour snort. ''No word about how Striker and Phoenix Force are doing in Europe, but they're all in France now.''

''Yeah,'' Blancanales replied. ''I wish them luck, but frankly I'm more concerned with what we're doing right here. Those guys already scored one big blow against the terrorists. So far, we haven't even been able to find the bastards.''

"Well, this is the only solid lead so far,'' Turrin said. "The combined efforts of the FBI, NSA, police in D.C., Virginia and Baltimore, as well as CIA, Secret Service and British Intelligence weren't able to do likewise.''

"That won't count for much if our lead turns out to be a dud,'' Schwarz stated. "What are we going to do if this turns out to be a washout?''

"What are you asking me for?'' the Fed replied with a shrug. "All we can do is try something else and hope.''

Voices from the speaker to the laser mike caused the conversation in the van to stop abruptly. They'd heard voices from the house since the laser beam had been fixed on a window, but the Crusaders had previously spoken only English. The Able warriors and Turrin didn't understand Arabic, but they recognized it when they heard it. At least, they were fairly sure they recognized it.

"Does that sound like Arabic or Farsi?'' Blancanales inquired.

"Hell, I don't know the difference between the two,'' Turrin admitted. "Could even be Turkish or Sanskrit for all I know.''

"We're getting it on tape,'' Schwarz stated. "It can be translated later. One of those voices is slightly muffled, and I think I hear some static in the background.''

"Maybe that's from our equipment,'' Turrin suggested.

"No static from a laser mike," Schwarz insisted. "I think one of those voices is coming from a two-way radio transceiver. Probably shortwave."

"You think the terrorists have contacted the Crusaders?" Blancanales inquired. "If that's true, we have to find out where that radio frequency is coming from."

The Arabic voices from the speaker stopped as suddenly as they'd begun. Someone inside the house asked what the message was about, and a strong, confident male voice replied in English.

"It's almost time, my brothers and sisters," the Crusader commander announced. "That blasphemy of a mosque will be destroyed and the infidels will feel the fury of God."

"That must be Ali Simba-Mtu," Turrin remarked. He'd read the Baltimore police records on the African Crusaders and knew Simba-Mtu was the leader of the outfit.

Turrin also recalled that Ali Simba-Mtu had formerly been known as Leon Brown before he'd adopted a name that was part Muslim and part Swahili. Brown was a career criminal and had served eight years in the Maryland state prison for armed robbery and attempted murder. He'd converted to Islam and joined the Hanafi Muslims while in the joint.

"Yeah," Blancanales confirmed. "We've heard him all day. The guy talks a lot, but he mostly lectures the others about being ready for the revolution and how whitey, Christians, Jews, infidels and assorted nonbelievers have to pay for their crimes of oppression against blacks."

"Not all blacks," Schwarz added. "Simba-Mtu and his pals seem to hate Afro-Americans who don't fit their concept of 'Crusaders' more than any other ethnic group. I've been hearing them complain about Uncle Toms and Christian 'niggers' and Black Muslims who aren't part of the African Crusader movement. In short, these guys are just down on anybody who doesn't belong to their particular fanatic group."

"Maybe they're willing to accept Arab or Iranian terrorists as being okay dudes," Turrin commented. "Any idea what they mean about a 'blasphemy of a mosque'?"

"Nope," Pol admitted, "but we'd better find out because whatever it is, they're talking about destroying it. That means it could be the next target of the terrorists.

POLICE COMMISSIONER Lake's office seemed to be shrinking. The guy who called himself Leonard Justice and Special Agent Theodore Anderson of the FBI had returned. They brought along another Justice Department officer named Eric Deckker, a big-shot section chief from Washington. Three other men also joined the Feds.

They didn't look like federal agents. The big blond guy looked strong enough to arm wrestle gorillas for a hobby. The shorter man reminded Lake of a former middleweight boxer who could still lick most men twice his size, and even the gray-haired member of the trio seemed to be a hardass. They dressed in loose-fitting clothes, but Lake knew they were packing heat. Whoever they were, these three were tough guys nobody in his right mind would want to take on.

Turrin, Blancanales and Schwarz told the others what they'd learned from the surveillance of the African Crusaders' base. Lyons had heard it before. He gazed out a window and scanned the street below.

"The FBI and NSA have been monitoring private radio broadcasts in five states since this mess started," Anderson stated. "They picked up the message you guys heard on the laser mike. The foreign language got their attention. I don't think they've translated it yet, but NSA is working on it and should—"

"We already translated it," Schwarz informed him. "The language is Arabic. Simba-Mtu learned Arabic after becoming a Muslim. He reads it fluently and speaks it pretty well. The other person spoke Arabic with an indistinct accent. Probably not the guy's native tongue, but apparently his first language is similar to Arabic. Might be Farsi, Pushtu, Kurdish, something like that."

"You managed to get that translated and evaluated faster than the National Security Agency?" Deckker asked, stunned by this claim.

Schwarz didn't explain that all he had to do was feed the taped data from the conversation into the computer terminal in the wonder wagon. This link with Stony Man computers presented the task of translating and analyzing the tape to Aaron Kurtzman. The Bear and his machines had had the answer in a matter of minutes.

"Congratulations," Deckker remarked, and cast a sharp gaze at Turrin. "I don't know what outfit you're the liaison for, but its people are damn good. Did they already determine where the broadcast to Simba-Mtu and the Crusaders came from?"

"NSA sort of shared that with us," Blancanales replied with a slight smile. "The radio waves were traced to the D.C. area, but no exact location was pinpointed."

"Looks like your fancy technology isn't perfect," Commissioner Lake commented with a degree of satisfaction.

"We never claimed it was," Turrin assured him. "Unfortunately we've still got a gang of killer fanatics out there and we only have a vague idea where the bastards are located or what their next target will be."

"What about the translation of the Arabic message?" Anderson asked. "Doesn't that help identify the target?"

"Afraid not," Blancanales answered. "The caller just told Simba-Mtu to be ready for the Crusaders' role in the holy war. Simba-Mtu assured him they were prepared, and the voice said that was good. Then they said they'd be going after the main target one week ahead of schedule."

"Great," Deckker muttered with disgust. "The problem is, we don't know when the original date of the terrorist hit was. They might have intended to carry it out a month from tomorrow or a week from today."

"We have to assume they're going to strike soon," Lyons announced as he turned from the window and joined the conversation. "They might even do it today."

"You might not know what to do now," Lake said with a sigh, "but I do. We know the African Crusaders are involved with the terrorists. They might even be the terrorists. The message could be from one of their agents in D.C. My point is, we know about them and we know they have enough illegal arms to justify arresting every member of their cult."

"Wrong move, Commissioner," Blancanales said. "You raid their house, and you'll just nab the African Crusaders that are there and tip off the others that we're closing in. They'll be even more difficult to find if that happens."

"They'll be more careful about communications, too," Schwarz added. "Unless they're dumber than a house brick, they'll realize we eavesdropped on the Crusaders' conversation with the guy in D.C."

"Maybe we can get the Crusaders to sell out the terrorists in the capital," Anderson suggested. "One or more of them might be willing to cut a deal."

"We can't rely on that," Lyons said. "Let's not worry about the African Crusaders right now. We know who they are and where they are. They're under surveillance twenty-four hours a day. Ali What's-his-name is..."

"Simba-Mtu," Blancanales supplied.

"Thank you," Lyons said with a mock bow. "Ali and his group can't make a move without us knowing about it. When and if they do, they can lead us to the other terrorists. We can take care of them later. Right now they're more valuable to us as a possible source to the rest of the enemy forces."

"You might be right," Lake admitted reluctantly. "But we still don't know what the terrorists' target is. There might not be enough time to prepare action against them if we wait for the Crusaders to lead us to the lunatics."

"Well, we know it has to be a big target," Schwarz stated. "The terrorists know their comrades in England got their butts kicked. They need a major strike to compensate for that loss. No offense to the city of Baltimore, but I think D.C. is a more likely choice for a hit."

"That's okay with me," Lake assured him. "Washington is welcome to that kind of attention."

"Thanks a bundle," Deckker snorted. "There must be a hundred different potential targets in the district that would appeal to these maniacs. The Israeli embassy, the Pentagon, the White House..."

"The Pentagon is actually in Arlington, Virginia," Anderson remarked.

Deckker glared at the FBI agent and was about to reply, but Blancanales cut him off quickly.

"Simba-Mtu referred to a 'blasphemy of a mosque,'" he reminded the others. "That means it's either a religious building they regard as a blasphemy of Islam or a building that is designed in a manner similar to a mosque."

"They might strike at a mosque of a Muslim denomination they're opposed to," Turrin commented, "but that doesn't seem likely since jihad is trying to get wide support from various Muslim sects."

"A mosque usually has two or more minaret towers nearby, and the building itself is noted for having a great dome topped with a cupola—" Schwarz began. He stopped in midsentence when he realized what famous D.C. structure fit that description.

"The Capitol Building has a huge white dome with a cupola and the Statue of Freedom at the pinnacle,"

Blancanales said, proving he, too, had drawn the same conclusion.

"So we know where they plan to strike next," Lyons concluded. "Now we just have to figure out how to stop them."

CHAPTER SIXTEEN

The slopes of Champagne were famous for vineyards and the production of fine white wine even before 1665, when a monk named Dom Pérignon discovered a way to add effervescence to the wine. Champagne remained one of the finest areas in the world for grapes and high-quality wines. It was usually a peaceful, almost quaint setting compared to Paris. Tourists knew Champagne to be a site to visit for the gentler side of France.

Mack Bolan saw Champagne as yet another battleground, and he saw little of the countryside from the back of the army truck as it rolled along a lonely road. Calvin James and Gary Manning accompanied the Executioner in the rig.

Several French paratroopers were also in the truck. They were members of the Eleventh Parachute Division, a special forces regiment. Bolan and Phoenix Force realized they were lucky to have the Eleventh Parachute Division called in to assist their mission. The vineyard of Armand Gelee was almost certainly the terrorist base they had come to France to find. Sûreté and Pierre Bertin had been embarrassed after Interpol computers confirmed that "Gelee" was actually Marcel Arnaud, a notorious member of the French Red Brigades. Like its Italian counterpart, the FRB had engaged in kidnapping, murder and various

forms of sabotage. The Brigade also financed many of
its operations with money acquired by robbing banks
and ransom payments made by the families of kidnap
victims. Arnaud had been one of the most cunning
and ruthless terrorists in the organization.

The manhunt for Arnaud had once extended across
Western Europe in the early 1980s. His face had been
on wanted posters in police and Interpol offices in five
countries. However, the man seemed to have disappeared and was believed to be hiding out at a terrorist
training camp in Yemen. Other villains took his place
on Interpol's most-wanted list. Arnaud was written off
as "one that got away."

No one expected the veteran terrorist to return to
France with a false identity as an investor from
Guadeloupe. The authorities hadn't been suspicious
of "Armand Gelee," and they hadn't objected when
the newcomer bought a vineyard that had gone belly-
up the year before. They hadn't paid much attention
to the guy until Bertin contacted the Interpol section
of Sûreté to run a check on him.

Marcel Arnaud was a few years older, a bit slimmer
and he sported a mustache and a suntan, but there was
no doubt he had come back to France as Gelee. This
was an unexpected discovery, but it seemed to fit a
pattern Stony Man had found since the mission began. Everyone seemed convinced the terrorism was
state sponsored by Iraq or possibly a combination of
Iraq and Iran. However, Bolan was intrigued by the
fact both Khemit and Arnaud were formerly believed
to have been at a terrorist camp in South Yemen.

Putting the pieces of a puzzle together could wait
for a better time, the Executioner realized. First they

had to take care of the terrorists who presented an immediate threat. Bolan was equipped for the occasion. He carried the Beretta 93-R and Desert Eagle in shoulder leather, as well as the M-16 with M-203 launcher attached. Calvin James also favored the M-16 assault rifle with the grenade launcher accessory, but carried a silenced Uzi, as well as a Walther P-88 holstered under one arm and a Blackmoor Dirk in a sheath under the other.

Gary Manning's choice of arms was somewhat different. A crack rifle marksman, the big Canadian carried an FAL assault rifle with a Bushnell scope. The big 7.62 mm ammo used in the Belgian-made rifle packed plenty of knockdown force. Manning seldom needed more than one shot when he had a target in his sights.

The Phoenix Force warrior carried a Walther P-88 in a shoulder rig and a Stony-M rocket launcher in a special holster on his hip. The ''Stony-M'' was the name Manning and Kissinger had given their newly developed magazine-fed rocket launcher. Since Manning had been one of its inventors, it was appropriate that he be the first to use the weapon in actual combat. The demolitions expert also carried a backpack loaded with an assortment of explosives.

The French paratroopers were armed with 5.56 mm FAMAS assault rifles. Unlike most military rifles, the magazine well to the FAMAS was located between the buttstock and the pistol grip. The front and rear sights were protected by a carrying handle that extended from the tip of the forearm stock to the top of the buttstock. Nicknamed the ''Bullpup,'' the FAMAS was a sturdy weapon and only seventy-five centimeters in length.

The troopers also carried MAB 9 mm pistols, bayonets and grenades. They wore fatigue uniforms and red berets, but they would exchange the headgear for helmets when they reached the enemy base. Bolan and the Phoenix pair were dressed in close-fitting blacksuits. The assault force was ready for action. Each man realized he would probably see plenty of it before the night was over.

THE VINEYARD LOOKED like hell. Untended and unwatered, the grapevines had shriveled and died. The lifeless crop resembled a network of mangled weeds stretched across the plantation. A tall wire fence surrounded the area, and armed sentries patrolled the perimeter. The main house was two stories high with an extended wing at the east and west ends.

Two smaller buildings had formerly served as areas for vinification—the process of converting grapes into wine—and storage, and cars and trucks were parked near the structures. The buildings had apparently been converted into improvised barracks for the terrorists residing at the vineyard. Bolan and the others could only guess how many opponents might be inside the three buildings.

The Stony Man commandos and the French paratroopers viewed the plantation from ridges overlooking the valley. Bolan's group set up at the flank to the north of the vineyard. Another team of soldiers, commanded by Yakov Katzenelenbogen, David McCarter and Rafael Encizo, were positioned at the south flank. A full moon and a plethora of stars in the blue-black sky shed ample light on the scene to allow them to observe the setting without the use of night-vision gear.

The Executioner checked his wristwatch. He'd synchronized watches with the Phoenix commandos and knew Katz would have his men in position at the prearranged time. The French paratroopers were well trained and professional. They knew what they were supposed to do and assumed their roles with little need of instruction.

"Fence is electrified," Gary Manning whispered as he used the Bushnell scope to scan the compound. "It's about four meters high. Won't be easy getting over it without getting fried in the process."

Bolan nodded. They'd researched the vineyard based on available information. The fence wasn't a surprise, but they didn't know it had been electrified. The possibility had been considered along with other security measures the enemy might have taken to fortify the base.

"I can see the cables," James stated, peering through a pair of binoculars. "They extend from the fence post at the east and west corners to a shack near the billets. Suckers didn't bother to hide the lines underground."

"Maybe they did it on purpose to be sure everybody would remember the fence was charged," Manning theorized. "The generator must be in the shack. Diesel powered. Separate from the main electrical source. Might also be used as an emergency means of electricity if the main power goes out."

"Can you take it out?" Bolan asked. He already knew the answer, but wanted confirmation from the Phoenix demolitions expert.

"Sure," Manning replied, "but we still have to take care of the sentries. I haven't spotted any surveillance cameras, rifle mikes, heat sensors or guard dogs. Hopefully that means they haven't invested in any fancy alarm systems, either."

"Nothing is sure until it happens," James commented. "If we touch the fence or take out the generator, it might set off an alarm and alert the entire camp that they're under attack."

"Calculated risk," Bolan decided. "Unless everybody's asleep, they'll know something's going down a minute or two after we move in anyway."

"Too bad we can't wait awhile," James said with a sigh. "I can't say I like taking on an enemy base without knowing more about it. Especially since you said there was a cannon at the base in England."

"That's exactly why we have to act now," Bolan told him. "If they have a cannon, they might use it against a target if we don't put them out of business right now."

"They might use it against us if they figure they've got nothing to lose," Manning reminded the others. "Artillery isn't designed for close combat. It would be awkward to use if we're right on top of them. Of course, if they have a shell loaded with chemicals, they can detonate it in a final effort to take us with them to the grave."

"Yeah," Bolan said, "I know."

The Executioner was painfully aware of the risk. This was one of the reasons he'd requested only a dozen French paratroopers to participate in the raid. They maintained radio contact with the paratroopers' commander five kilometers away. A battalion of Eleventh Parachute Division troops could be summoned to the vineyard if reinforcements were necessary. This would include four gunships, armed with enough firepower to utterly destroy the enemy base.

Bolan, Phoenix Force and the paratroopers didn't want to annihilate the terrorists. They needed living enemies to interrogate and whatever evidence they could find at the vineyard to help track down the rest of the terrorist conspiracy. The Stony Man warriors had decided to accept the greater risk of facing the enemy up close and personal in order to try to accomplish these goals. If the terrorists used a "doomsday device," at least the number of French allies killed would be a minimal number and the paratroopers' commander could avenge them with a massive air strike that would guarantee none of the fanatics would leave the base.

"Well," James said with a shrug, "I guess we just have to play the game with the cards fate deals us in a situation like this. You can go crazy trying to figure out everything that could happen in a combat zone."

"Speaking of crazy," Manning said, "McCarter's probably chomping at the bit to get into a fight with these guys. We'd better get on with this before he breaks his leash."

"We have three sentries to take out," Bolan began as he checked the silencer attached to the muzzle of his Beretta. "That's what we can see on patrol. They've probably got the equivalent of a sergeant of the guard on duty in one of the buildings, as well as the other guys assigned to guard duty tonight. It isn't very late in the evening, so most of them are probably still awake."

"Most of the whole camp is probably still awake," James added, shaking his head. "This is gonna get messy, man."

"Let's try to keep it from getting any messier than necessary."

"Okay," James agreed, and began to screw a silencer to the threaded muzzle of his micro-Uzi. "We'll be quiet as long as possible."

Manning had already fixed a silencer to the muzzle of his FAL rifle. The Canadian slipped out of his backpack and opened it to select the proper explosive for the job.

"Guns can be muffled," Lieutenant Martens remarked. A young officer in the Eleventh Parachute Division and fluent in English, he had approached the Stony Man trio and heard part of their whispered conversation. "How do you intend to set off explosives without making noise?"

"Very carefully," Manning replied as he stuck a pack of gray puttylike material in a pocket.

"Are your men ready?" Bolan asked Martens. "We need your best riflemen at the ridge to supply cover fire. The guys with the bolt cutters had better be ready when we are."

"Yes," the lieutenant replied in an annoyed tone. "All is taken care of. We're waiting for you to make the next move."

"You won't have to wait much longer," the Executioner assured him. He turned to Manning and James. "Let's go."

THE SENTRY TURNED UP the collar to his jacket. He'd
spent most of his life in desert climates, and although
the night could be bitterly cold he felt the chill more
intensely in France. This was due to his imagination
more than the wind that swept across the vineyard.

The rustle of movement among the tall grass beyond the fence drew the guard's attention. He'd heard
such sounds before, and the cause had always been a
hare or a pheasant that wandered close to the vineyard. This time the sound was louder and seemed to be
caused by a larger creature.

Not alarmed, but still aware of possible danger, the
guard went to investigate. He was afraid his comrades would mock him if he seemed to be frightened
by something that proved to be no more threatening
than a stray dog. The man came from a culture that
placed great emphasis on saving face and manly
honor.

His attention was fixed on the area where he'd
spotted the movement. The sentry didn't see Calvin
James hidden behind a cluster of bushes, although he
passed the Afro-American's position.

James watched his opponent, peering through the
branches of the shrubs. He almost hesitated, repulsed
by what he had to do, yet aware it was necessary.
James raised his silenced Uzi, pointed it at the sentry
and squeezed the trigger. A 3-round burst flew from
the muzzle of the sound suppressor. One bullet struck
a wire link in the fence. Sparks ignited and blue coils
of electrical flames crackled along metal. The remaining slugs passed through the fence and slammed
into the side of the sentry's skull, the man's head
snapping sideways from the force of the bullets.

Another guard saw his comrade crumple to the ground, but he didn't live long enough to yell an alarm or use his weapon. Mack Bolan took out the sentry with a single shot. From a prone position, the Executioner triggered his Beretta and propelled a round neatly between the links of the fence and scored a deadly bull's-eye in the guard's forehead.

The third sentry collapsed a fragment of a second after the second man fell, the fiberglass shaft of a crossbow bolt jutting from the back of his skull. Bolan nodded with grim satisfaction. The assault team commanded by Katz was obviously right on schedule.

The sentries had been taken out with a minimum of noise. The special subsonic 9 mm ammunition used for the silenced weapons reduced the usual crack on the high-velocity round breaking the sound barrier. The crossbow made even less noise. There were no shouts or alarms to be heard within the enemy camp. So far, the plan was working as smoothly as any experienced warrior would dare hope.

Gary Manning emerged from the tall grass near the fence post linked to the electrical cables. The demolitions expert placed his FAL rifle on the ground as he knelt by the fence and removed the packet of plastic explosives from his pocket. It was a CV-38 charge, precisely measured for the task. Manning placed it by the base of the post and set the timing mechanism to a detonator. Then he gathered up his rifle and moved back a safe distance.

The explosion was barely as loud as an average-sized firecracker, and the post seemed to hop up from the ground beneath the glare of the subdued blast. Fire spit from the end of the cable as it whirled away from the post, and electrical sparks sputtered as the cable was severed. Manning took from his pocket a small chain the size of a dog's choker collar and tossed it into the fence. No sparks were generated when metal touched metal. The fence was no longer electrified.

Soldiers rushed to the fence and used bolt cutters to snip wire links. Manning used the buttstock of his rifle to push back fencing broken by the post, then made a large-enough gap to slip through the barrier. He was the first member of the assault force to enter the enemy compound.

James was next, still holding the silenced Uzi in his fists. Manning held the FAL, butt braced against his hip as he scanned the vineyard.

"Better check the generator and make sure there isn't an emergency backup system that might kick in," Manning whispered.

"Shit, man," James rasped. "Why didn't you mention that before?"

"Didn't think of it until now," the Canadian admitted as he headed for the shack.

"Great," James muttered, and followed Manning to the building.

CHAPTER SEVENTEEN

Rafael Encizo stood guard, micro-Uzi in his fists, while two paratroopers cut through the fence. David McCarter had already cocked the bowstring to the Barnett Commando crossbow and fitted another bolt in the groove. The Briton was familiar with the weapon and had used it many times in the past. The dead sentry with a bolt lodged in his skull testified to McCarter's lethal accuracy.

"Saunders and Johnson are inside," Encizo whispered to Katz. The Cuban was the only member of Phoenix who didn't speak French, and he had to rely on his teammates to communicate with the paratroopers. "We'd better hurry."

"Nobody is taking a nap," Yakov Katzenelenbogen assured him.

The one-armed Israeli held a micro-Uzi in his single fist, silencer-equipped barrel laid across his prosthesis. He realized they had to move quickly. Every man in the assault force was aware of this. Katz didn't translate Encizo's remarks for the French soldiers, confident the pair working on the fence were cutting it as fast as they could.

"Maybe we should have pole-vaulted over this thing," McCarter complained, even less patient than his Cuban partner.

Katz understood their concern. Manning and James were inside the compound, and the other Phoenix warriors were eager to join them. However, they couldn't allow haste to make them careless. Too much was at stake.

The soldiers finished cutting through the fence and removed a section three meters wide and almost two meters high. Encizo and McCarter immediately took advantage of the opening and slipped inside, followed by Katz and two paratroopers. They noticed another section of wire fencing had been removed by the soldiers with Bolan's group. The Executioner himself stepped through the gap, silenced Beretta in one fist.

More figures appeared at one of the billets. Four men walked from the building. Three carried assault rifles, and the fourth wore a side arm on his hip. The three Phoenix commandos and the paratroopers crouched by the shadows near the fence for concealment. Bolan had also spotted the enemy and dropped to the ground to avoid detection.

The terrorists glanced about the compound, apparently more puzzled than worried. Their attitude suggested they hadn't heard the silenced gunshots or the CV-38 explosion. Katz guessed the men were probably sentries about to replace the guards on watch. The other guy was probably the watch commander.

That meant they were looking for the sentries who were supposed to be on duty. Katz realized they'd soon notice the bodies of the dead guards or the damage to the fence. Encizo drew the Tanto knife from his belt sheath and held the weapon low to hide the metal blade with his thigh. No one had to tell the Cuban what had to be done. Katz nodded his agreement, and both men crept forward.

McCarter sucked in a tense breath and assumed a kneeling position. He slowly raised the skeletal metal stock of the Barnett and placed the padded end to his shoulder. The soldiers looked at McCarter, but he gestured for them to stay put. The Briton peered through the telescopic sights mounted to the cross-bow and waited, finger poised by the trigger.

Encizo and Katz moved forward, knees bent and bodies low. The Cuban wanted to get close enough to use his knife, but realized this was impractical. Their opponents were already suspicious and would soon be aware they were in danger. Older, slower and con-scious that he was less adept at stealth, Katz followed behind Encizo, Uzi held ready.

Then their luck went bad.

One of the terrorists saw the movement among the shadows. He shouted an alarm and unslung his rifle. The guy's face suddenly burst apart. The back of his skull exploded as the 7.62 mm slug exited after knif-ing through his brain.

The other terrorists gasped and shouted when their comrade fell. One man swung his rifle toward the shack, guessing the direction the shot had come from. A blur of movement streaked from the shadows. The gunmen barely glimpsed the projectile before it struck the rifleman in the heart. The fiberglass shaft of a crossbow bolt protruded from the man's chest, the feathered end bobbing slightly due to the impact.

Encizo charged forward and closed the distance be-tween himself and the remaining gunners. Katz jogged after him, aimed the Uzi at the terrorist to the left and fired a 3-round burst. The silenced machine pistol coughed rapidly, and the targeted gunman toppled backward, a trio of bullet holes in the center of his chest.

The guard commander was alone and drew a pistol from his hip holster. Encizo dived into the terrorist before the man could use his side arm. Both men crashed to the ground, the Cuban on top. The pistol fired, but the shot went harmlessly into the sky.

Encizo grabbed the guy's gun hand and pinned it to the ground. His other fist held the Cold Steel Tanto, and he plunged the knife between the terrorist's ribs. When his opponent struggled and cried out in agony Encizo flipped the knife and grabbed the handle in an overhand grip. Then he drove the blade hard into the man's heart and terminated his suffering forever.

THE SOUNDS OF BATTLE alerted the base that it was under attack. Rifle barrels shattered windows, and voices yelled orders from within all three buildings. Bolan decided it was time to unleash some serious firepower. He raised the M-16 and triggered the M-203 launcher. A 40 mm grenade rocketed across the compound and smashed through an already broken window of one of the billets.

The shell exploded and blasted out a large section of the wall. Wood, plaster and pieces of mangled human bodies hurtled from the building. Katz and Encizo rushed for cover, taking advantage of the distraction created by the explosion. McCarter and the two paratroopers moved to a rusted hull of a tractor for shelter. The Briton discarded the crossbow and unslung a micro-Uzi.

"Well, things are getting interesting," McCarter remarked.

"Eh?" a puzzled paratrooper inquired.

"I'll explain what it means later," McCarter answered, switching from English to French. "You two have greater range and accuracy with those FAMAS rifles than I do with this short-barreled baby submachine gun. Hold your fire unless you have a clear target. Don't want to draw any more attention to this site than necessary."

"We have adequate cover from rifle fire," the second soldier said with a nod, "but a grenade or a rocket launcher would destroy this tractor and us with it."

"Exactly," McCarter confirmed. "Bear that in mind and let the other blokes handle the bulk of the strafing fire. They're outside the compound and less vulnerable to counterattack."

The Briton moved to the edge of the tractor and waited for a lull in the shooting. One of the paratroopers asked what he was doing. McCarter glanced over his shoulder and displayed a crooked grin.

"I can't do any good with a short-range weapon unless I get closer to the enemy," he explained. "You chaps take care. Good luck."

"Thanks," the soldier replied. "Take care!"

McCarter nodded in response. He concealed his amusement at the Frenchman's warning to be careful. The British ace realized little was accomplished in a battlefield by being careful. Caution wasn't a strong trait in his character, but McCarter tried to avoid being reckless. He didn't always succeed.

The Phoenix fighter bolted from cover and raced across the compound to the billets struck by Bolan's grenade shell. Automatic-rifle fire erupted from the remaining buildings. Bullets slashed air near the Briton and tore into the ground by his running feet. McCarter held his fire, aware it would be useless and the muzzle-flash of the Uzi would only serve to attract enemy fire rather than discourage it.

He spotted Katz and Encizo crouched by a military-style truck rig and headed for their position, running a zigzag pattern to present a more elusive target. A bullet tugged at the fabric of McCarter's field jacket. He dived forward and hit the ground in a shoulder roll. The Briton kept tumbling across the ground as slugs ripped chunks of dirt near his moving body.

"You really are loco," Encizo remarked as McCarter rolled to the truck.

The Briton glanced up at his fellow Phoenix Force commandos and grinned. Katz shook his head and sighed. McCarter assumed a kneeling stance beside his partners.

"How are we doing so far?" he inquired as he peered around the hood of the vehicle to scan the area.

"Body count is in our favor," Encizo replied through clenched teeth. "Whatever comfort that might be."

"Better than the other way around," Katz observed.

The cover fire from the French paratroopers raked the buildings with steady 5.56 mm fury. The soldiers concentrated on the windows as targets, which forced the enemy to stay down and prevented them from returning fire. Bullets chipped wood and smashed what little glass remained in the window.

The building hit by the M-203 round leaned at a crooked angle. The terrorists within had moved away from the gap in the wall and counterattacked from an open door and the windows. Some gun-toting figures raced from the building, apparently deciding it was better to risk being shot in the open than remain in the barracks and have it bombed to bits.

"Heads up, gents!" McCarter called, and pointed his Uzi at a group of advancing terrorists.

The Briton opened fire, and two gunmen collapsed to the ground. Two other terrorists bolted from the line of fire while a third dropped to a kneeling position and returned fire with an Italian-made Beretta M-12 subgun.

McCarter ducked behind the rig as bullets pelted the metal frame of the truck. One round skidded across the hood and sliced air centimeters from McCarter's left ear. Even the bold Briton flinched from such a close call.

The two terrorists who had bolted to avoid McCarter's line of fire ran along the length of the truck to try to ambush the Phoenix warriors. Katzenelenbogen was waiting for them at the rear of the rig. The Israeli crouched low and opened fire.

The stream of 9 mm slugs cut the enemy across the upper torso, and the rounds bored upward to tear into hearts and lungs. Both men were driven backward by the force of the impacts. Fatally wounded, they were rendered senseless by massive shock to vital organs before they hit the ground.

"More will follow," Katz announced as he turned to address his Phoenix partners. "Let's go for the best defense."

McCarter and Encizo knew the best defense to be a strong offense. They nodded their agreement and followed Katz around the rear of the truck. The commandos hoped the paratroopers saw them and held their fire as the trio dashed for the besieged building.

The terrorists were preoccupied with the barrage of gunfire from outside the camp and concerned about another grenade attack. Their attention focused elsewhere, they paid little mind to the direction from which the three Phoenix fighters approached. The warriors reached the rear exit to the structure. Katz moved to the side of the door while McCarter and Encizo took grenades from their belts.

A gunman suddenly charged through the door, a Skorpion machine pistol in his fists. He was startled to discover Katz waiting at the threshold. The Phoenix commander saw the young man's eyes widen and his mouth fall open. The steel hooks of the Israeli's prosthesis clawed into the terrorist's wrist above the Czech minichopper.

Katz slammed the Uzi into the side of his opponent's face as he locked the metal talons of the prosthesis around the guy's wrist. Bone cracked and the man's fingers opened to drop the Skorpion. The guy's head rolled, dazed by the blow and the pain in his broken wrist. Blood trickled from his mouth, but he still tried to raise his uninjured arm to strike back at Katz.

The Phoenix fighter moved in and rammed a knee to the opponent's groin. As the guy doubled up with a gagging moan, another terrorist appeared at the doorway. Katz glimpsed the second guy and saw him raise a gun barrel. The Israeli immediately pointed his

Uzi and triggered a short burst. The silenced machine pistol spit three rounds, and the terrorist toppled backward. Then Katz hit his first opponent with an elbow to the back of the neck, using his abbreviated right arm. The guy collapsed unconscious as Katz jumped away from the door.

A salvo of automatic fire snarled from inside the building. Katz narrowly managed to avoid the stream of bullets. He glanced over his shoulder and saw that Encizo and McCarter had pulled the pins from their grenades and prepared to throw the explosives at windows.

"Now would be an excellent time, gentlemen," Katz said tensely as he moved back to avoid ricochet rounds that sizzled past his position.

The British and Cuban commandos hurled the grenades in unison. The metal eggs sailed into a first- and second-story window simultaneously, the twin explosions rocking the building a split second later. Dust and debris showered down on the Phoenix trio, but Katz ignored this, ducked his head and dived through the doorway.

The Israeli kept to a crouch and lunged into the room—slamming into a dazed terrorist who had been stunned by the violent concussion of the grenade blast. Katz's shoulder caught the guy in the stomach, pushing him backward into a wall. The Phoenix commander quickly swung up the Uzi and rammed it across the terrorist's collarbone. The blow doubled up the stunned man. Katz followed through with a knee to the man's jaw. The guy slumped to the floor.

Rafael Encizo darted through the doorway, followed by David McCarter. A ribbon of smoke drifted from the Cuban's Uzi as he scanned the room, gun barrel moving in harmony with his head. They'd entered a chamber once used for storing and bottling wine. At least one figure bolted behind a row of wine kegs for cover.

McCarter saw the motion and fired at the kegs, the bullets gouging out large splinters of wood. Encizo ran to the kegs and gestured at McCarter with an arm wave. The Briton held his fire to avoid hitting his partner. Katz knelt by a pillar support to the ceiling beams and held his Uzi ready. No more of the enemy remained in sight.

Encizo moved to the end of the barrel row opposite their concealed enemies. The Cuban noticed that a low gate held the kegs in place. Leather bands were attached to the gate and hooked to the wall. He drew his knife and placed its sharp steel on the strap at his end of the row. The blade easily sawed through leather, and the band snapped apart. The gate hung loosely, and the kegs shifted toward Encizo's position.

"I get the idea, mate," McCarter whispered, although he knew Encizo couldn't hear him.

The British ace drew the Browning Hi-Power from shoulder leather. McCarter was more accurate with the pistol than with the Uzi. He gripped the Browning in both hands, took careful aim and squeezed the trigger.

The shot was challenging, yet McCarter struck the intended target—the well-placed bullet hit the leather strap at the end of the row of kegs where the terrorists were located. The band snapped and the gate fell open. The barrels rolled loose and rumbled across the floor.

Two astonished terrorists stood dumbfounded as their cover suddenly vanished. They were fully exposed, and the Phoenix warriors were ready for them. McCarter's Browning and the Uzis of Katz and Encizo blasted the pair without hesitation. One terrorist managed to return fire with an MPiK rifle. A version of the Soviet AK-47, the assault rifle spit a wild burst of 7.62 mm rounds in the general direction of David McCarter. The Briton dropped to the floor as bullets slashed air above his head.

Although his heart had already been stopped by two bullets, the terrorist's finger remained on the trigger as he fell. A steady stream of MPiK rounds raked the floor. McCarter's body jerked from the impact of slugs striking his flesh. Encizo fired another burst into the fallen gunman in a frantic effort to stop a dead man from pumping bullets into his friend.

The death grip on the MPiK finally relaxed, and the finger slipped from the trigger. The shooting ended. The sounds of battle raged outside, but Encizo and Katz were more concerned about their fallen partner at the moment. They rushed to McCarter as a pond of crimson slowly formed beneath his still form.

MACK BOLAN LOADED his M-203 with another shell, then launched the grenade at the main house. It hit the rooftop and exploded with a brilliant glare. Tiles were thrown in all directions. A section of the roof collapsed, and windows on the second story burst apart.

The Executioner ejected the spent shell casing and inserted another 40 mm round. He aimed with care and fired. The grenade lobbed neatly through the opening of the front door of the building. The shell erupted and spewed forth noxious CN/CD tear gas. The fumes were contained inside the house, and the constant gunfire from the paratroopers prevented the terrorists from fleeing the house.

Bolan took a gas mask from the case on his hip. He made certain the straps were firmly in place and the rubber mask snug around his face. He took a deep breath through the plastic filters and raced toward the house. Several French troopers had also entered the compound and followed Bolan's example. They jogged toward the main building as the others kept the enemy busy with steady cover fire.

A pair of figures appeared at the doorway to the house. Both men wore *keffiyeh* headdresses, the scarves drawn across their noses and mouths in an effort to protect them from the effects of the tear gas. They had moved a long-barreled light machine gun to the threshold. A metal box was attached to the right side of the frame, and the barrel was supported by a bipod.

Bolan recognized the weapon. It was a Czech-made Model 59 or a machine gun quite similar to it in design. With plenty of firepower and a cyclic rate of 800 rounds per minute, the Model 59 was a fearsome weapon that could easily chop down the assault force members if the terrorists could bring the machine gun into play.

The Executioner thrust the muzzle of his M-16 at the doorway. The lens of the gas mask restricted vision somewhat, but he had no trouble finding his targets. He fired the assault rifle and nailed the closest opponent with a burst of 5.56 mm slugs. The machine gunner collapsed across the frame of the M-59.

The second terrorist didn't waste time trying to move the corpse to reach the trigger mechanism to the machine gun. He immediately dropped to a kneeling position and dragged a pistol from his belt. It was a good move, but not good enough. Bolan triggered the M-16 again, and the guy's head snapped back, cored by two rounds.

Bolan reached the main house and fired another salvo as he charged the threshold. Bolan slammed a kick to the door and felt it smash into a terrorist lurking behind it. He saw several opponents in the front room. Dazed and weakened by the explosions and tear gas, they were slow to react to the threat that appeared before them. Without missing a beat the warrior sprayed the terrorists with the remaining rounds in the magazine. None survived.

The door creaked as the terrorist behind it made his move. The warrior turned to face the threat and thrust the buttstock of the M-16 into the attacker's chest. The blow stamped the guy's breastbone and knocked him backward into a wall. Bolan followed through with a chop to his opponent's face. The terrorist slumped unconscious to the floor.

Bolan found shelter at the end of a long couch. He discarded the empty M-16 and drew the Beretta. The 93-R was better suited for close quarters than the long-barreled weapon. He swung the Beretta around the edge of the sofa and opened fire on a pair of gunners who carried MAT-49 subguns.

A 3-round burst struck one man in the center of the chest and sent the guy hurtling across the room. His partner managed to return fire with a French chopper, but the spray of bullets missed the Executioner and ripped into the wall behind him. Bolan pumped another trio of parabellums into the attacker, and the gunman fell across a pair of previously slain comrades.

The immediate threat had been terminated, but Bolan heard angry voices and pounding footsteps approaching from other parts of the house. He also saw a pair of French paratroopers enter the room. Their faces were concealed by gas masks, but Bolan identified them as allies by their uniforms and FAMAS rifles. The pair scanned the room, apparently surprised to discover the only enemies present were corpses littered across the floor.

"Troopers!" Bolan called out, using some of his limited French vocabulary. "Over here."

The paratroopers were startled when they heard Bolan's voice. They turned toward the sound, rifles held ready. The Executioner stayed down, aware their adrenaline was pumping and they might react to any moving target with gunfire. However, the troopers held their fire, and Bolan rose slowly. The soldiers recognized the tall man in black and nodded to convey this.

"Cover the stairs and the west flank," Bolan ordered. "We'll have company any second now."

The Executioner's prediction came true even as he finished the sentence. Three terrorists descended the stairs as another pair appeared from the west archway. Bolan swiftly trained his 93-R on the figures at the stairs and triggered a long burst. A stream of parabellums cut across the first two opponents.

The dying pair tumbled down the stairs in a thrashing heap of tangled arms and legs. The third man de-

cided he wasn't eager to die for God after all and
bolted up the stairs. He almost made it. Bolan nailed
the guy with another burst. The man screamed as he
lost his balance and toppled down the risers to land
beside the bleeding bodies already at the foot of the
stairs.

The French troopers confronted the two new arrivals. The terrorists wore gas masks, and one of the
French soldiers hesitated, unsure if the men were
friend or foe. This mistake proved fatal as the terrorists opened fire with automatic weapons. The paratrooper folded up, his abdomen shredded by bullets.
Another round bored into his skull and burned
through his brain.

The second French warrior returned fire and blasted
one man with a burst of FAMAS slugs. Bolan swung
his 93-R toward the remaining fanatic and fired another salvo. A lens shattered on the terrorist's gas
mask as a parabellum plunged through the Plexiglas
barrier to puncture an eye socket.

Bolan heard the approach of more footfalls despite
the ringing in his ears from the gunshots in the confined area. He whirled to confront four shapes that
appeared from the east wing. The Executioner's finger began to close on the trigger, but he recognized the
uniforms and weaponry of the French paratroopers
and held his fire.

The paratroopers shouted something in French that
was too fast for Bolan to follow. Their heads bobbed
in a positive manner, and the warrior hoped this meant
he'd hear good news when somebody got around to
translating what they were talking about.

"Our troops have taken both wings to the house and dispatched what resistance they encountered," a voice finally explained in English. "Most of the enemy had to be killed, but we managed to take a few prisoners."

"Good," Bolan replied. "Search the house carefully. Make sure there aren't any terrorists hiding in closets or pantries. Don't forget they might have set up some booby traps. I'm going outside."

"I do not think the terrorists have much fight left," a paratrooper declared with more confidence than justified at that moment.

"They've got enough left to use the cannon if they have one here," Bolan reminded the troops. "And we have to assume they've got one."

GARY MANNING and Calvin James advanced from the generator shack. The Phoenix pair had contributed to the rifle fire that kept the enemy pinned down during the battle. The fighting gradually subsided as the terrorist forces were beaten down by the well-coordinated strategy of the assault force.

Manning had used his exceptional ability as a sharpshooter and sniper to pick off terrorists with precise bullet placement. James's marksmanship wasn't as impressive as the Canadian's, but he had also taken out several opponents with well-placed bursts of 5.56 mm rounds. The enemy fire had been reduced to little more than token efforts. The main house and one of the storage buildings had been captured.

The only remaining structure was damaged, and only sporadic enemy fire erupted from the broken windows and dismantled door. However, a long, thick barrel of a massive weapon appeared at the threshold. The Phoenix pair immediately recognized a cannon although they only saw part of the howitzer-style weapon.

"Shit," James rasped as he dropped to the ground. "I was afraid this would happen."

Manning nodded. They were well aware the enemy probably had such a cannon. They'd hoped the weapon would be disassembled, just as the one in England had been. No such luck, Manning thought as he drew the Stony-M rocket launcher from the belly holster.

"You sure that's the way to handle this, man?" James asked, tilting his head at the weapon in Manning's hands.

"We don't have time to debate this," the Canadian said as he knelt by his partner and aimed the Stony-M.

Manning triggered the launcher. A stream of white smoke streaked from the missile that shot toward the enemy building. The rocket hissed through the opening and sliced above the barrel of the cannon. It exploded inside the storage house, and the payload went off with a powerful blast. The cannon lunged forward and fell into view, a bloodied figure draped across its breech.

Manning launched another rocket, and the second exploded within the structure. The battered walls and supports to the billets gave way. The roof collapsed and crashed down on terrorists still inside.

"Let's go mop up," Manning announced in English, then in French.

The French soldiers jogged to the wreckage, weapons held ready. Manning and James walked to the cannon. The metal was dented and marred by the explosion. The Canadian demolitions expert found the breech handle and yanked it back to examine the chamber. A large shell had been loaded.

"I didn't think they were bluffing," Manning commented. "Wonder if this warhead is loaded with poison gas or germ warfare."

"That's why I questioned your wisdom firing those goddamn rockets at the sucker," James told him. "What if you'd set off the shell when you hit this thing?"

"That's why I didn't aim at the cannon itself," Manning explained. "There was still a risk, of course, but I figured the cannon would have to be pretty sturdy. Not likely it would burst apart or detonate the round unless I hit it directly with a rocket. I intended to stop the crew from firing it. The tactic worked. So did the Stony-M launcher."

"Yeah," James commented. "Doesn't make me glow with confidence when you're using weapons never tested in genuine combat before."

"Well, you're usually around when I'm in combat," Manning replied with a shrug.

Mack Bolan and several paratroopers approached from the main house. The Executioner was relieved to see that the cannon had been neutralized. He nodded to the Phoenix pair, expressing his thanks.

Katz and Encizo emerged from the third building. The battle was over, but the pair appeared grim. The other Stony Man commandos realized something was wrong. James dashed to the Israeli and Cuban warriors.

"Better take a took at David," Encizo said. "He's been hit pretty bad. We did what we could for him, but you're the team medic."

"Crazy Englishman better not die on me," James said as he headed into the building.

Katz looked about the remains of the enemy base. There was no doubt as to the victor, yet the Israeli's concern for a fallen teammate dampened his satisfaction with the success of their raid.

"I know how you feel," Mack Bolan assured the Phoenix commander, "but we still have a job to do. Let's start rounding up prisoners for interrogation and search for evidence in the debris."

"Right," Katz agreed with a weary nod. "This is no time to get sloppy."

"No time is the right time for that," the Executioner replied. "Life and death are our business. David knows that."

CHAPTER EIGHTEEN

Mohandra whirled the heavy Indian-club weights in a set of *zohahn* exercises. The other Iranian advocates of the Shiite form of physical exercise and meditation had already completed their hour of strenuous workouts. Mohandra always continued for another hour alone.

Klauss Zeigler and Arnoldo Lipari watched the muscular Iranian, unimpressed by the man's strength and endurance. Mohandra might be as powerful as a bull, but muscles didn't make him bulletproof. The European terrorists could stand ten meters away from the man and blow him away with their machine pistols before he could get close enough to get his hands on them.

Zeigler and Lipari weren't worried about Mohandra, but they realized he was only one of a hundred fanatics loyal to Hawran. The Europeans comprised only twenty members total. Jiro, a Japanese Red Army veteran who specialized in teaching the terrorists hand-to-hand combat, would probably side with Zeigler and Lipari if he thought they had a chance of overthrowing Hawran or escaping from the island base. However, the German and Italian hadn't formed a friendship with Jiro, and the Japanese had formerly worked with Palestinian factions. They weren't sure they could trust him.

"Bonjour," Kaborya greeted as he approached the pair. He knew both men spoke French and continued to communicate in that language. "You don't look very happy today."

"Do we have a reason to be happy?" Zeigler asked bluntly.

"You heard," Kaborya commented as he turned to watch Mohandra swinging his clubs.

"Of course," Lipari replied. "Our bases in England and France have been destroyed. Unless the operation in America is successful, all our work for the past year will be for nothing."

"And the capitalist forces of our combined enemies may hunt us down and attack this base," Zeigler added grimly.

"There's no reason to believe the enemy knows where we are," Kaborya insisted.

"There was no reason to believe they could learn the location of our bases abroad," Lipari reminded the Palestinian, "but they have done so, haven't they?"

"Yes," Kaborya was forced to admit. "Perhaps the unit in America will succeed. They should be carrying out their mission even as we speak."

"That's small comfort considering the enemies can still learn we're here," Zeigler declared. "We've known you for some time, Kaborya. You're no more eager to be a martyr for this holy war than we are. I doubt you even believe in God, let alone want to die for Him."

"What I believe in isn't important," the Arab answered. "We have to accept the reality of our situation. Major Hawran is in charge here. Like it or not, we all agreed to his plan and now we're in too deep to back out."

"I don't suppose we could poison the water supply," Lipari suggested, seeing the flaw in this notion even as he spoke. "No. They wouldn't all drink water at the same time, and when the first Iranians become ill the rest would assassinate us immediately."

"They've always been suspicious of us," Zeigler agreed. He turned to the Palestinian. "You got us into this mess, Kaborya. What do you suggest we do now?"

"I'll talk to Hawran," Kaborya said reluctantly. "Meantime, I advise you not to make the Iranians any more suspicious than they already are. Hawran's people know about the news from the front, as well. They're not apt to turn against their master or abandon his cause, but they'll turn on you Europeans if they have the slightest reason to think you oppose them."

"Just where do you stand, Kaborya?" the Italian asked, an eyebrow cocked high. "Are you on our side or Hawran's?"

The Arab smiled and replied, "I'm on my own side, gentlemen. That means I'll support either side depending on which offers me the greatest chance for survival. Don't count on me to back you if you decide to move against Hawran in a manner I consider suicidal."

"Staying here could be suicidal," Zeigler insisted. "You'd better remember that sometimes the most dangerous choice of action is to do nothing."

"The most dangerous action is to aggravate the person in the best position to kill you," Kaborya told the Europeans. "You'd do well to remember who that person is."

MAJOR HAWRAN WAS HOLDING a meeting with his advisers concerning strategy. Kaborya found the Iraqi commander discussing plans in the war room, and he realized this wasn't a good sign. He'd always been privy to Hawran's machinations in the past, but the major hadn't included Kaborya this time.

Whatever else might be said about Hawran, the Iraqi wasn't capricious. He wouldn't have assembled his advisers on a whim and overlooked Kaborya by accident. The Palestinian recognized Hawran's communications officer, as well as experts in chemistry and missile systems among the advisers. Mohandra, Hawran's most trusted Iranian follower, wasn't present. The muscle man was little more than Hawran's pet bodyguard and a go-between for the major and his Iranian recruits. Hawran's Intelligence officers were all fellow Iraqis. Kaborya had been the only exception, and it was obvious Hawran no longer regarded him as a valued confidant.

"Good day," Kaborya greeted as he approached the group.

"What do you want?" the communications officer demanded.

"I want to know what this is about," Kaborya replied. He glanced at the wall map and noticed several red flags pinned in a region of the Persian Gulf. "Looks like you're going on to the next phase, Major."

"I didn't call you to this briefing because there was no need for you here," Hawran stated as he stepped from the platform, arms folded on his chest. "This is a military operation that doesn't involve the questionable covert contacts of your international terrorist comrades."

"You're criticizing my contacts throughout Europe and the United States?" Kaborya asked, stunned by the remark. "Many of them worked undercover in those countries for more than a year without attracting the attention of the authorities. What makes you so certain the failures in England and France were their fault and not that of those brainwashed Iranians?"

"Because I know the men I conditioned for so many years," Hawran insisted. "They followed orders without question. They believed every command as if it came from the mouth of God...."

"You mean they believed in you?" Kaborya inquired. "Just as the Iraqi people were supposed to believe in Saddam Hussein. We saw what that got them."

"We might have need of your associates in the future," Hawran began. His tone was quiet, but an edge to his voice warned that his temper was strained. "For that reason, I'll overlook this insubordinate behavior."

Kaborya almost replied to this threat, but he recalled his own warning to the Europeans and held his tongue.

"We haven't heard about our operation in the United States," he reminded Hawran. "They might yet be successful."

"Whether they are or not," Hawran stated, "we're going ahead with the attacks on the American and other so-called allied naval vessels in the gulf. We've had two serious setbacks. If we don't strike swiftly and achieve another victory, the momentum of our holy war will suffer. We must continue to attack and keep the enemy off balance and filled with fear."

"Speaking of fear," Kaborya began. "None of you has any concern about the possibility the authorities will locate this base?"

"Are you and your European friends getting nervous?" one of Hawran's advisers asked with a smirk. "You had formerly told us those infidels had execrated the governments of the West. Perhaps they haven't denounced their countries and politics. They might have even influenced you with their weakness and cowardice."

"There's no need to insult Kaborya," Hawran told his aide. "He has done his job as well as possible. That might not be good enough, but we'll deal with that later. Now we have to change tactics and targets. This strategic vicissitude simply does not require your presence, Kaborya."

The Palestinian knew there'd be nothing gained by arguing with Hawran. The major had made up his mind, and he clearly had no intention of changing it. Hawran's attitude had become steadily more dictatorial since the operation had begun. The godlike power he wielded seemed to warp Hawran. He was beginning to believe in the infallibility of the holy war he preached to the Iranians.

Kaborya left the meeting. He was even more worried about what would happen in the future and unsure what to do under the circumstances. The Palestinian felt as if the entire world were slowly closing in around him. Hawran, the Iranians and even the European terrorists posed as great a threat to Kaborya as the Americans, British and French who were certainly stalking them. He suspected he was already a walking dead man. All that remained was to wait and see who finally put him in a grave and shoveled in the dirt.

CHAPTER NINETEEN

Jack Grimaldi circled the sky a few miles beyond the city limits of Washington, D.C. His Bell 206A helicopter was a TV station sky-cam and bore the station call letters painted on the side of the chopper carriage. The aircraft didn't attract much attention at seven o'clock in the morning. It was commonplace to see media helicopters, scanning the freeway to report traffic and weather conditions.

The Stony Man pilot watched the lines of vehicles below. Most were cars headed for Washington. Hundreds of people commuted from their homes in Virginia and Maryland to jobs in D.C. An occasional bus or delivery truck traveled the roads, as well as a few motorcycles and mopeds. However, Grimaldi was interested only in three vehicles—a canvas-top deuce-and-a-half truck, a battered four-door Ford and an equally mistreated old Chevy sedan that accompanied the rig. The trio looked like a miniature paramilitary convoy to Grimaldi. The vehicles also fit the description of the cars and truck that had left the Baltimore area three hours earlier.

The convoy had first been sighted by the federal agents and police involved in the surveillance of the African Crusaders in Baltimore. They had reported that the cars had briefly visited the Crusaders' house and left with the truck as a new addition. All three headed toward D.C., adopting an irregular and rather winding route to reach their destination.

The vehicles had been tracked by police, FBI and Justice department units along the way. Leo Turrin had personally supervised the surveillance and made certain all involved kept a low profile to prevent tipping off their quarry. Now they were almost at the capital, and Grimaldi's role as "spy in the sky" came into play.

He gathered up the microphone and switched on his radio. Grimaldi called out his code name of "Cloud Nine" and reported the position of the convoy. The voice of Rosario Blancanales replied from the radio, telling Grimaldi the message had been received "loud and clear." He then signed off.

"Yeah," the pilot muttered, but he had already returned the mike to its cradle. "Good luck."

Grimaldi passed over the road ahead. Roadblocks had been established to redirect traffic to another road where a line of sawhorses and men dressed in construction clothes and hard hats waved vehicles into a single left-hand lane. It looked innocent to Grimaldi, but he wasn't sure how paranoid the enemy would be. He banked the helicopter and left the area.

"OKAY," POL REMARKED as he emerged from the back of the Stony Man assault van. "They're headed this way."

Carl Lyons looked at his partner and nodded. The Able Team leader wore a gray coverall and yellow helmet. Blancanales donned his own hard hat to complete his disguise as a member of the road construction crew.

"Looks like we guessed right," he remarked. "After we figured the Capitol Building was the target, it was just a matter of using the logical information about the routes into D.C. to extrapolate which the enemy would use."

"Lucky us," Lyons remarked. "I know you and Gadgets are on your toes, but make sure the other guys know this is coming down. We don't want anybody caught napping when the convoy arrives."

Special Agent Anderson approached the pair. The FBI agent looked awkward in his road-worker disguise, his dark features brooding and grim. Lyons and Pol had already guessed the Feds had picked up the radio report and knew the terrorists were only minutes away.

"This is really it," Anderson remarked, his voice tense, "isn't it?"

"You got it," the Ironman replied. He pointed at the big steamroller and trucks by the roadblock. "You got your people with automatic rifles back there?"

"Just like you said," Anderson confirmed. "They're staying out of sight until needed. They're the best sharpshooters the Bureau could get on short notice."

"Okay," Lyons continued. "It's unlikely the convoy will try to break through the roadblock. The steamroller and trucks will be too tough to crash through. We want them to use this lane. That way we can separate the enemy from civilian vehicles and isolate them as much as possible on the freeway."

"Stray bullets might still hit innocent bystanders," Anderson said in a solemn tone. "I wish we could have come up with a better method that would be less risky."

"We've reduced the risk to civilians as much as possible," Lyons insisted. "You know damn good and well we couldn't move on the enemy convoy when it was between Baltimore and D.C. because it might have been a decoy to draw us out."

"It might still be a decoy," Anderson said glumly.

"Yeah," Lyons agreed, "but we can't let it go any farther. Unless we're totally wrong about the target the terrorists have selected, and the African Crusaders and the imported terrorists have played us for suckers, these sons of bitches are coming to Wonderland to blow the hell out of the Capitol Building."

"I'm just saying—" the Fed began.

"There's no more time for talking," Lyons said, a hard edge to his voice. "Get in position and be ready for the convoy. End of discussion."

Anderson wisely moved on to check with the other agents. Blancanales headed for the roadblock to join the sharpshooters. Lyons took a position along the line of sawhorses at the right-hand lane of the road. Schwarz remained inside the Stony Man wonder wagon. He'd helped build it and knew the equipment better than the other Able Team warriors.

They didn't have to wait long. The trio of vehicles rolled into view along with a number of civilian automobiles. The lead cars were waved to the left lane and obediently drove in that direction. Lyons stood on the line formed by a row of plastic cones. He waved his arm to urge the traffic to continue as he tried to watch the enemy convoy from the corner of his eye.

The first car was the Ford four-door. The driver rolled down the window and called out to the men by the roadblock. He was light skinned with blond hair, and he spoke with a guttural accent. The guy wasn't what the Feds expected. They thought the terrorists would be swarthy and dark. The FBI might have anticipated that black Americans from the African Crusaders would be driving the vehicles, but they didn't expect to see a guy at the wheel who resembled an Olympic ski champ from Sweden.

"What's wrong here?" the driver demanded.

"Just construction, mister," Anderson replied, and pointed to a signal banner at the left lane to the road. "You'll only be delayed a minute or two."

The driver hesitated. The deuce and a half was behind it, trailed by the Chevy. Other traffic began to assemble in back of the convoy. Horns announced frustration as drivers quickly became impatient. Lyons felt the muscles in his stomach knot. If the terrorists suspected the roadblock was a trap, they might start shooting or even fire the cannon in desperation. Civilians would certainly be victims if that happened.

Only a few seconds passed, but the time seemed to drag sluggishly as the nerves of Able Team and their allies grew taut. Finally the Ford pulled into the left lane. Lyons glanced into the windows of the car as it passed. The driver was as blond as Lyons himself, but the others inside the vehicle were dark men. They wore hats and had turned up collars to prevent showing much of their faces to the construction crew.

The truck followed. Lyons didn't try to look inside the cab, aware that too much interest in a passing vehicle might trigger the enemy into violence. The Chevy crept behind the rig. The Able Team warrior didn't see the driver and passengers clearly because the windows were tinted. He wondered if that meant the glass was reinforced and bullet resistant. That wouldn't make their job any easier.

Anderson held up his sign and kept traffic from following the convoy onto the left lane. A construction truck rolled forward to form a solid barricade in case a hasty driver decided to ignore instructions. Angry car horns responded to the maneuver, but Able Team and the others didn't care how much the civilians protested. Better to be pissed off than dead.

Schwarz backed the big black van into the left lane to block the convoy. The Ford came to an abrupt halt, and the deuce-and-a-half nearly hit the rear fender. Lyons pulled down the zipper to his coveralls and slipped a hand inside to touch the grips of his Colt Python.

The Chevy stopped behind the truck. Lyons barely glanced at the car. His attention was fixed on the canvas flap at the rear of the deuce-and-a-half. The Able Team leader suddenly bolted for the rig. He heard voices shout something in a language he didn't understand, and a car door opened behind him. Lyons didn't look back at the Chevy. He had to trust Pol and the others to cover his back as he raced to the truck.

A figure appeared from the passenger side of the Chevy, carrying an Ingram MAC-10 machine pistol. Blancanales broke cover and charged forward, pointed the H&K MP-5 and squeezed the trigger. He nailed the enemy gunman with a burst of 9 mm parabellums before the guy could aim the Ingram at Lyons.

The impact of the high-velocity rounds drove the terrorist back into the frame of the Chevy. The gunfire seemed to ignite both sides into action. All hell broke loose.

CARL LYONS HAD REACHED the rear of the truck, ignoring the gun battle all around him. He knew if Blancanales and the sharpshooters from the Corps couldn't protect him from the gunners in the Chevy, he wouldn't be able to save himself. The Ironman ripped back the canvas as he climbed onto the tailgate.

The deuce-and-a-half was loaded with a howitzer-style cannon mounted on a heavy cart, its barrel set in a horizontal position. At least half a dozen sets of eyes stared back at Lyons. Lean, tough and filled with anger, the terrorists looked as if they held Lyons personally responsible for everything unpleasant they had ever known in their entire lives.

The closest man reached for an M-16 assault rifle near his feet. However, Lyons's concern turned to another terrorist who already held a Mini-14 rifle in his fists. The Able commando snap-aimed the big Magnum revolver and shot the guy in the chest. The .357 Magnum slug smashed through the terrorist's heart, the force hurling him back into another pair of opponents who were trying to train weapons on the invader. The Mini-14 clattered on the floorboards as Lyons climbed over the tailgate.

The man who had reached for the M-16 started to raise it from the floor. Lyons grabbed the barrel with one hand and shoved it upward. His other fist held the Python and pointed the muzzle at a third opponent,

who was about to open fire with an Ingram MAC-10.
Lyons triggered his weapon faster and pumped two
158-grain bullets into the torso of the man with the
Ingram.

Punched back by the .357 grand slam, the gunner
fell as he triggered the subgun. The Ingram sprayed a
harmless volley of parabellum slugs through the canvas ceiling. The M-16 also spit out a short burst and
punched more holes in the tarp as Lyons held the rifle
barrel at bay. The terrorist with the M-16 tried to yank
it from Lyons's fist, but couldn't.

Frustrated, the terrorist attempted a butt stroke.
Lyons moved with his opponent and shoved the rifle
across the guy's chest, which pushed the man back
into a bench and a support rib to the canvas frame.
Lyons rammed a knee into the guy's groin before the
terrorist could regain his balance. Breath whooshed
from the gunman's mouth in a painful wheeze as his
testicles seemed to have been slammed up under his
lungs. Lyons quickly slapped the barrel of his revolver across the terrorist's skull.

The man dropped senseless as another terrorist
lunged forward, a large Puma hunting knife in his fist.
Lyons opened fire and blasted a Magnum round
through the attacker's stomach. The momentum of
the knife-wielding man carried him into Lyons. The
Able commander avoided the poorly aimed blade and
pumped another .357 missile into the man's solar
plexus.

More dead than alive, the terrorist still collided with
Lyons. The dead weight struck the Able warrior's
gunhand. The Colt Python roared and blasted a
harmless round into the floorboards. The Ironman

cursed under his breath, but managed to retain his balance. He grabbed his opponent's shirtfront and felt the man sag. Lifeless eyes stared at the commando. Lyons held the corpse's shirt in his fist and thrust his other hand between the dead man's legs, revolver still in his grasp.

He scooped up the slain terrorist and charged toward another pair of men. Lyons hurled the corpse, and the body slammed into one gunner who was about to fire a pistol at the Able Team leader. The other man sidestepped the attack. Lyons pointed the revolver and watched the guy duck for cover behind the cannon.

The terrorist didn't realize Lyons's Magnum was empty.

Pushing the dead man aside, the fanatic tried to point his Taurus pistol at Lyons's chest. The Ironman lashed out a boot and kicked the gun from the would-be killer's grasp. He followed with a left hook to the side of the opponent's jaw. The terrorist's head bounced from the punch, and blood oozed from his mouth. Lyons swung his arm and chopped the butt of the Python on the top of the dazed man's skull.

He turned to face the cannon, where his remaining enemy was located. The barrel of an M-16 poked above the massive frame of the artillery piece. Lyons dived to the floorboards as the rifle fired a short burst. He heard bullets strike flesh and a moan from the guy he'd slugged over the head. The terrorist rifleman had wasted his own comrade.

Lyons rolled to the cannon and quickly grabbed the barrel of the assault rifle with both hands. He gripped the warm metal firmly and pulled hard. The terrorist gunman grunted as he was yanked into the steel cannon frame. Lyons rose and whipped a back-fist to his opponent's face. The guy lost his hold on the rifle and crumpled to the floor of the truck, unconscious.

Lyons opened the cylinder of his Python, dumped out the spent shell casings and fished a speedloader from his pocket.

The Able commander discovered he was breathing heavily and he felt a frosty chill travel along his spine. No man was immune to fear, and Carl Lyons was no exception. The fierce battle inside the deuce-and-a-half had been brief but terrifying. Lyons had come within inches of death. His training and reflexes had overcome fear during the fight. Now he felt the effects of the stress after the battle.

"Don't lose it, man," Lyons cautioned himself as he inserted the six .357 shells into the chambers of the open cylinder.

His hands were steady as he reloaded the revolver. Lyons turned the speedloader knob to release the cartridges, then closed the cylinder. The Colt Python was fully loaded and ready for combat once more. So was Carl Lyons.

The sound of shooting outside the truck warned him that the battle wasn't over. A bullet ripped through canvas and struck the steel howitzer. It ricocheted against the cannon and tore another hole in the tarp. Lyons dropped to one knee, aware that more stray rounds could pierce the truck cover at any moment and the next bullet might find him instead of the cannon.

An explosion rocked the vehicle. Lyons braced his free hand on the floor boards to prevent being thrown on his face. He kept low as he moved to the rear of the vehicle and carefully peered through the gap in the canvas.

The Chevy had been destroyed—an explosion had torn the vehicle apart. The fuel tank had ignited, and flaming gasoline surrounded chunks of metal and burned the remains of three or more corpses. Fire also reached the truck. Lyons felt the blaze as canvas burned along the opening.

"Oh, God," he whispered tensely when he recognized the motionless figure sprawled on the ground near the charred remains of the enemy car.

Rosario Blancanales lay on his side. Lyons saw blood near his head, but couldn't tell if his partner was dead or alive. The fury of the gunfire that continued told Lyons the enemy was far from defeated and something had happened to change the way the battle was unfolding.

Something Able Team and the FBI had failed to foresee.

CHAPTER TWENTY

Reinforcements had arrived. Unfortunately for the Stony Man warriors and their allies, the reinforcements were additional terrorists.

Two cars appeared on the road parallel to the combat lane. The vehicles had come from the direction of Washington, D.C., and parked along the shoulder of the road. Terrorists emerged from the cars, armed with assault rifles and at least one grenade launcher. The latter weapon was used to lob a 40 mm shell at the FBI agents and sharpshooters stationed by the construction vehicles. The round missed its mark and hit the Chevy, which was already blown apart.

Lyons evaluated the situation from the rear of the truck. The enemy had thrown them a curve. Able Team had anticipated the terrorists might have backup, but they'd expected this would come from the direction of Baltimore, not D.C.

There was nothing to be gained by chastising themselves for the oversight. Lyons figured they had to deal with the reality of the situation and worry about what they should have done after the danger was over. He gathered up an M-16 and pulled back the charging handle to be certain a round was in the chamber. He searched the pockets of a dead terrorist to find a spare magazine.

He stuck the extra ammo in a coverall pocket and returned the Python to the holster inside the one-piece garment. The commando took a deep breath, moved to the tailgate and climbed from the rig.

He spotted the new arrivals positioned by the cars at the opposite road. The terrorist backup team used their vehicles for cover and fired rifles at Able Team and their federal allies. One guy held a weapon with a short, thick barrel, which Lyons recognized as an M-79 grenade launcher.

The FBI agents returned fire. Bullets struck the cars of the enemy, and one gunman dropped his rifle and clapped both hands to his face as blood spurted from his split skull. Lyons pointed his confiscated M-16 at the terrorists' position and sprayed a short burst as he jogged to Blancanales. The Ironman dropped to the ground next to the still form of his partner.

"Pol!" Lyons rasped, hoping for a response.

There was none, but Lyons noticed Blancanales was still breathing. He bled from several wounds, including at least one head injury. Lyons realized there was little he could do at the moment. He was even reluctant to move Blancanales because he didn't know if the fallen warrior had suffered any neck or spinal damage.

SCHWARZ HAD ALSO BEEN busy during the battle. He used the big black van to block the path of the convoy, pressed remote buttons to open the sliding door and activated the robotic arm attached to the micro-Uzi. The gun turned on the Ford to point at the terrorists who charged from open doors of the vehicle.

"Don't look like they plan to surrender," Schwarz commented when he saw the angry figures produce a variety of weapons.

A wave of automatic fire pounded the armor-plated van and bounced against bullet-resistant glass. Gadgets responded by triggering the remote-control box. Nine-millimeter rounds spit from the Uzi. The Able warrior operated the control dial and moved the robotic device along its track. Parabellums continued to pound a steady stream of high-velocity slugs into the chests of three opponents.

The impacts hurled the terrorists across the hood of the Ford. The two remaining opponents dropped to the ground to avoid the Uzi fire. Schwarz grunted with grim satisfaction as he peered through the eyepiece to the periscope. Not a bad start, he figured.

He grabbed his H&K submachine gun and worked the remote to activate the brake pedal. The van rolled back three yards as Schwarz switched off the robot Uzi. The enemy gunmen fired at the side of the vehicle and the windows to the front of the rig. Bullets hammered the tough glass, but didn't even scratch the surface.

Schwarz opened the trapdoor on the floor of the van and stealthily slipped through it to crawl under the vehicle. He slithered to the rear of the vehicle, MP-5 cradled in his arms. The enemy fire was directed toward the side of the rig and the front of the van. Neither opponent expected Schwarz to attack from the opposite end of the big black rig. They didn't notice him until he opened fire from his new position.

A well-aimed burst of H&K rounds slammed into one prone opponent. Parabellums shattered the guy's skull and snapped his spinal cord at the base of his neck. The terrorist's body jerked in a feeble death spasm as his comrade turned to face the attacker at the rear of the van. He wasn't fast enough. Schwarz nailed him with another burst of MP-5 slugs.

Bullets struck the edge of the van. Ricochets screeched past Schwarz's head and forced the commando to retreat. He glimpsed the source of the new threat. A terrorist, armed with an Ingram machine pistol, had emerged from the cab of the deuce-and-a-half to fire at the Able Team warrior.

"My turn," Schwarz whispered as he pressed the button to the Uzi robot device.

The microchopper at the door of the van opened fire as the mechanical arm moved along its track. Schwarz swung his MP-5 around the corner of the rig and triggered another volley at the gunman, who was suddenly caught in a lethal cross fire. Half a dozen 9 mm slugs sliced into his flesh. The MAC-10 rattled out a wild burst of bullets as the guy's bloodied form was thrown back into the cab of the truck.

Another grenade shell exploded between the trapped enemy convoy and the construction vehicles used for cover by the FBI agents and sharpshooters. Shrapnel burst in all directions. Schwarz heard a scream, but he couldn't tell where it came from. The truck trembled, and numerous tears in canvas revealed the effects of shrapnel on the vehicle.

Schwarz feared the enemy on the opposite road might be trying to target the truck deliberately. A grenade round might explode the cannon warhead and release whatever chemical payload was stored in the artillery shell.

Schwarz knew there was a way he could take out the enemy quickly and effectively. He climbed into the van and moved to the periscope. He located the pair of enemy automobiles and fixed them in the cross hairs. The Able warrior removed the box seat at the back of the van to unsheath the mortar fixed to the floor of the rig.

"Let's give these sons of bitches a surprise they won't live to remember," he muttered as he trained the mortar on target.

The shell was launched through the van's open sunroof. It hurtled high above the road and sailed toward the startled gunmen positioned by the two cars. Two terrorists broke cover and tried to flee from the descending projectile. Lyons stopped one with a burst of M-16 rounds; FBI riflemen gunned down the other.

The mortar shell landed with a mighty explosion, the blast demolishing both enemy vehicles. Smashed metal was strewn across the road. Gas tanks blew and secondary explosions increased the spread of debris. Gasoline was set ablaze, and a sheet of fire covered a large area. There was little doubt that the terrorists who'd used the cars for cover had perished along with their vehicles.

"Holy shit!" Agent Anderson exclaimed as he stared at the burning wreckage. "What the hell was that?"

"A Sunday punch," Lyons replied. He knelt beside Blancanales and placed two fingers to the fallen commando's neck.

"Is he alive?" Schwarz asked, running from the van to join his partners.

"Yeah," the Able commander said with a nod, "but his pulse is weak and he's obviously lost a lot of blood. He's not going to make it unless he gets medical help, pronto."

"I'll call for an ambulance," Anderson announced.

"There's already one on the way," Schwarz told him. "I punched the medical emergency code to the computer in the van. Figured we'd need medical personnel here to tend the wounded among the terrorists even if none of our people were injured."

"You guys think of everything," Anderson remarked.

"Not quite," Lyons said glumly. "We didn't anticipate that the backup team would come from D.C. Should have guessed the bastards would have somebody already in place in a city they targeted for terrorism."

"Well, we still stopped 'em cold," the Fed insisted. He was ecstatic that he'd survived the gun battle and the enemy had been defeated. Anderson liked the sensation of victory and didn't want it diminished.

"Yeah," Lyons confirmed. "We stopped them. The cannon is in the truck, like we figured. Better contact Lake and the Feds in Baltimore. Tell them they can move on the African Crusaders' base now."

"We've got plenty of evidence to link them with this conspiracy," Schwarz added. "Ali Simba-Mtu and his followers are going to find themselves facing a shitload of criminal charges for their part in this business."

"But it's over, right?" Anderson inquired. "I mean, the African Crusaders will be arrested and any of the terrorists who survived here will stand trial, too. That's it, isn't it?''

Carl Lyons and Gadgets Schwarz didn't answer. They were concerned about their fallen teammate. The sound of helicopter rotors announced Grimaldi had returned. More choppers appeared in the sky: flying ambulances with veteran medics among them.

''Hang on, pal,'' Schwarz told Pol as he held the unconscious commando's hand. ''We're not going to let you die.''

Lyons glanced at the deuce-and-a-half. He found some sense of satisfaction that they'd stopped the terrorists and captured the cannon that would have been used to attack the Capitol Building. Concern for Blancanales remained paramount in his mind. Lyons also knew the mission might be over as far as Anderson and the FBI were concerned, but Stony Man Farm and its fighting men still had a lot of work left to do.

It wasn't finished. Not yet.

CHAPTER TWENTY-ONE

"Bloody hell," the Briton complained as he tried to sit up in the bed. A sharp pain in his side made him abandon the effort.

"You must not move about," the French army doctor insisted as he stood by the bed. "You might break the sutures. We removed two bullets from you, and you must give the wounds time to heal."

"He's right," Rafael Encizo stated. "You're lucky to be alive, amigo. Gave us quite a scare."

"I bet I did," McCarter replied. He managed a thin smile in spite of the pain. "How would you blokes be able to get along without me?"

"Guess we'll find out," Manning said with a shrug. "Looks like we'll have to wrap up this mission without you. Hell, David, if you wanted some time off, you didn't have to go to such extreme measures to get it."

The Phoenix Force members exchanged the good-natured ribbing because they were relieved McCarter was going to recover from the wounds he'd suffered during the raid on the terrorist base at the vineyard in Champagne. The British ace had been lucky. Bullets had cracked a rib and caused some tissue damage, but no vital organs had been hit. Thanks to Calvin James's medical skill and fast action by the French paratroopers, McCarter was expertly treated for his wounds and rapidly delivered to the military hospital outside Paris.

"How did our side do?" McCarter asked as he glanced about the hospital room, hoping to see a pack of cigarettes.

"Pretty good," Encizo replied. He looked at the army doctor. "Who gave you authorization to handle medical care for our friend in this case? Please understand, I don't doubt your qualifications..."

"I understand," the doctor said with a nod. "This is a matter of security. My authorization came from army Intelligence and Pierre Bertin of Sûreté. I believe you know him."

"We do," Manning confirmed. "However, some of the details of our mission are restricted even from Sûreté."

"I can leave the room if you wish to speak privately," the doctor assured them. "Just be certain your friend doesn't get out of bed. Don't let him have a cigarette, either."

"Neither of us smokes," Encizo said. "Don't worry."

The doctor nodded his approval and left the room. McCarter muttered something about not being allowed to smoke, but **real**ized Manning and Encizo didn't sympathize with his nicotine habit.

"Six French paratroopers were killed and a dozen wounded in the raid," Manning told the Briton. "Katz, Mack and Cal are all okay. They're not here because they're busy interrogating prisoners."

"Did you manage to take many of the terrorists alive?" McCarter asked as he tried to prop himself up on an elbow.

"We took twelve terrorists alive," Encizo said. "We had to kill almost three times that number. Some of the survivors are too badly injured to interrogate. The wounded enemy are here at the hospital under heavy guard. So are the majority of the French troops hurt in the battle."

"Great," McCarter commented. "Maybe we can form a bridge club if we stay here long enough. How many terrorists are still healthy enough to question?"

"Three or four," the Canadian commando answered. "Cal is making the decision on who's fit enough to hold up under injections of scopolamine. You know what he's like. Cal will kick ass in combat, but when enemies are injured and captured, he regards them as patients. He won't stand for anything that might jeopardize their health."

"Admirable trait," McCarter said, "but I don't know if we can afford to handle these blokes with kid gloves. We still don't know where the enemies' main headquarters is located or how many of those human cockroaches are still lurking in the international woodwork."

"Yeah," Encizo agreed, "but we'll get them, David. For now you've got to stay put and heal your wounds. Afraid you'll have to sit out the rest of this mission."

"Sure," the Briton said with a sigh. "I just hope I don't die of boredom in this place. You chaps be careful when you go out there again."

"We'll be as careful as we can. Don't worry. We'll be back," the Cuban assured him.

BOLAN WATCHED Calvin James prepare the prisoner for interrogation. He took the pulse, blood pressure and used a stethoscope to check the subject's heart. Only after he was satisfied with the information about the captive's health did James insert the needle of a syringe into a vial of scopolamine.

"This guy's in good physical condition," James announced as he measured the dose of truth serum. "Aside from the bump on his head, there's nothing wrong with him. He's about 155 to 160 pounds. The dose has to fit the person's body weight and other conditions."

Bolan nodded. He knew scopolamine was potentially dangerous. A dose that was too great could be fatal, and too small a dose could be ineffective. James was a qualified chemist, as well as a former hospital corpsman with the navy SEALs, and had earned medical degrees since he'd left the service. The black warrior had also acquired a great deal of in-the-field experience in the use of scopolamine since he'd joined Phoenix force.

Scopolamine was the most reliable and effective truth serum. It wasn't infallible, but James was familiar with the telltale signs that suggested a subject was resisting the effects of the drug and lying under the influence. He was also a skilled hypnotist and recognized posthypnosis in a subject. This was a method used by some Intelligence agencies to relay false information when a captured agent was interrogated with truth serum or sleep deprivation. James knew what to watch for and could spot posthypnotic programming.

Yakov Katzenelenbogen stood next to Bolan as they waited for James to inject the scopolamine into the arm of the terrorist. The subject was strapped to a chair and already groggy from a mild sedative. James held the man's arm firmly and inserted the needle into the vein at the crook of the guy's elbow.

"Yankee—pig—" the prisoner said in a slurred voice. He tried to spit at James, but the saliva glob landed on his own pant leg.

James stepped away from the subject and moved to Bolan and Katz. The prisoner's head began to weave, and he cursed under his breath. He struggled slightly, but the efforts soon subsided. James glanced at his wristwatch.

"Give the drug two more minutes to be sure it takes effect," he advised. "We know this dude speaks some English, but it's best to interrogate a person in his native language when— Hell, you know how this works."

"Yeah," Bolan confirmed. He turned to Katz. "You're the master linguist, Yakov."

"I just hope he speaks a language I know," the Israeli replied with a sigh. He waited two minutes and approached the man strapped to the chair.

"What's your name?" Katz asked in Arabic. He repeated the question in a loud, firm voice when the man failed to answer.

"Jabir Ramad al-Ahmed," the subject replied in a dazed manner. He sounded as if he was talking in his sleep.

The guy had responded to the question. Katz continued to interrogate him in Arabic. He asked, "What nation is your home, Jabir?"

"Jomhori-e-Islami-e-Irân," Ramad answered.

Katz didn't understand much Farsi, but he recognized the words "Islamic Republic of Iran." The Phoenix commander asked if Ramad spoke Arabic fluently. Ramad replied that he had been born and raised in west Iran. Arabic had been his first language.

"Good," Katz said, relieved they shared a common language. "Why are you and your comrades in France?"

"To strike at the infidels," Ramad replied. "To bring the Islamic holy war to the land of one of our enemies and to strike at the Great Satan country of the United States of America."

"That's why you attacked the U.S. Embassy?"

"Yes," Jabir answered.

"Did the government of Iran order you to carry out this mission?" Katz inquired.

"Our orders come from the great commander who represents the Ayatollah, President Saddam Hussein and God Himself," Ramad declared with a smile.

"This great commander must be quite a man," Katz said, wondering if the prisoner was hallucinating. The notion that someone was a conduit for the leaders of both Iran and Iraq, as well as God, didn't seem to make sense. "What is this great man's name?"

"He is called Major Karim Hawran," Ramad answered. "I met him as a prisoner, but he showed me the light to see the holy war had to embrace both the Shiite teachings of the Ayatollah and the doctrine of Islamic unity of Saddam. Then, on one glorious day, the major freed me from the prison walls to become one of his elite warriors against the infidels."

Katz absorbed these remarks and tried to assimilate the information. "This major taught you about Saddam? Is he an Iraqi?"

"He is a Muslim, and that is all that matters."

"I understand that," Katz replied, choosing his words with care, "but how can I learn from Major Hawran if I don't know where to find him and study what he has to teach?"

Ramad nodded, satisfied with Katz's statement. "The major is no longer in Iraq," he explained. "We left there before the Americans and their allies came to the gulf to attack Iraq."

"So you were in Iraq and you were in prison?" Katz asked, putting together the pieces of the puzzle. "That means you were captured during the Iran-Iraq war in the 1980s."

"We Iranians were wrong to fight Iraq," Ramad said with a frown. "Muslims must unite to fight the infidels and the traitors who side with the West. Kuwait and Saudi Arabia are traitors to Islam. Egypt, Qatar, the United Arab Emirates and others have also betrayed us."

"I understand. The major taught you well. Where may I find this great man of wisdom and action?"

"There is an island somewhere between Yemen and an African country in the Gulf of Aden. Do you know the islands of Abd al-Kuri and Socotra?"

"Not really," Katz admitted. "I assume these islands are in the Aden Gulf. Can I find them on the map?"

"You can. But both are part of Yemen. The major's island is smaller. It's in the area of the other islands, but it isn't Yemeni territory."

"Does the major have connections in Yemen?" Katz asked, recalling the terrorists they'd encountered who were known to be associated with training camps in South Yemen.

"I believe so," Ramad answered. "We went to Yemen when we first left Iraq. Major Hawran and Kaborya took us to a camp where others were already in training. Some of these were infidels, Europeans. I didn't trust them, but the major said these men were necessary for our holy mission. We needed the Westerners in order to infiltrate Western nations."

"That makes sense," Katz said. "What did Major Hawran plan to do after you completed your terrorist assignments in France?"

"He didn't tell us more than we needed to know for our assignments. He said it would be best that way, and we needed only to have faith in God and the holy war."

"That makes sense, too," the Phoenix commander remarked. He approached Bolan and James as he fished a pack of cigarettes from his pocket.

"I didn't understand a word, but it seemed like a heartfelt conversation," James remarked. "Learn anything of interest?"

"Struck the jackpot," Katz replied. He used the steel hooks of the prosthesis to draw a cigarette from the pack. "The prisoner told me the name of the leader of the terrorist conspiracy and a general location of the main base."

"How general?" Bolan asked. "A country? A city?"

"An island in the Gulf of Aden," Katz stated, and took out his lighter. "From the description, it must be off the coast of Somalia."

"Good enough," the Executioner said with a nod. "We'll find the base. Let's just hope we can do it before the terrorists make their next move."

CHAPTER TWENTY-TWO

"Congratulations," the President of the United States said. "I've learned that your people were successful in their work overseas, as well as here in America."

Hal Brognola listened to the President on the hot line at Stony Man Farm. The Commander in Chief sounded pleased and enthusiastic. Brognola hated to tell him it was premature to celebrate.

The big Fed hadn't expected to hear from the President so soon. He'd planned to contact the Man in the Oval Office with a progress report, but he'd been too busy. Brognola was at the hub over every Stony Man operation. Barbara Price had been coordinating various Intelligence agencies in Europe with the Stony Man warriors' mission. Leo Turrin was the main go-between for the Farm and federal and local law enforcement involved with Able Team's work in the States. Aaron Kurtzman continued to man his post at the computer room, gathering and sending information.

Brognola had to cope with handling everything else. He had to carry this prodigious burden and act as go-between with the White House and various government agencies, as well. It was an onus that could break the back of an elephant, but he'd borne it for years. Nobody held a gun to his head to accept the role as director of Stony Man Farm. He knew it would be tough and demanding. Brognola figured it was part of the job and he wasn't one to whine.

"Well, sir," Brognola began with a sigh, "I appreciate the call, but I'm afraid the situation is still reinfecta at this time."

"Reinfecta?" The President's voice conveyed a frown.

"Yeah," the big Fed answered. "You know, the business isn't really finished because we haven't accomplished our ultimate purpose."

"I'm familiar with the term. But I do have sources of information other than your group. The reports from them have been very favorable. In fact, they seem to feel the business was completed with total success."

"The operations in the United States and Europe succeeded, but we still have to take care of their headquarters."

"Have you located this site?" the man in the Oval Office wanted to know. "Is it a private enterprise or connected with a government?"

"We have a pretty good idea where it is. We should be able to pinpoint the exact location soon. I'll probably need your help to get cooperation from certain authorities. They might not be willing to assist us without some pressure from your office."

"You'll get it," the President assured him. "Whatever you need, you can count on it from my end."

"Good," Brognola said. "We're still trying to find out if the headquarters is privately run or sponsored by a foreign government. So far, the evidence suggests the former."

"I hope you're right." Terrorism directly linked to a government would lead to political headaches the President would just as soon not have to deal with. "What else can you tell me at this time?"

"Not much," Brognola admitted. "I'll know more myself later. Don't worry. I'll meet with you directly when I have some definite information."

"That sounds fine," the President stated. He wished Brognola good luck and hung up.

THE ELEVATOR DOORS ROLLED open. Brognola had ridden up from the War Room in the basement level to the computer room on the first floor. Kurtzman was waiting for him at the threshold.

"Got a pot of coffee brewing," the Bear announced. "Come on in and have a cup."

"No, thanks," Brognola replied. "I think I might be getting an ulcer, and a cup of your coffee could kill me."

"So put some extra cream in it," Kurtzman suggested. "Interpol came up with positive ID on some of the terrorists Able Team took out earlier today. One of them was a member of the German Red Army Faction who dropped out of sight in 1986 and was believed to be in a camp in South Yemen."

"Yeah, that seems to be a pattern. Any news on Blancanales's condition?"

"I don't have a computer linkup with the hospital," the Bear answered. "Schwarz is there with him. We'll get a call when he knows how Pol is doing. Blancanales is tough. Not easy to kill a man like him."

Brognola grunted and nodded. He knew everybody died eventually. They'd buried more than one of their own since Stony Man was created. The fact any of them were still alive was a small miracle.

"The FBI and Justice Department are holding the terrorist prisoners for interrogation," Kurtzman explained as he rolled his chair across the room. "The National Security Agency and the CIA found out what happened, and they're claiming this should be their jurisdiction because the incident concerns international sabotage. They're pretty bent out of shape and figure they got left out in the cold on this."

"Life is tough. Is Leo still coordinating the FBI and Justice personnel involved?"

"Yeah," the Bear confirmed. "Getting some flak on that, too. Some high-mucka-mucks are demanding to know who the hell Leonard Justice is and why he ranks being in charge of such an important operation. The Bureau is particularly annoyed because they figure they're getting upstaged and used by Justice."

Brognola guessed Turrin was dealing with this problem by telling the federal brass to get off his back and let him do his job. If they made things too difficult, Turrin would contact the Farm, and Brognola in turn would contact the President. The FBI and Justice boys would back off double-quick after the man in the White House told them Leonard Justice had his personal authorization to command the situation.

A buzzer sounded above a closed-circuit television screen. The Bear glanced up at the TV and saw a helicopter hover over a line of treetops. Jack Grimaldi was returning to the Farm.

Kurtzman's attention turned to a computer printout sheet that shuffled from one of his machines. The Bear steered his wheelchair to the data sheet and scanned the information. He nodded, pleased by what he read.

"The Baltimore police, FBI and BATF raided the African Crusaders' headquarters approximately half an hour ago," Kurtzman announced. "The combined forces of the local cops and Feds surrounded the house and ordered the Crusaders to surrender. There was a brief exchange of gunfire before the Crusaders gave up. No officers or federal agents were injured or killed in the encounter."

"That's great," Brognola agreed. "Any information about how many Crusaders were hit?"

"Two," Kurtzman answered as he finished reading the sheet. "Simba-Mtu and his top lieutenant. Apparently they started shooting at the cops, who responded with automatic rifles and threatened to blow the place up if they had to. Some of the African Crusaders had women and kids in the house. They wanted Simba-Mtu to surrender. When he refused to do so, they killed him. The second-in-command tried to protect his boss, so they shot him, too. Then they got out the white flag."

"Not bad news," Brognola commented. "Another loose end that's been taken care of. Let's see what Jack has to tell us."

"Lyons is probably with him," Kurtzman stated. "You go ahead. I'm going to stay here in case some more information comes in."

Brognola punched in the numbers to the coded access door, left the computer room and headed for the entrance hall. The front door opened, and Jack Grimaldi entered, followed by Carl Lyons and Gadgets Schwarz.

"I thought you were at the hospital," Brognola said, directing the remark at Schwarz.

"That's a hell of a welcome, Hal," Gadgets complained, but he was clearly in a good mood. "No reason for me to stay at the hospital. I don't want to disturb Rosario if he decides to start hitting on the nurses."

Brognola smiled with relief. "Sounds like Blancanales is going to be okay."

"He caught some shrapnel and took quite a bruising," Schwarz explained, "but the doctor said there were no broken bones, internal bleeding or other serious injuries."

"You should have seen the blood from the Pol's scalp wound," Lyons remarked. "Looked a lot worse than it was."

"Well, Rosario did lose a fair amount of blood," Schwarz stated. "Enough that he needed a transfusion, and he'll be laid up in the hospital for a few days. Nothing to worry about except we're one man short now."

"Two men short," Brognola replied. "McCarter stopped a bullet or two in France. He's in a hospital, too. He's not hurt badly, considering what happened. Still, with a broken rib and a hole in his side, McCarter isn't going into combat for a while."

"They'll have to use restraining straps to keep that crazy Englishman in bed," Grimaldi remarked.

Nobody argued with that statement. They all knew McCarter.

"This news still takes the dark cloud off my day, fellas," Brognola announced. "Everything sounds pretty positive right now. Phoenix Force and Bolan took out the terrorist camps in England and France. You guys stopped the enemy in D.C., and the cops raided the African Crusaders. Simba-Mtu has gone to that big lion cage in the sky, by the way.''

"I think he'll find out God isn't too happy with him after all," Lyons commented. "So what's next on the agenda?"

"We think we've located the main base of the entire terrorist network," Brognola explained. "Striker sent us a coded message after interrogating some prisoners. Apparently the leader is an Iraqi army officer who recruited a large number of Iranian POWs as his followers."

"You mean during the Iran-Iraq war?" Lyons asked with surprise. "Son of a bitch started planning that long ago?"

"Why the hell would Iranian POWs want to follow one of their captors?" Grimaldi wondered aloud.

"Look, I don't know," Brognola replied. "What matters now is the terrorists have an island stronghold in the Gulf of Aden. One prisoner recalled occasional visits by a black African VIP of some sort. That suggests the island is part of Somalia and someone with the government—or at least a branch of it— knows the terrorists are there."

"Great," Schwarz said with a groan. "So we have to take on the Somali government?"

"No," Brognola assured him. "Stony Man won't take it on. The President will. All you guys have to worry about is an island full of bloodthirsty fanatics and professional killers."

"I see," Lyons replied. "Business as usual."

CHAPTER TWENTY-THREE

Klauss Zeigler raised the club. The slender Japanese opponent's stoic expression didn't change as the German threatened him with the stock. Zeigler had squared off with Jiro numerous times in the past. On several occasions he'd tried to use a club against the martial-arts instructor. He'd never been able to touch Jiro with a stick.

The German terrorist decided to try to catch his opponent off guard. He feinted with the club in an overhead position and quickly changed the attack to a lunge, hoping to ram the stick into Jiro's belly. The Japanese wasn't fooled by this distraction. He sidestepped the thrust and grabbed Zeigler's wrist above the cudgel.

Jiro pulled, increasing Zeigler's momentum. He twisted the captured wrist as his free hand caught Zeigler's elbow. A foot swept into the German's ankle. He tripped and fell face-first to the mat. Jiro easily disarmed the European, sat on his back and smacked the mat a few centimeters from Zeigler's head to make it clear he could have bashed in the other man's skull.

"I never was any good at this sort of thing," Zeigler complained as Jiro helped him to his feet. "Give me a decent automatic weapon or some explosives. All your judo and karate and whatever else you know won't do you any good then."

"What if you don't have a weapon?" Jiro inquired. They conversed in English because neither spoke the other's native language.

"I always have a weapon," Zeigler insisted.

Jiro sighed and shook his head. They'd discussed this before, and he didn't care to waste time explaining that one can run out of ammunition and firearms can jam. An explosive can only be used once and may even fail to detonate. Yet, if a person's body was a weapon, he could never be truly unarmed.

"Why don't you tell me what you want?" Jiro inquired, and folded his arms on his narrow chest. "I suspected something was odd when you requested a private training session."

"You didn't believe I needed to brush up on my hand-to-hand combat skills?" Zeigler asked.

"I know you well enough to realize this shortcoming doesn't worry you," the Japanese explained. "You want to talk to me, but you don't want Major Hawran or the others to hear. Correct?"

"That's right," Zeigler admitted.

"It might not be wise for you to speak," Jiro warned. "Or for me to listen."

Zeigler glanced about the dojo. The small martial-arts gymnasium was empty aside from the two men. Yet Zeigler was afraid someone might be listening to their conversation. He also wondered if Jiro could be trusted to keep what he said confidential.

"You know the operations in France, England and the United States of America have failed," Zeigler began. "All our people are either dead or prisoners."

"I'm aware of that," Jiro assured him. "And I know Major Hawran is planning some new action. An attack on U.S. Navy vessels in the gulf."

"The man only knows how to launch offense actions," Zeigler stated. "Instead of attacking a new target, Hawran should be moving on to a new base of operations. The enemy will find us eventually if we stay here."

"So you want to leave?" Jiro asked with a smile. "I don't think Hawran and his Iranian friends would look kindly on any effort to leave this island. Just where do you think you'd go if you do leave? Don't expect either Somalia or Yemen to protect you."

"I'm aware of that," Zeigler stated. "But I think we'll die here like sheep in a slaughterhouse if we remain."

"What do you suggest?" Jiro inquired. "Mutiny? I wouldn't dishonor myself by such behavior. When we agreed to join Kaborya and Hawran, we essentially gave our word that we wouldn't betray the jihad."

"Gave our word?" Zeigler repeated as if astonished by Jiro's remark. "Just like you gave your word to follow the dogma of the Japanese Red Army and I swore allegiance to the Baader-Meinhof gang? Don't you realize we were used? The KGB manipulated us because it served the interests of the Kremlin to have us stir up unrest in West Germany and Japan. The capitalist governments took advantage of our actions to enforce greater restrictions on the public. Our cell leaders became more concerned with personal ambitions than any political goals. We were betrayed, Jiro. They dishonored us."

"So why are we here?" Jiro asked. "You didn't object when this mission began. The opportunity to leave the Yemen camp and carry out activities against the imperialists appealed to you until our cause suffered these setbacks."

"Losing close to a hundred of our forces is more than a setback," Zeigler insisted. "This jihad is absurd. You know that as well as I do."

"What does Kaborya say?" the Japanese asked. "We followed him when we joined this cause. Does he also feel we've made a mistake?"

"He's being evasive," the German said. "Kaborya knows how vulnerable we are here. He doesn't want to go against Hawran."

"But you do. You're so desperate for an ally you even turn to me. I'm not your friend, Klauss. I never have been."

Jiro suddenly unfolded his arms from his chest. A hand slashed a cross-body stroke and chopped Zeigler in the face. The unexpected blow to the cheekbone stunned the European and knocked him backward three steps. Jiro unleashed a kick to the abdomen. The edge of his foot stuck Zeigler below the navel. He doubled up with a gasping groan.

"I'm not a traitor, either," Jiro rasped as he wrapped an arm around Zeigler's neck.

He secured a headlock with his right arm and planted his left hand on Zeigler's shoulder. Jiro's right hand grabbed his own wrist to secure the viselike grip around Zeigler's neck. The German rammed a fist under Jiro's ribs. The Japanese hissed in pain and twisted with all his might.

Bone cracked. Zeigler heard the sound of vertebrae popping in his own neck. Pain bolted through his spinal cord to the brain. The immense shock rendered him unconscious, but the last flickering thought in the German's mind was the knowledge that Jiro had killed him.

The Asian lowered the limp body to the mat. Zeigler's head rolled loosely on the broken stem of his neck. Jiro looked down at the corpse. His expression remained calm as he stepped over the still figure of Klauss Zeigler.

THE VOICE OF THE CRIER calling from the summit of the minaret sounded across the island. More than a hundred Iranian Muslims knelt on prayer rugs, facing Mecca.

Arnoldo Lipari took advantage of the situation to meet with several other Europeans at the terrorist base to discuss the crisis that had developed since Hawran's forces had suffered defeat after defeat.

"You said Zeigler would be here," a German terrorist remarked.

"He's trying to convince Jiro to join us," Lipari explained. He turned to a trio of fellow Italian Red Brigade veterans. "Our best chance to survive is to leave this island before the combined forces of the United States, England and France find this place and destroy it."

"How do we leave? Iranians guard the airstrip and the boats."

"We decide whether it would be more feasible to steal a boat or a helicopter," Lipari answered. "If we have to, we'll build rafts and set to sea on them."

"What do you think the Somalis will do if we arrive on their coast?" a French terrorist asked, and shook his head. "We'll be lucky if they just shoot us on sight."

"We might do better if we head for Abd al-Kuri or one of the other Yemeni islands," Lipari answered. "The government of Yemen doesn't want to be associated with Hawran. That's why we had to leave the old camps."

"Sounds desperate and foolish to me," the German said. "What about Kaborya and the other Palestinians? They got us into this. How do they feel about Hawran now?"

"Kaborya isn't taking a firm stance either way," the Italian explained. "Hawran is trying to blame Kaborya and all of us for the failures so far. Kaborya thinks it will take very little to convince Hawran to slaughter the lot of us. The rest of the Palestinians are either emulating Kaborya or they believe in this Islamic holy-war nonsense and they're loyal to Hawran."

"Those Muslim idiots have probably finished their rituals by now," the German commented. "We'd better continue this debate another time. The savages tend to get suspicious when we get together."

"I wonder why," the Frenchman remarked dryly.

Lipari and the other Italians filed out the front of the barracks. Some of the others would leave by the back, and a few would remain in the building. Lipari glanced at his wristwatch and wondered what had happened to Zeigler. He must have had trouble convincing Jiro to join them, Lipari decided. The Japanese was an odd character, and none of them knew him well although they'd all spent years together at the training camps in Yemen.

Major Hawran materialized from the communications building, accompanied by Kaborya and two Iraqis. He held a Stechkin machine pistol in his fist, and his fellow Iraqis carried AK-47 assault rifles. All weapons were pointed at Lipari and his companions. Kaborya looked at the Europeans and shook his head sadly.

"You made a very bad mistake, gentlemen," Hawran announced in English. "Kaborya, perhaps you should translate this into French or Italian to be certain they understand."

"I don't think that's necessary," the Palestinian said grimly. "The meaning must be obvious."

"Arab pig!" Lipari grated, the insult hurled at Kaborya. "You betrayed us to save yourself!"

"I wouldn't be interested in saving anyone else," the Palestinian admitted. "You and Zeigler made a very stupid decision. All I did was prevent myself from being pulled down with you."

"Did you tell him you suggested we plant microphones in the European barracks so we could eavesdrop on their conversations?" Hawran inquired. Kaborya and Lipari had spoken in French, and the Iraqi officer wasn't certain what they said.

"Let's just get this over with," Kaborya urged, switching to Arabic.

Gunshots erupted. Screams mingled with the bursts of automatic fire. Lipari realized the other European terrorists had been ambushed by Hawran's men. They were being executed by the impromptu firing squads. The Italians knew they'd be next. There was nothing to lose and only one thing left to hope for. Lipari reached for the pistol on his hip.

Major Hawran triggered the Stechkin. The Russian machine pistol snarled, and a trio of slugs smashed Lipari's breastbone and ripped his lungs and heart. The AK-47 rifles chattered metallic songs of death as the echoes of Hawran's Stechkin still hung in the air. The other Italians toppled to the ground beside Lipari.

"No wonder my people didn't complete their missions in Europe and America," Hawran said through clenched teeth. "They were forced to work with scum like this!"

He sprayed the fallen figures with another volley until the clip ran dry. Chunks of flesh burst from the lifeless bodies of the slain Europeans. He returned the Stechkin to the holster on his belt and stepped over the pile of corpses.

"So much for the insurrection," Major Hawran said with a cruel smile. "Now, let's finish preparations to launch our attack on the enemies stationed in the Persian Gulf."

CHAPTER TWENTY-FOUR

Abu Yuman was eager to meet Mohammed Mabettet. He didn't know why he'd been chosen to represent the Republic of Yemen, but Mabettet had apparently requested him personally for the meeting at the city of Abha in the southwest area of Saudi Arabia. The Saudi was a high-ranking official in his country and a close friend to King Fahd himself.

Relations between Yemen and Saudi Arabia had been frayed for many years. Occasionally there were improvements, but problems occurred that kept the countries on shaky terms most of the time. Yemen's refusal to condemn Saddam Hussein's invasion of Kuwait or to support UN sanctions against Iraq hadn't endeared the government to the Saudis. Yemen was even less popular with the West for the same reasons. Yemen needed to mend some fences and improve relations and international trade.

Yuman hoped this might be a big first step toward that goal. He was a deputy minister with internal affairs—not a likely choice to be asked to meet with a powerful Saudi official like Mabettet, but Yemen wasn't going to question that as long as a chance for improved relations existed.

A government limousine met Yuman at the airfield outside Abha. He was taken to the city with VIP treatment as the morning sun rose high in the blue-

and-white sky. The limo eventually pulled into a carport of a small building near an oil refinery.

Three men waited for Yuman at the archway to the port. He recognized Mohammed Mabettet. A large man with a round face and strangely gentle features, the Saudi was well-known throughout the Arab world. Dressed in white robes and a matching *keffiyeh,* the man was an impressive figure.

The other men with Mabettet puzzled Yuman. They appeared to be white Europeans or perhaps Americans. One man wore a baggy dark suit and a necktie that hung loose beneath the open button at his throat. The other man was big and athletic. He looked tough enough to break a camel's neck with his bare hands, but the bulge under his jacket revealed the man carried something more effective than muscles.

"Greetings," Mabettet said. "I understand you speak English, Abu Yuman. Let's converse in a language my friends understand."

"These men are your friends?" Yuman inquired suspiciously.

"Of course. They're Americans. When Kuwait was invaded and Saudi Arabia threatened by the legions of Saddam Hussein, Americans came to help us. I fought in the war, you know. The Americans fought with great skill and courage. I welcome them as my friends."

"I wasn't told Americans would be present at our meeting," Yuman replied. He felt a degree of xenophobia toward non-Arabs in general and Americans in particular.

"It's a surprise," Hal Brognola announced as he took a cigar from his pocket. "Come on, pal. Let's talk."

"What's this about?"

"I'll explain everything inside," Mabettet assured him.

"Meter's running," Brognola stated. He realized the Arab might not understand the slang expression. "We don't have time for idle chitchat. Okay?"

"First I'd like to call my country's embassy," Yuman insisted.

"You're not calling anyone until we talk," Mack Bolan said in a stern yet quiet voice. "Get inside the building, or I'll help you move."

Yuman believed the man was serious. He doubted Bolan would be gentle if he "helped" him inside. The Yemeni followed them through the entrance. The men walked along the narrow hallway to a door guarded by two Saudi paratroopers. At Mabettet's nod, one of the sentries opened the door.

Yakov Katzenelenbogen and a middle-aged black man sat at a conference table in the room. Mabettet invited the others to be seated. Yuman felt uncomfortable and slightly frightened. He noticed that the gray-haired man with an artificial arm appeared calm, but the black man looked as distressed as Yuman felt.

"May I introduce Mr. Kismaayo from the country of Somalia," Mabettet announced. "This is Mr. Yuman from Yemen. These other gentlemen are using assumed names, and there's little point in introducing them. Who they are isn't important, but they represent the American government and they are sanctioned by the President of the United States."

"No one mentioned Somalia or the United States would be represented at this meeting," Yuman complained. He cast an accusing glance at Kismaayo as if the African were somehow to blame for his situation.

"My government sent me to discuss relations with Somalia and Saudi Arabia," the black man stated, offended by Yuman's attitude. "I don't know what this deception is about, but I don't appreciate these tactics."

"That breaks my heart," Brognola scoffed. "The United States government doesn't appreciate Somalia giving sanctuary to a small army of international terrorists plotting a conspiracy against the United States of America, Great Britain and France."

"What are you talking about?" Kismaayo demanded as he stared at the big Fed, as if questioning the man's sanity.

"You speak Arabic, correct?" Katz inquired. "I'll be happy to translate if necessary."

"I understand English," the African replied. "I don't know anything about terrorists in my country aside from the hoodlum radicals trying to overthrow our government in Somalia."

"A lot of people would like to see your government pulled down," Brognola declared. "Somalia isn't going to win any awards for enforcement of human rights. Oppression and torture are common practices according to Amnesty International and other sources. It's sort of embarrassing for Uncle Sam to be associated with regimes like your government. How would you like it if the U.S. decided to cut off foreign aid to Somalia and pull our military personnel out of the bases there?"

"The American people wouldn't be upset," Bolan added. "Most don't even know where Somalia is. Just about every American would rather see their tax money used at home than helping to back up your country."

"America has those military bases in Somalia to protect their own interests in the region," Kismaayo insisted.

"I think we can get along without them," Brognola said with a shrug. "Hell, we can count on Saudi Arabia to help us protect our interests in this region."

"Absolutely," Mabettet agreed. "We Saudis are also wise enough to realize every fanatic who declares a holy war isn't fighting for Islam. A good Muslim will fight for a just cause. That has nothing to do with following the dogma of a power-hungry lunatic who disgraces our religion by associating it with his own ambitions."

"What does this have to do with Yemen?" Yuman asked.

"Because the terrorists were formerly stationed in your country," Brognola explained. "The Office of Naval Intelligence confirms that fishing and cargo vessels passed through the blockade in the Persian Gulf to arrive at Aden in August of 1990. That fits information we acquired from interrogating terrorist prisoners. The men we're up against were on board those vessels."

"They joined forces with international terrorists already camped in Yemen," Katz added. "Considering your position in the internal security ministry of Yemen, I'm surprised you didn't know about this already."

"I know of some refugees in Yemen," Yuman answered. "What they might have been doing wasn't my concern as long as they didn't present a threat to my country."

"Refugees?" Bolan said dryly. "Did you decide any of these refugees might be undesirable and evict them from Yemen?"

"That has happened on occasion," Yuman admitted. "Some might have found sanctuary on an island off the coast of Somalia. We might even have observation posts at our own islands in the Gulf of Aden that have watched for problems from a possible base in the area that might present concerns for the national security of Yemen."

"What are you saying, Mr. Yuman?" Kismaayo demanded, stunned by the Yemeni's remarks. "You're supporting these absurd claims that terrorists are carrying out a conspiracy against the West from Somalia?"

"I'm not saying I know any precise details about such things," Yuman replied. "However, I wouldn't want Yemen accused of sheltering terrorists or failing to cooperate in the West's efforts to locate and deal with such a threat."

"And we appreciate your cooperation," Brognola managed to say with a straight face. "Okay, Mr. Kismaayo, we want some cooperation from you, too."

"The Somali government isn't involved in harboring terrorists," the African insisted. "I swear by the Koran and the honor of my family, I know nothing about this."

"You're with the Somali Ministry of Foreign Affairs," Bolan began. "Maybe you don't know any details. I'm not one to question a man's word without reason, and I believe you to be a man of honor.''

''I appreciate that,'' Kismaayo replied. ''I don't want my country connected with terrorist outlaws, either. Why would I refuse such information if I could help?''

''Especially since the terrorists are processing chemical and biological weapons at their island,'' Brognola remarked. ''If the wind blows the wrong way, gas from such chemical plants could blow across the Somali coastline.''

''Are you sure these plants really exist?'' Kismaayo asked with a frown.

''We're sure,'' Bolan confirmed. ''We're also sure somebody in your government, the military or a combination of both must know what's going on. The terrorists wouldn't be able to occupy the island otherwise.''

''You're a highly placed official,'' Katz began. ''You know those in power in your country. Who would be interested in making a deal with a renegade Iraqi officer commanding a holy war?''

''Some might advocate such support if they thought the individuals involved could succeed and get assistance from a powerful country,'' Kismaayo admitted. ''A country that could send enough troops or even mercenaries to reinforce our military in order to reclaim the Ogaden region.''

''Ogaden?'' Katz remarked, and raised an eyebrow. ''That's part of Ethiopia.''

''I'm impressed by your grasp of geography,'' Yuman commented.

"Many Somalis believe Ogaden is rightfully part of our country and not Ethiopia," Kismaayo stated. "We tried to take control of it once in 1978. The Ethiopians and Cuban troops stationed there drove us out. Some Somalis admired Saddam when he invaded Kuwait, claiming it to be part of Iraq. They related to this and found it an inspiration for the hopes of one day capturing Ogaden."

"Which one of his admirers would be most apt to assist a well-organized terrorist outfit?" Bolan asked.

"I have an idea who might be responsible," Kismaayo replied. "I need to call Mogadishu. May I use a phone here?"

"Make your call, Mr. Kismaayo," the Executioner agreed. "Just be careful who you talk to and what you say. The enemy is unpredictable and cunning. They might have arranged line taps of the phones of government personnel in Somalia. If the terrorists suspect they're in danger, they'll be inclined to lash out with desperation and fury. Somalia is the closest target, and we don't know what sort of weapons might be at the island base."

"If you're right, how do you plan to deal with these terrorists?"

"Just help us find them," Bolan replied. "We'll take it from there."

CHAPTER TWENTY-FIVE

"Bear in mind this is based on memory and I never had the opportunity to precisely measure distance," Captain Gedka explained as he pointed at the crudely drawn map laid across the tabletop.

The Somali army officer had been summoned to Abha. Gedka had been mentioned by one of Kismaayo's cronies when the official made a series of calls to Mogadishu. The captain was working as some sort of go-between for a top-secret operation at an island and a group of Gedka's superiors, which consisted of both ambitious establishment government members and military hawks.

Captain Gedka was willing to cooperate when Kismaayo spoke with him at the Abha conference room. He'd been uncomfortable with his role in the affair from the beginning. He loathed Major Hawran and felt his superiors were making a serious, possibly ignominious, mistake. He welcomed a chance to cut himself away from the tentacles of Hawran's contrivances. He was assured his own involvement in the past wouldn't be held against him because he was simply following orders.

The faces at the conference room changed. Bolan, Katz and Brognola remained. Gedka and Carl Lyons replaced the others who formerly met in the room. The Somali captain spoke some English. When his vocabulary failed, he switched to Arabic and Katz translated for the others.

"The billets are strategically placed in circular formations so that every side to the island is covered by troops," Gedka explained. "These are large tents, but the men are well armed with automatic weapons. They also have explosives. Hawran was secretive about the arms at the base. However, I know they set up chemical-processing buildings here."

He pointed at a pair of circles at the outer southern portion of the map. Bolan noticed the chemical site was near the enemy port. The terrorists obviously used their boats to deliver shipments of chemicals and transported these the short distance to the processing area.

"The chemical plants are located in a ravine," Gedka continued. "I don't know exactly what chemicals they have, but I'm sure the substances they're creating are toxic and very dangerous."

"Yeah," Lyons commented. "We didn't figure they were making synthetic oyster sauce. About how many terrorists are stationed at the island?"

"I don't know the exact number," Gedka answered. "Perhaps as many as two hundred."

"That's enough," Bolan said. "What about security? Do they have surveillance cameras? Radar? Sonar? Mine fields or booby traps? Anything we'll have to deal with?"

"There are radar and radio dishes mounted on the communications building," the captain answered, pointing at the drawing on the map. "I haven't seen any cameras, and I don't believe there are booby traps or mine fields. However, guards patrol the island.

They're armed with assault rifles. Some also have guard dogs. Large black-and-brown animals with sleek heads and great teeth. Very aggressive animals."

"Sounds like Doberman pinschers," Lyons said.

"Did the captain see any evidence of cannons or artillery shells?"

Katz repeated the question in Arabic to be certain Gedka understood. The African glanced down at the map as he spoke.

"I didn't see anything of that sort, but I would suspect the most likely place for cannons and ammunition would be near the headquarters building. It's a large structure of adobe brick, easily the strongest and largest building on the island. The tents by the headquarters don't seem to be barracks, but they're guarded. The cannons might be there."

"Hawran would probably want the greatest weapons in his arsenal close by," Lyons guessed. "What about this guy? Figure he's the type to get everybody killed and set off chemical gas in the air if he figures he lost the game?"

"Would he rather die than surrender and take as many people with him as possible when he goes?" Brognola offered another version, which he hoped would be easier for Gedka to understand.

"Major Hawran is quite intelligent, but arrogant," the African answered. "I don't think he'll surrender. His pride is probably too great for that. He's a man with *waba yo* in his veins."

"Okay," Brognola said with a sigh. "What does that mean? Ice water or something?"

"Sorry," Katz replied with a shrug. "I don't know. It isn't an Arabic term." He asked Gedka to explain the word.

"It is Somali," Gedka explained. "It refers to the poison found in certain dogbane trees and shrubs in my country. *Waba yo* is used on arrowheads by some primitive hunters in Somalia."

"So Hawran has poison in his veins," Bolan commented. "I assume that means he won't give up and will sacrifice as many lives as possible if he thinks there's no way out."

"Major Hawran carries death inside him," Gedka declared in a stern tone. "He will spread death as if a contagious disease. I think he wants to do this. Death is Hawran's only concept of victory."

"Then he's going to get a personal victory," Lyons said with a cold smile. "And his last."

"But how many others will die in the process?" Brognola wondered aloud.

THE SEA HAWK HELICOPTER descended smoothly from the sky. Captain Lester watched the aircraft from the deck of the USS *Narwhal*. The commanding officer of the mighty submarine had received a top-secret crypto message twelve hours earlier that ordered the *Narwhal* to leave its previous patrol area in the Persian Gulf and rendezvous with an unidentified party in the Gulf of Aden.

Lester didn't know the Sea Hawk would be arriving until an hour before it appeared in the sky. He wasn't sure what was going on, but his orders were coming from the fleet commander himself. It was big, whatever it was.

The amphibious landing gear of the chopper touched down on the water near the submarine. Sailors set out in rafts to meet the helicopter's passengers. Bolan, Schwarz, Manning and Encizo boarded one raft, Lyons, Katzenelenbogen and James another. The Stony Man commandos climbed a rope ladder to the deck of the submarine.

"I'm Captain Lester," the *Narwhal* CO announced. He noticed none of the men saluted. This suggested they were probably civilians, which was a breed he didn't like aboard his vessel.

"Call me Pollock," the Executioner replied. "We have to go below and talk, Captain."

Lester looked at the tall stranger. The guy was dressed in a field jacket, fatigue pants and boots. Maybe he was technically a civilian, but "Pollock" had the demeanor of a military man. Lester recognized one of his own.

The other six visitors were also veteran warriors. Captain Lester would have realized this even if they hadn't been armed. They were tough, serious men. Even the middle-aged guy with the slight paunch and an artificial arm looked as if he could still kick ass if he had to.

"All right," the captain said with a nod. "Follow me, gentlemen."

Lester escorted them through the sail-deck hatch, then they descended the ladders to the control deck below. The captain led the Stony Man unit to a conference room near his own quarters. He quietly sealed the hatch.

"This is soundproof and completely secure," the Navy officer assured them. "Now, I'd like to know what this is about."

"We have the coordinates to an island located off the coast of Somalia," Bolan began. "We need the *Narwhal* to pass approximately ten kilometers from this island."

"Simply pass by it?" Lester asked with raised eyebrows. "I doubt you need a nuclear submarine for that."

"Well, we also want to leave the sub and head for the island," Lyons explained.

"We need to travel underwater," Encizo added. "Of course, ten kilometers is a pretty long swim, and we have to carry a fair amount of gear, as well. That means we'll need seven sea sleds."

"What makes you think we have sea sleds?" Lester asked.

"You have thirty sea sleds aboard this vessel," Schwarz stated. "Originally you had thirty-four. Two were damaged during a training exercise in the Persian Gulf two months ago, one was lost at sea and the other is being repaired."

"I'm impressed," Lester admitted, startled by how accurate their information about his submarine appeared to be. "Your Intelligence sources must be top-notch."

"They're the best," Katz stated. "That's why the *Narwhal* was chosen for this job. You and your submarine were the best available in the region. We got a computer printout on your career, the capabilities of the vessel and special weapons and gear."

"Including the sea sleds," Lyons contributed to the conversation. "We also know you have Polaris missiles and a full load of torpedoes."

"What the hell?" the captain asked with a frown. "We going to war again? Against who?"

"This mission is top secret," Bolan began. "That means this is on a need-to-know basis. My idea of how much you need to know might not be the same as the President and the director of my organization."

"You have my word," Lester promised. "Tell me where I stand and what you need."

The Executioner nodded. He was a shrewd judge of men and decided the best way to get good results from a man like Captain Lester was to tell him as much as possible and leave out the bullshit.

"The island is a terrorist base," Bolan explained. "The enemy there is the brain center for the terrorism that recently occurred in the United States, England and France. We're going in to shut them down."

"Just you seven?" Lester asked, astonished by the news. "You ought to have a battalion with air support to back you up."

"You'll have to be our air support," Bolan stated. "We're going in alone because a battalion of troops couldn't hit the shores unnoticed. We can't fly in because they have radar. They might have sonar, as well, so we can't go in by boat. Since the enemy has a chemical-processing center, we don't want to shell the place or use other indiscriminate bombing. That could send poison gases all across the Gulf of Aden."

"So how are we your air support?" the captain asked.

"If the mission goes wrong," the Executioner explained, "you'll have to hit the island with Polaris missiles. Some have conventional warheads with high explosives instead of nuclear payloads. Use the conventional missiles to attack the southern portion of the island. That's where the chemical plant is located."

"But you said that could cause contamination and spread toxic fumes into civilian areas," Lester said. "That's why you said you were going in to deal with it personally."

"Yeah," James answered. "That's the way we want to handle this because it would present less threat to any innocent parties in the area. However, if we can't manage that, it'll be less hazardous for the neighboring populations if you guys level the plant with missiles. That would probably bury the processing center and cover the chemicals with debris. Not a perfect way to restrain contamination, but better than allowing the terrorists to either detonate the chemicals for deliberate destruction or take the stuff in cannisters and leave the island to use it for future acts of terrorism."

"That brings us to another role for you and your men," Katz told the naval captain. "Some terrorists might manage to get to the boats or helicopters on the island. If they try to escape, you'll have to torpedo the boats or shoot the choppers from the sky."

"You won't have to do this all alone," Bolan assured the captain. "We'll give you some radio frequencies and code names. Contact these after we pass the island. Six frigates and at least a dozen gunships will head for the area to back you up if the *Narwhal* has to fight."

"The ships and combat choppers will be British, French and Saudi Arabian, as well as American," Lyons added. "We're getting international cooperation on this one."

"The terrorists have at least one cannon located in the center of the island," Bolan explained. "It's a howitzer-type weapon. Range is limited to a few kilometers, but you'll want to take it out before any military personnel hit the beach on foot."

"All right," Captain Lester said. "We'll get you some diving gear and prepare the sleds."

"I brought my own Emerson closed-circuit breathing apparatus," Encizo remarked. "Like to use my own gear whenever possible."

"Got mine, too," James added. "But the others will need diving gear. We'll help select it."

"You two are the experts," Bolan agreed. "We'd better get ready now. It'll be dark in a couple hours. We want to reach the island by 2100 hours."

CHAPTER TWENTY-SIX

Mohammed Mabettet handed Hal Brognola a cup of hot tea. The big Fed thanked his Saudi host, although he personally favored coffee.

"I've made certain my other guests are comfortable," Mabettet announced as he removed his *keffiyeh*. "Mr. Yuman is annoyed that he's being detained. However, I think it wise that he not return to Yemen until your friends have completed their mission."

"Let him bitch when he gets home," Brognola agreed.

"Bitch?" Mabettet said with a frown. "That's a female dog or an insult to a woman. Is it not? I know one insults a man by saying his mother is such a woman. I don't understand the term as you use it, sir."

"Complain," Brognola explained. "Bellyache. Whine. That sort of thing."

"You Americans do some very strange things with the English language," Mabettet remarked with a sigh.

"Yeah," the big Fed admitted, "I guess so."

He was tempted to point out that the Saudi did some pretty strange things with the decor of his office. The room was big enough to use for a basketball court. The terrazzo floor was made of genuine marble, and Mabettet's coffee table was hand-carved teak with a silver pot and fine china cups. The guy's desk was a ghastly contrast of aluminum and glass. Mabettet's leather-bound books were stored in a handsome oak case, but his cabinets were Formica. The Koran sat on a separate wooden stand, near a wide glass window, facing Mecca. Brognola sat on a sofa made of brown vinyl, facing an entertainment center complete with color TV, stereo and videocassette player.

Mabettet had been very cooperative when Brognola and the Stony Man commandos had arrived in Saudi Arabia. He also displayed the Muslim tradition of hospitality by doing his best to make Brognola feel at home as his guest.

However, the big Fed's thoughts were with the seven Stony Man warriors. They were somewhere in the Gulf of Aden, aboard the USS *Narwhal*. The pilot of the Sea Hawk stated that he'd seen the submarine submerge as he headed back to home base. Bolan and the combined members of Phoenix Force and Able Team were getting ready for the assault on Major Hawran's island stronghold.

Brognola didn't like the odds. The Executioner and the six warriors with him were the best men for the job, but they'd be grossly outnumbered. Captain Gedka said there could be as many as two hundred terrorists at the island. The enemy was heavily armed with a fearsome cannon and chemical weapons, as well as conventional instruments of war. Regardless of how skilled and professional the Stony Man unit might be, they were taking on one hell of a stronghold.

It would have been a suicide mission for almost any other combat unit. It might prove to be too much for even Bolan and the other commandos to handle. Brognola had argued that they ought to wait for reinforcements, but the Executioner insisted that there was no time to wait. He and the members of Able Team and Phoenix Force stated that the mission required a small number of skilled experts to move in stealthily. Seven men would be better than seven hundred for this task.

Brognola realized they were probably right.

"Mr. Kismaayo and Captain Gedka seem less eager to return to Somalia," Mabettet continued as he poured himself a cup of tea. "Perhaps they think it will be easier to confront the members of their own government and military who conspired with Major Hawran after the terrorists on the island are defeated."

"They shouldn't have too much trouble after it's confirmed the place was crawling with international bad guys," Brognola commented. "Somalia might be tempted to complain about us carrying out a military-style operation on one of their islands without consulting the government, but they won't want the embarrassment of being connected with Hawran's group. Kismaayo and Gedka will save the Somali government a lot of headaches when they expose the guys responsible for doing business with the terrorists. Hell, those two will be heroes when this is over. I won't be surprised if Kismaayo is elected prime minister and Captain Gedka is promoted to full colonel."

"Right now I'm more concerned about the terrorists," the Saudi admitted. "I pray God will watch over your friends and protect them in their mission. Yet I also confess I worry about the ramifications if they don't succeed. The terrorists may strike in Saudi Arabia next if what you say is true. My country was also part of the coalition forces against Saddam Hussein."

"Yeah," Brognola said. "The United States, England and France have already been targets. Hawran and his boys would have gotten around to Saudi Arabia eventually, but they're as good as extinct. My people will either take care of the bastards, or the combined firepower of the frigates, gunships and the USS *Narwhal* will blow the island apart."

"I wish there was more we could do, my friend," Mabettet commented. "If I thought I'd be more useful in the combat zone, I'd go myself."

"Well," Brognola began, "I read the file on you and I know you took a large dose of shrapnel in the back during Operation Desert Storm. You've already proved your courage. Fact is, neither one of us is suited for battlefields anymore."

"Sometimes it feels like it takes more courage to stay out of the actual fighting and work in the background as coordinators and planners," the Saudi remarked.

"Yeah," the big Fed agreed. "Ain't that the truth."

MAJOR HAWRAN personally supervised loading the cannon onto one of the fishing vessels. The big gun was wheeled down a slope to the berm by the port. His men followed instructions and moved the cannon along the narrow earthen shelf to the gangplank of the boat.

A crew of six Shiites hauled the cannon onto the port side of the boat to the deck. Hawran knew each man well. He'd diagnosed each as suffering from an inferiority complex and a neurotic fear of failure, which was capped by a death wish.

They were perfect candidates for the mission Hawran had assigned them. He'd groomed them for such a suicide mission for almost ten years. He'd exploited their weaknesses, deliberately made them depend on him as their messiah and father figure. During training exercises, the Iraqi never seemed to be quite satisfied with their performance. Yet he never actually ridiculed them. Instead, he had his fellow Iraqi officers belittle the chosen Iranians to help ensure their mental condition would remain insecure and pliable for Hawran's purposes.

The cannon was moved aft and concealed by a pile of fishing nets. Hawran addressed the crew.

"You all know how vital this mission is," he began. "You're going to strike a blow against the Great Satan of the United States of America. You'll accomplish what the entire army of Iraq was unable to do. You'll deliver death and terror to the enemy."

"Death to the Americans!" one of the Iranians exclaimed.

Hawran expected such an outburst. He waited for the Iranians to chant their battle cry in unison three times before he spoke again.

"Indeed," Hawran declared in a loud, clear voice. "Death to the Americans. The United States supported Shah Mohammad Reza Pahlavi. The Americans helped the shah stay in power and oppress the people of Iran. Some of you were only children when the shah's secret police, the SAVAK, terrorized your country. Yet I'm sure you all remember these butchers. SAVAK broke into homes and carried innocent people away to be tortured and murdered. The Americans were responsible for the shah and SAVAK. You defeated their pawn in Iran and began the Islamic holy war. It was continued by Saddam Hussein. His armies fought the traitors of Islam, as well as the infidel nations of the West. Now the holy war has become our responsibility.''

Hawran pointed east as he continued. ''You'll strike another blow against the American persecutors. They wait for you in the Persian Gulf. Confident and arrogant in their battleships and aircraft carriers, the Americans believe technology can protect them from any threat.''

He stared at the Iranians and added, ''But nothing can protect them from the will of God. We are His instruments. We cannot fail.''

The extremists cheered and chanted. Hawran again patiently waited for the noise to subside. He decided he'd pumped the execration of the Americans long enough and appealed to the Iranians' belief that they were carrying out a sacred mission for the holy war. It was time to send them on their way.

''My prayers and hopes go with you all,'' Hawran told them. ''I'm confident you'll crush our enemies and achieve Paradise as righteous warriors of Islam.''

Major Hawran descended the gangplank. Kaborya and Mohandra were among the men who stood at the berm. The Palestinian kept his thoughts to himself as he watched the Iranians aboard the fishing boat. He considered them to be a collection of hopeless idiots too stupid to realize they were being sent to die for Hawran's personal ambitions.

Not that Kaborya cared what happened to the Iranians. His only concern was for his own survival. He'd hoped the conspiracy would allow him to claim some revenge against the British and the Americans for their actions in the Middle East, which he considered to be part of the tragedy of the Palestinian people. However, Hawran's schemes had only succeeded in getting a lot of people killed and resulted in the humiliating defeat of the terrorists stationed in America and Europe.

Perhaps the attack on the United States naval forces on patrol in the Persian Gulf would be a major victory for the terrorists. Kaborya thought this was feasible, but they could only count on such a tactic working one time. Then they'd have to change strategy or disband. The latter would be the more pragmatic move, but Kaborya realized Hawran wouldn't agree to this.

The only chance they had to survive was to leave the island and move to a new location unknown to any of the terrorists already captured by the other side. Kaborya had no doubt the Americans and the Europeans would be able to squeeze information out of the prisoners. Soon they'd find Hawran's island stronghold.

Even if they fled, Kaborya figured it would only be a temporary solution. Too many forces worked against the terrorists. The Intelligence networks of at least three countries would continue to stalk them. The majority of Hawran's people were too unstable to be trusted to maintain security. Hawran himself was making careless mistakes due to his own delusions of grandeur.

Kaborya's grand plan was to regain the trust of Hawran and the others. The fact that he'd helped the major uncover the plot by the Europeans in their camp had increased their faith in him. In a month or two Kaborya hoped the Iraqis and Iranians would decide it was no longer necessary to watch him.

When this happened, Kaborya would escape from Hawran's camp and get as far away as possible. He'd figure out what he would do in the future after he'd fled the major's insane conspiracy. At least then he would have a future.

"It's good that our brothers are taking the fight to the enemies in the gulf," Mohandra stated with a nod of approval. "The American military is restricting the mobility of Muslims in the region. They should pay the price for this arrogance."

"They will," Hawran replied. "The infidels won't expect us to strike in the gulf."

Mohandra nodded again. Kaborya glanced at the huge muscle man. He suspected the Iranian would agree with anything the major said.

Hawran glanced at his wristwatch and tried to estimate how long it would take the fishing vessel to reach the Persian Gulf.

"Kaborya," the major began, "what can you tell me about the Comoros? You have connections with various groups throughout the world. Perhaps they can yet be useful to us."

"Comoros?" Kaborya replied, surprised by the question. "I'm not even sure where it is."

"It's a very small African nation consisting of three main islands and several smaller ones. The Federal Islamic Republic of Comoros is located in the Mozambique Channel. That's the southeast portion of Africa, nearly three thousand kilometers from here."

"So it must be between Mozambique and Madagascar," Kaborya remarked, revealing he wasn't totally ignorant as to geography.

"Quite so," Hawran confirmed. "Until 1975 Comoros was still a French-controlled property. Since it achieved independence, Comoros has had a great deal of political turmoil. Coups and attempted coups. Typical· for African countries. In 1989 President Ahmed Abdallah Abderemane was assassinated."

"You've obviously studied this country with some interest," the Palestinian remarked. "What have you got in mind?"

"We'll need to leave this island base soon," Hawran explained. "Comoros may be a good area to relocate part of our network. It's an Islamic country, and a large number of the Comoros population are Arabs. The official language is called Shaafi Islam. I think it's similar to Swahili with some Arabic mixed into the vocabulary. French is a common second language."

"None of that means the Comoros government or even factions of it would welcome us to set up operations there," Kaborya said. However, he was surprised and pleased to hear Hawran planned to move to a new location. "We might do better to head for Libya or even Syria."

"But we'd probably have less chance of being detected if we traveled to the Comoros, and it would be more practical for the boats. Perhaps the best tactic will be to divide our forces and send some to Libya, Tunisia, Algeria and maybe an exploratory team to the

Comoros to see if conditions are favorable there. At least if the enemy comes for us, it will be unlikely they'll catch us all.''

"So you think the Americans and Europeans will strike here?''

"I know they will,'' Hawran confirmed, his expression grim. "It may take them some time to find us, but I know they will.''

He was amused by the startled expression on Kaborya's face. Apparently the Palestinian thought he was too dense to realize the danger to their base had escalated after the series of failures in the United States and Europe.

"When will we start to leave here?'' Kaborya inquired.

"At dawn. You might start packing tonight.''

The major didn't reveal that his survival instincts seemed to scream at him to run as fast as possible. He sensed that dawn might not be soon enough. Yet Hawran suspected this was simply his own fears exaggerating the risk to the base. He wouldn't allow his personal insecurities to panic him into rash action. He couldn't afford to appear frightened or lacking in supreme confidence.

He'd try to maintain his mask of self-assurance, but Hawran guessed he wouldn't get much sleep that night.

CHAPTER TWENTY-SEVEN

Rafael Encizo steered the sea sled with ease as he led the Stony Man assault force through the dark waters of the Gulf of Aden. The Cuban was the most experienced diver among the Stony Man forces, and the others bowed to his expertise.

The Phoenix Force pro peered through his face mask and studied his surroundings. He barely glanced at the sled's control panel. It was a simple machine, similar in design to a modified snowmobile powered by an insulated engine with a propeller located safely beneath the diver's carriage. The sled was steered by handlebars, and a headlight illuminated the path as the sled cruised forward.

The other six Stony Man commandos followed behind Encizo. All had done some diving in the past, and they'd been trained for underwater operations. Katz and Schwarz were the least experienced of the group. The one-armed Israeli was accustomed to using the steel hooks of his prosthesis to do what his right hand had formerly done, but using the metal "fingers" underwater was difficult because the hooks were wet and slippery. However, Katz kept up with the others in spite of this disadvantage.

Lyons was a strong swimmer, but found the sled awkward and unfamiliar. His fellow Able Team veteran seemed to take comfort in the fact he was operating a machine. Schwarz had no trouble handling such a simple contraption after he'd been underwater for a few minutes. Manning had trained with Encizo and James with similar equipment and had less difficulty with his sled. Calvin James was superbly skilled in underwater work of all kinds. He brought up the rear of the group in order to assist anyone who might encounter trouble with the sleds or diving gear.

Encizo signaled to the others to stop as he shut down his sled. He lowered the machine into a cluster of sea ferns along a sloped surface of granite and coral. The rest of the Stony Man team followed his example and parked their sleds. Encizo gently paddled his feet and headed for the surface.

His head broke the surface. Water drops misted the lens to his diving mask, but Encizo still saw the island less than a hundred meters from his position. The shoreline was dotted with dark rock formations along the sand, and there were no fences or guards in view. It appeared to be an ideal spot to enter the enemy turf.

Encizo waited for the lens to clear so he could get a better view of the island. He continued to breathe through the mouthpiece of the Emerson regulator unit. The Cuban knew he still had more than half an hour of air in his tanks. No hurry, he thought as he studied the island.

He descended under the water to join his teammates, gesturing that it was okay above and gathering up his gear from the sled. He carried the sealed waterproof bag in one fist and held his spear gun in the other.

He headed for the shore, using his fins with as little noise as possible. The Cuban reached the sandy rim and started to rise from the water. Movement among the rocks caught his attention. The bark of a large dog warned Encizo of the threat even as the figure cleared the dark ridges of stone. A great black-and-brown Doberman scrambled into view, sand flying beneath its paws. White teeth gleamed from its gaping jaws, lips curled back to display the fanglike incisors.

Encizo heard a man say something in a language he didn't understand. The sentry didn't know what was bothering the animal until he saw Encizo standing knee-deep in water.

The guard released the dog and unslung an AK-47 assault rifle. The Doberman charged for Encizo, jaws snapping like a steel bear-trap. The sentry reached for the cocking knob of his rifle.

Encizo raised the spear gun. Faced with two lethal opponents, he made a snap judgment and selected a target. He triggered the weapon. The spear bolted above the head of the attacking Doberman, its pointed ears barely flinching as the projectile hissed past. The sentry uttered a groan of pain and surprise. The steel point of the spear had struck him in the chest and pierced his heart.

The AK-47 dropped from the guard's hands. He grabbed the shaft of the spear and tried to yank it from his flesh. His punctured heart quickly drained him of strength, and the guy fell to his knees. He fell back on the sand, twitched slightly and died.

Encizo slashed the empty spear gun at the attacking Doberman, which moved like a blur of murderous hair and sinew. The gun missed the beast by scant centimeters, and the dog lunged for Encizo's throat. The Cuban raised his arm to shield himself and brought the barrel of the spear gun accidentally into the path of the dog's snapping jaws. Teeth clamped around the frame of the weapon.

The Cuban wrapped his legs around the animal's torso and continued to hold it at bay with the spear gun. He was breathing hard and let the mouthpiece fall from his teeth. Paws clawed at the rubber wet suit, trying to rake Encizo's flesh.

Man and dog tumbled into deeper water. Encizo pinned the beast and forced its thrashing head under the surface. The animal fought in desperation. He held the dog down until water filled its nose and mouth. Finally the dog struggled with less strength. Encizo kept it pinned beneath the water until he was sure the dog had drowned.

"Jesus," Lyons rasped as he emerged from the water and watched Encizo slowly rise from the slain dog. "I thought you said it was okay up here."

"What are you complaining about?" the Cuban asked, gasping for air. "It's okay now... since I took out the guard and his four-legged friend."

Lyons grunted and headed for shore, rubber bag slung over a shoulder. The rest of the Stony Man unit followed. They rose from the water like warriors from Atlantis.

"Get your gear out pronto," the Executioner instructed. "Better be ready for company."

As if to confirm Bolan's warning, a chorus of barks and snarls erupted from the beach. The men hastily clawed at the sealed bags to open them. Three more Doberman attack dogs splashed into the shallows.

"Holy shit!" Schwarz exclaimed as one of the dogs charged for him.

The bursts from Katz's micro-Uzi took the dogs out of play.

MACK BOLAN TOOK the Beretta 93-R from his gear bag and headed for cover behind a rock formation. He realized human opponents would soon come to see what the dogs were after. The ultrasensitive noses and ears of the Doberman pinschers had detected the intruders at the shore. The less keen senses of the terrorists hadn't located the Stony Man unit, but the enemy would have to be very stupid not to follow the dogs.

Bolan figured they wouldn't be lucky enough to be dealing with stupid men.

Lyons and James also raced for the rocks, confident the other commandos would cover the opposite flank in case danger approached from that side. They climbed the rocks, easily securing hand- and footholds among the craggy surface. The two men mounted the stony formations to the peak, using the elevated position to peer down at the four figures that approached the beach.

The terrorist sentries carried Kalashnikov rifles at port arms. At least one had a two-way radio on his belt. They wore green-and-brown-spotted camouflage fatigues, and two men sported *keffiyeh*s instead of caps.

James slipped between two conical stones, about three meters above the marching terrorists. He looked at Lyons and tilted his head toward the enemy below. Lyons nodded and moved closer. James took a short breath and jumped.

He leaped onto the back and shoulders of the last man in the group. The unexpected impact drove the guy to the ground, and James heard the terrorist groan as they both hit the sand. The Phoenix fighter sprawled on his side and pointed his Uzi machine pistol at the men still on their feet. The terrorists turned abruptly when they heard the thud of bodies colliding.

James didn't give them time to aim their AK-47s. He trained the silenced Uzi on the closest terrorist and opened fire. A volley of 9 mm slugs stitched the guy from crotch to throat. No sooner did the guy pitch backward than Lyons triggered his MP-5, blasting another enemy gunman before the terrorists realized James wasn't alone.

The fourth enemy gunner bolted for cover and tried to swing his assault rifle at the Stony Man pair. He was unsure which commando to fire at, but pointed the AK-47 at James because the man presented a better target. However, he was unaware that Bolan was stationed at the opposite end of the rock formation. The Executioner had heard the subdued reports of the silencers and swung around the edge of the stone monoliths.

He fired the Beretta 93-R and cut the enemy gunman across the spine and the base of the skull with a trio of 9 mm rounds. The terrorist was dead before he even realized he'd been hit.

James started to get to his feet, but he caught a blur of movement next to him. The man he'd jumped on had recovered from the blow and now struck out at his attacker. Doubled fists slammed into James's forearm and knocked the Uzi from his grasp.

"Asshole!" James exclaimed as he retaliated with a quick punch to the man's face.

The guy staggered from the blow, but lashed out with a booted foot. He kicked James in the chest as if trying to kick open a door. The blow sent the Phoenix warrior hurtling back into the rock formation. The terrorist hissed with anger. He grabbed the hilt of a sheathed combat knife and drew the long, curved blade.

James shuffled away from the rocks. He'd been in knife fights before, and he didn't want to be pinned with his back to a wall, unable to move. His Blackmoor Dirk was sheathed and strapped to his ankle, but James knew he couldn't draw the blade quickly enough to avoid leaving himself vulnerable to the wicked steel in his opponent's fist.

Lyons and Bolan aimed their weapons at the knife man. They held their fire because the terrorist was too close to James and they feared hitting the Phoenix warrior. Bolan snapped an order for James to drop to the ground so he wouldn't be in the line of fire. The Phoenix fighter either failed to hear or chose not to obey.

James sunk his bare foot into the sand as he faced his opponent, hands poised in a karate fighting stance. The knife-wielding terrorist crouched low, blade held underhand and pointed at the American's belly. James suddenly snapped his leg forward and flung sand from his instep into the face and eyes of his opponent.

Enraged and half-blind, the terrorist lunged. James sidestepped the attack and avoided the knife thrust. He slammed a kick to the man's gut and quickly grabbed the wrist above the knife. James pulled the captive arm and whipped a knee to the man's battered abdomen. The terrorist groaned and started to double up. A right cross rendered him unconscious.

"Next time I tell you to get down," Bolan began as he approached, "you'd better damn well do it, Cal. Carl and I could've taken him out."

"Well, we got this one alive," James offered as an explanation.

"Then cuff him and gag him," the Executioner replied. "Put him out of view behind the rocks. Make it quick. We still have a lot to get done tonight."

CHAPTER TWENTY-EIGHT

The Stony Man warriors prepared for battle. Bolan assembled his M-16 with M-203 grenade launcher. He slid the Beretta into a special holster rig designed to accommodate the extra bulk of the silencer. He also carried the .44 Magnum Desert Eagle in a hip holster.

Katzenelenbogen also wore a shoulder holster under his right armpit, a Walther P-88 pistol in the leather scabbard. He carried his micro-Uzi on a long shoulder strap, and the weapon dangled near his left hip within easy reach of his hand. A ballistics knife was hooked to his belt.

Lyons didn't feel truly secure until the Colt Python was holstered under his arm. The big ex-cop also carried a Stony-M rocket launcher, as well as the H&K chopper. Schwarz was armed in a similar manner, but had an M-16/M-203 instead of a rocket launcher.

James carried the same assault rifle and grenade launcher combination in addition to the micro-Uzi and Walther pistol. Encizo didn't favor rifles. He preferred to work close and carried an MP-5 subgun, as well as the Phoenix Force standard side arm and machine pistol. Manning wore a backpack loaded with explosives and carried an FAL assault rifle, an Uzi and a Walther P-88.

All seven men packed grenades, combat knives and garrotes. James carried a full medical kit, and the others had smaller first-aid packets suited for their limited knowledge. Schwarz had unfurled a crude map based on information they'd acquired on the island.

"Okay," Bolan said as he examined the map with a penlight, using a palm to shield the glare. "We've already gone over this. You guys know the objectives and which targets are most critical. This is a tough assignment, but we can do it. Each man has to handle his assigned target first and foremost. Make sure it's completely terminated and controlled before rushing off to help the others. Understood?"

Six heads nodded.

Bolan nodded in turn. It was time to go into the lion's den.

THE PORT WAS small and simple. Three trawlers were docked at the cove, as well as two smaller motor boats. Encizo also saw that a fishing vessel was moving away from the island, heading east, toward the Persian Gulf. He watched the boat through binoculars and noticed a suspicious lump of netting on the decks, but couldn't identify it.

Only one guard patrolled the pier, but Encizo noticed there were more men aboard the larger vessels still docked. A forebay extended from the cove, its water used to power turbines for the main electrical source of the island. The Phoenix fighter saw two guards stationed by the generator center. He evaluated the situation, slithered from under the shrubs he used for concealment and crept down the hill to join Manning and James at the base of the slope.

He reported what he'd seen, but couldn't give an accurate count of the number of terrorists at the boats or the generators. The fact that one of the fishing boats was already out to sea presented an unexpected problem. The USS *Narwhal* and other naval vessels would be on watch for any boat coming from the island, and they'd been instructed to destroy any terrorist craft they encountered.

If the fishing boat was torpedoed close enough for the terrorists on the island to hear the explosion or if the men aboard the vessel managed to radio the base to say they were hit, Major Hawran would realize the island was under attack. The Stony Man unit would be in a very hazardous position.

"Well," Manning whispered to his partners, "I don't see that there's anything we can do about a boat that's already gone. No way we can stop the Navy forces from blowing it up, either. All we can do is go ahead with the plan the way we've already worked it out."

"Yeah," James agreed. "The port and the generators are secondary targets. We've got to take care of the big one first."

"Better not forget the back door," Encizo warned. "There could be twenty or thirty terrorists on those boats and in the generator center."

"We can't forget anything," Manning stated as he fitted a customized silencer to the barrel of his FAL rifle.

They followed a dirt path from the dock and the forebay to the chemical-processing section half a kilometer away. The building was made of adobe brick and flanked by metal silos. Pipes connected the silos with the building, and other tubes protruded from the silos to trenches.

The stench of sulfur was overpowering. The two sentries posted at the chemical plant stood about eight meters away from the building and tried to remain away from the stink carried on the breeze. Their watch duty was unpleasant and boring. If they'd heard the dogs barking twenty minutes earlier, they didn't appear to regard this as a warning of possible danger.

James and Encizo crept from the shadows behind the sentries. The terrorists were more concerned with being able to breathe clean air than protecting the plant. The Phoenix pair had little difficulty approaching the men without being detected. Encizo's target was closer, and he closed the distance stealthily, Tanto Cold Steel knife in his fist.

He pounced, grabbing the sentry with one hand and clamping the palm around the guy's mouth while striking swift and deep with the point of the knife. Encizo held the man as the body convulsed in a violent death spasm. He lowered the corpse to the ground even as he heard the other sentry shout something in Farsi.

The second guard saw his comrade go down and started to unsling his rifle. Calvin James realized there wasn't time to creep closer and take out the guy quietly with the Blackmoor Dirk. He bolted forward in a flying leap while the sentry's attention was still focused on Encizo.

His boot slammed into the back of the man's head, the kick landing with bone-jarring force. The guard collapsed, stunned and only semiconscious. James dropped to a kneeling position, knife ready to deliver a deadly strike. But it wasn't necessary to kill the guy.

James chopped the butt of the Dirk behind the fallen man's ear and knocked him unconscious.

Manning approached as James used plastic riot cuffs to bind the guy's wrists and ankles. Encizo wiped the blade of his knife on the shirt of the sentry he'd killed and returned the blade to its scabbard. The Canadian pointed his FAL at the building in case more opponents appeared. However, there was no movement outside the plant.

"I hate to harp on this," James whispered as he retrieved his rifle from the bushes, "but they've probably got vats of chlorine, cyanide, various types of acid and maybe tanks of concentrated hydrogen and oxygen gases."

"That means we can get poisoned, blown up and burned to a crisp all at once if we're not careful," Manning commented with a nod. "We understand that, Cal. We also know that the silos and barrels there could be filled with poison gas or other deadly chemicals."

"We'll try not to hit anything with bullets," Encizo assured his comrade. "I just hope nobody inside is suicidal."

"Hell, from what Gedka told us, everybody on this island is suicidal except us," James muttered. "And we can't be wrapped too tight or we wouldn't be here."

"Take it up with your analyst," Manning suggested. "You and I will take the front. Rafael, cover the back."

The Cuban headed for the rear of the plant. James and Manning carefully moved to the front entrance. The loud humming of an air-conditioning unit drowned out other sounds as they pressed forward.

The interior of the building was certainly hot and stuffy because processing chemicals required extreme levels of heat. Air filtering was also necessary to prevent asphyxiating the personnel working inside the plant. The noise of the air conditioner would certainly block out any sounds made by the Stony Man assault team, thus far.

Manning peered into a window. The glass was thick, and closed shutters concealed the activity within. However, light appeared between the slats. The place wasn't deserted. The Canadian checked the door, found no alarms, coded access panels or evidence of booby traps. The door was steel, and it wouldn't be easy to blast open with CV-38 low-velocity explosives. This certainly couldn't be done without alerting the people inside. Also, Manning had no idea what might be on the other side of the door. A hundred different kinds of alarms, traps and signal devices could be there, undetectable from outside the building.

No way to do this subtly, the Canadian thought. There was one possibility, and he decided to try it first before getting out explosives to blow the door. Manning grabbed the door handle, turned it, pushed gently and it opened. The heavy security door wasn't even locked. The guys working on the chemicals had obviously done so without much interference by the others at the island base. They didn't have to worry about untrained people wandering in, and they must have had enough confidence in Hawran's defenses for the entire stronghold to allow their own security of the plant to become lax.

Manning slipped inside the building, FAL in his fist, stock braced on a hip. The room he entered was large, but filled to capacity with columns of vats, metal tanks and piping. A man dressed in shorts and T-shirt stood by the vats, watching temperature gauges and marking information on a clipboard.

Another man sat by a small metal desk. His head was bowed slightly, and he appeared to be sleepy. Neither man noticed Manning or James as they entered. The Afro-American commando saw the situation and nodded to his partner. The big Canadian walked to the desk while James approached the man with the clipboard.

The drowsy man at the desk suddenly raised his head, eyes wide with surprise. He'd sensed danger too late. Manning quickly swept the barrel of his rifle across the guy's skull. The blow knocked the man forward with enough force to slam his forehead into the desktop.

The noise drew the attention of the clipboard man. He turned and saw James about to deliver a butt stroke with his M-16. The terrorist lunged before his attacker could carry through the blow. He grabbed the frame of James's rifle and tried to shove it under the black warrior's chin.

James immediately threw himself backward, moving with his opponent's push instead of trying to resist it. He folded a leg and landed on his buttocks. The Phoenix fighter raised his other leg and jammed the boot into the terrorist's midsection. James rolled back and straightened his leg to kick the guy over his head in a judo circle throw.

The terrorist crashed hard into the tile floor. Dazed, he rolled onto all fours and started to rise. Manning rushed forward and stamped the buttstock of his FAL behind the man's ear. The man slumped to the floor, unconscious. James got to his feet and started to examine the chemical vats. As Manning cuffed their prisoners, both men kept an eye open for more terrorists.

"Chlorine, sulfur, carbon," James commented. "Looks like they were brewing up some good old-fashioned mustard gas. They also have cyanide, lots of tanks of nitrogen and hydrogen. My guess is they were planning to whip up some aniline or maybe carbon tetrachloride or antimony trichloride."

"That's what I figured, too," Manning commented with weary sarcasm. "I take it those are all used for poison gas?"

"They're all potentially lethal if inhaled or absorbed through the skin," James explained. "I'm going to shut down the heat on the stuff being blended for future use."

"But are the chemicals here still dangerous?" Manning asked.

"Hell, yes. We can't safely dispose of all this. That'll require more time than we've got right now. We'll just have to make sure—"

A door opened to a room adjacent to the laboratory. James and Manning swung their weapons toward the figure at the doorway. A short, slightly overweight man with a trimmed beard stared back at the pair. He spit out an angry expression in Arabic and bolted past some vats and tanks.

The Phoenix commandos were reluctant to open fire for fear of hitting the volatile chemicals that surrounded them. Since the other guy chose to run instead of fight, this suggested he wasn't armed. Manning raced after the fleeing figure while James stayed at the lab in case more terrorists appeared.

The man was familiar with the building and quickly made his way among the maze of vats, crates and furnaces. Manning chased him, dodging the obstacles in his path. The terrorist managed to reach a door at the rear of the building. He hit the bar handle, and the door swung open, slamming shut as Manning closed in.

Breathing hard, the terrorist grabbed a key ring on his belt and fumbled for the right key to lock in his pursuer. He didn't see Rafael Encizo stationed at the back of the building. The Cuban emerged from behind a silo and rushed the man at the door. He swung the MP-5 and hit the terrorist across the side of the skull with the steel frame. The blow knocked the man to his knees.

Manning kicked the door open, and it swung into Encizo. The unexpected blow struck the Heckler & Koch subgun from the Cuban's grasp. Manning charged through the threshold and thrust the butt of his FAL at Encizo's head. The Cuban warrior dodged the attack and drew his Walther P-88. Both men recognized each other before taking further action.

"Did you forget I was back here?" Encizo asked, his voice tense.

"I didn't expect you to be right by the door," the Canadian replied as he tilted the rifle across a shoulder.

The fallen terrorist shook his head to clear it and spotted the MP-5 subgun on the ground. He lunged for it, but Encizo followed the guy's movement and kicked him in the ribs to knock him away from the weapon. The man tumbled, rolled to his knees and tried to rise. Encizo backhanded the barrel of his pistol across the man's temple. The terrorist went down and stayed down.

"You haven't come across anybody else?" Manning asked as he stood watching while Encizo cuffed the unconscious terrorist.

"Just you and this idiot," the Cuban replied. He finished binding the man and retrieved his MP-5. "What did you and Cal find inside?"

"Enough dangerous chemicals to be pretty serious if this place gets hit by a rocket or grenade," Manning answered.

CHAPTER TWENTY-NINE

The jeep rolled along the dirt path, its headlights revealing some scatterings of tamarisk shrubs and tall grass, weaving slightly in the night breeze. An Iranian, promoted to senior sergeant by Major Hawran, held his AK-47 ready. The barrel was pointed at the sky, and his fist was wrapped around the pistol grip, index finger by the trigger guard.

Something was wrong. He was sure of that, but hadn't found any proof to support this theory. The guard commander had told him foot patrols along the coast hadn't radioed in their standard hourly reports. That wasn't uncommon because some of the guards simply forgot to do so. However, the terrorist NCO sensed that something had changed. The island was different. It was too quiet.

His driver didn't seem to share his feelings. The man was dense, in the sergeant's opinion. He didn't have the spiritual awareness of the NCO. The senior man believed he was in closer touch with God and more sensitive to his environment than most of his comrades. The driver probably thought he was paranoid, but the sergeant knew he was simply more enlightened. Yet it didn't require psychic powers to notice that the animal life was troubled by something, or that the roving patrol hadn't been able to find any of the sentries on foot or even one of their Doberman attack dogs. The sergeant felt his stomach knot as they continued to travel the length of the island.

"Hey!" a voice called out from the bushes in Arabic. "Help me!"

The sergeant told his driver to stop the jeep. He wasn't fluent in Arabic, but the language was similar to Farsi. He knew the person among the bushes was calling for help.

"See what's wrong," the NCO told the driver. "I'll cover you."

The other Iranian reluctantly climbed from the jeep and gathered up his Kalashnikov. He walked slowly toward the shrubs where the voice came from. The sergeant stepped from the vehicle and assumed a kneeling position, using the hood of the car for a bench rest.

"Help," the voice moaned softly as the driver approached the bushes.

The guy moved closer and tried to peer between the twigs and branches. He couldn't see anyone and stepped closer. The unexpected sputter of a silenced weapon broke the stillness. The driver saw the blinking glare of the muzzle and felt slugs smash into his chest. His heart burst, and his upper torso was filled with an abrupt aneurysm that rose into his throat. Blood spilled from the guy's mouth as he tumbled to the ground, his rifle still clenched in his fists.

The sergeant saw his driver fall, but failed to notice Bolan emerge from the shadows behind him. The Iranian's alleged sensitivity to danger didn't warn him that the Executioner held a garrote raised high and aimed at the NCO's neck. Bolan swung the steel sling over the man's head and pulled hard. The loop snapped tight as the warrior slammed a kick to the Iranian's elbow to strike the AK-47 from his grasp.

Bolan turned slightly and stood back-to-back with his opponent. He bent forward and hauled the guy off his feet, wire noose biting into flesh. The Executioner felt the terrorist struggle until the garrote throttled the life from him.

Katzenelenbogen stepped from the bushes, Uzi in his good hand. Bolan dropped the corpse to the ground and unwrapped the wire from the dead man's neck. The Stony Man warriors nodded with grim approval. The trick had worked, and their deadly skills had served them well once more.

"We should be roughly two kilometers from the heart of the enemy base," Katz whispered. "If we encounter another guard patrol, our best course of action might be to let them pass and deal with them later."

"Yeah," the Executioner agreed. "Our main concern has to be the major's headquarters."

The commandos moved on, and soon reached the heart of the stronghold. Rows of tents and some wooden structures comprised the barracks for the bulk of Hawran's private army. The Executioner and the Phoenix commander avoided these. They circled the edge of the terrorist compound and approached the small airfield. Two helicopters and a single twin-engine airplane sat on the tarmac.

The pair moved to a hangar and observed the buildings from the shelter. They didn't see any guards on patrol at the airstrip, but two were posted by the big brick structure at the center of the base. Actually the sentries appeared to be protecting the tent beside the headquarters building. The scene fit Gedka's description of the most likely place for the terrorists to be hiding howitzer-size cannons.

They'd found their main objective, but Bolan didn't want to leave the enemy aircraft operational. He glanced about the airfield to be certain no enemy eyes were watching. Shadows appeared against light from an open door to the hangar, and the men could hear voices inside the building. Bolan turned to Katz and tilted his head toward the door. The Israeli nodded.

The warrior crept along the wall to the door. He peered through the crack at the door hinges and saw two men dressed in mechanic's coveralls seated at a small card table playing chess. An AK-47 was propped against the wall near one of the men, and a pistol rested on the table near the other guy's right elbow.

Katz moved next to Bolan. The Executioner decided the best tactic was to hit fast and hard, but he didn't want to fire a shot. Even with the silencers, the report of a gun would echo within the hangar and might be heard clearly by the other terrorists at the base.

Bolan charged through the doorway. The mechanics looked up, startled, as the big warrior in black bolted toward them. The Executioner swung a boot and kicked the card table which tipped over and crashed to the floor as one man tried to grab for the pistol. The handgun landed on the floor among the black and white chess pieces.

The Executioner whipped his M-16 across the face of the guy who was about to grab the rifle, hitting him hard enough to knock him off his stool.

The other terrorist rose from his seat and lunged at Bolan. The warrior used his M-16 as a bar and slammed it under the attacker's forearms to deflect the groping hands.

Bolan hooked the buttstock of his rifle into the terrorist's ribs. The blow staggered the mechanic, and he stumbled into Katz, who quickly caught one of the man's arms and pinned it under his own left armpit. He jammed the steel hooks of his prosthesis and clamped them around the terrorist's throat.

Katz applied crushing force, puncturing the carotid artery and smashing the terrorist's thyroid cartilage. The man thrashed wildly as he realized he was choking to death. Katz kept his opponent off balance until the struggles ceased, then he lowered the limp body to the floor.

Although he'd suffered painful injury from Bolan's butt stroke, the other terrorist rose from the floor and seized the Executioner from behind, wrapping his arms around Bolan's upper torso in a bear hug. The Executioner immediately responded by thrusting a back-kick between the attacker's legs. The back of his heel struck the man squarely in the testicles.

Bolan heard a choked gasp when the kick connected. He continued the counterattack by snapping his head back into the Iranian's nose. The warrior easily broke free of the stunned man's grasp and slammed an elbow to the point of the other man's chin. The guy hit the floor again, this time unconscious.

"Tough neighborhood," Bolan commented as he cuffed the guy.

Katz moved to the hangar door and checked outside. No one had come forward to investigate sounds of the scuffle. The Israeli continued to stand watch while Bolan searched the building for more enemies.

"Those two were it," the Executioner announced finally. "How's it look out there?"

"I don't think anyone knows we're here."

"Okay. Cover me, Yakov."

The Executioner left the M-16 with his comrade and dashed to the nearest helicopter. He slipped underneath the aircraft's carriage, opened a pouch on his belt, removed a special limpet mine and attached it to the metal skin. The magnet held fast, and Bolan adjusted the selector mode on the dial.

The mine was another development by the Stony Man weapons team of Kissinger, Schwarz and Manning. It could be set to a timing mechanism or to respond to vibrations. Bolan set it for the latter mode. He left the chopper and moved to the next aircraft to repeat the procedure. He continued until all the enemy helicopters and the single plane were rigged with explosives.

He returned to the hangar and rejoined Katz. They considered the best way to handle the next objective, then made their way stealthily to the tent in front of the main house.

Bolan knelt by the tent while Katz stood guard, Uzi braced across his mechanical arm. The Executioner drew his K-bar fighting knife and inserted the point in the canvas. He cut a slit in the tent and peered inside. Two great iron-gray cannons stood on wheeled platforms. They had found the enemy howitzers.

Two men were also inside the tent, one by a small table with a metal teapot on a hot plate, another seemingly asleep as he lay on a cot near the entrance. Bolan carefully cut canvas along the bottom of the tent, increasing the slit and taking care not to make noise that might betray his presence.

The Executioner handed his M-16 to Katz and crawled through the gap in the canvas. He slithered to the closer cannon, using the massive barrel for cover. The guy at the table still seemed more interested in his teapot. Bolan held the combat knife in his fist and slowly crept toward the man's back.

A man near the entrance of the tent called out something in Arabic, prompting a reply from the man with the teapot, who poured tea into two small cups.

Bolan ducked behind a stack of crates. He didn't speak much Arabic, but knew that one of the guards outside the tent had said something about wanting a cup of tea. The other guy invited him to come in. A figure appeared at the flap to the tent, an AK-47 carried on a sling across his shoulder. The guard was handed a cup of tea, and he nodded his thanks.

This made the problem of taking out the terrorists more difficult. Bolan stayed low behind the crates and waited for teatime to end. He heard the men converse in Arabic, the tone of the discussion sounding informal and friendly. This suggested they didn't know the base was under siege.

An explosion rumbled somewhere in the distance. The terrorists were startled by the noise. The guard rushed outside while the tea maker woke the guy on the cot. As the man climbed out of his bed and reached for a stack of folded clothes, his companion grabbed an assault rifle.

Bolan waited for both men to leave. The fellow who'd just woken up pulled on a pair of pants and followed his comrade outside. The Executioner wondered what had happened. The explosion had occurred far from their position, perhaps even somewhere at sea beyond the island.

There was no time to dwell on idle speculation. Bolan took advantage of the absence of the terrorists to inspect the cannons. Katz slipped through the slit in the canvas to join him.

"Any idea what that explosion was?" Bolan asked, hoping the Phoenix commander may have overheard someone outside the tent.

"Not really. It was far away, but they heard it all over the base. People are coming out of tents and buildings to see what's going on, but I don't think anyone knows for sure what it might be."

"We might not have much time. Pry open one of those crates and see what's inside."

Katz followed instructions and used the hooks to his artificial limb to rip open a crate. Bolan opened the breech to the first cannon. There was no shell inside. He inspected the other cannon and found it was also unloaded.

"Artillery shells," Katz announced as he placed the first crate on the ground. "Obviously ammo for the howitzers."

Bolan glanced down at the big cartridge. The shell was the right caliber. One-hundred-and-fifteen-millimeter projectiles could deliver a deadly payload of chemical poison.

The Executioner set another limpet underneath the breechlock assembly to one of the cannons. Set to respond to vibrations, the mine would explode if anyone tried to open the breech to load it. The blast wouldn't detonate any of the shells unless someone managed to feed one into the breech before the mine went off. That wouldn't happen unless the limpet malfunctioned.

A figure suddenly dashed through the entrance. It was the terrorist who had formerly been sleeping on the cot—he'd returned to get his boots and shirt. The guy didn't expect to find two strangers in the tent tampering with the cannons. Although he hadn't taken time to don his shirt and footgear when he'd hastily left the tent to see what was going on outside, the terrorist had remembered to grab his AK-47.

The gunman started to swing the rifle barrel into play, but the Israeli's Uzi snarled and pumped a trio of 9 mm slugs into the terrorist before he could trigger his weapon. The silenced Uzi spit out a muffled series of reports, but the terrorist cried out loudly and toppled backward through the flap to the ground.

Excited voices announced that the dead man hadn't gone unnoticed. The bullet-torn corpse was an undeniable message that the threat to Hawran's stronghold wasn't restricted to the distant explosion.

"So much for being subtle," the Executioner rasped as he grabbed his M-16.

CHAPTER THIRTY

Bolan opened fire, spraying a sustained burst that stitched a ragged line of bullet holes in canvas. The strafing blast was fired blindly, but Bolan realized terrorists outside the tent would be pointing weapons at the opening after the dead man fell into view.

Katz fired his Uzi in the same manner, but aimed lower because he assumed the enemy outside would dive to the ground after Bolan's initial burst.

The Executioner moved to the tent entrance, thrust the barrel of his rifle through the opening, aimed at the front of the main house and triggered the M-203.

The 40 mm grenade bolted from the big bore of the launcher, striking the thick double doors to the building, and exploded. The blast tore apart the entryway and sent chunks of adobe and plaster raining down on the terrorists outside. The force of the explosion shattered glass from three windows and sent an unlucky terrorist tumbling from the sill.

Bolan charged through the opening of the tent, firing the M-16 on the run. Katz followed and backed the Executioner's play with his Uzi. A number of enemy gunners were sprawled on the ground, dead or injured. The terrorists who remained on their feet found themselves facing the Stony Man warriors.

Many fell before the onslaught of the pair's combined firepower. Several others dropped to the ground and attempted to return fire, but Bolan and Katz weren't easy targets and kept moving. A kneeling gunman tried to raise his pistol as the duo charged straight toward him. The guy was in Bolan's path, less than a meter away. The Executioner swung the butt of his M-16 and took the man out of play with a blow to the temple.

Bolan leaped up the steps to the main house, followed by Katz, who climbed the stairs backward, blasting away with the Uzi. The Executioner reached the smashed doors to the building, spotted two dazed figures inside and promptly hosed them with the last rounds of his M-16. He entered the house swiftly, Katz right behind him.

Bullets splintered wood from the doors, which hung from broken hinges. Katz gasped with pain as a shard of wood pierced his left cheek. He moved to the cover of the doorway, blood trickling down his face. Bolan pulled the pin from a grenade and tossed it outside. The M-26 fragger rolled down the steps to explode among the terrorists.

"Yakov?"

"I'm all right," the Israeli assured him as he removed the splinter from his cheek. "This neighborhood seems to be getting worse."

"I noticed," Bolan replied.

He rammed home a fresh clip and pulled back the charging handle to chamber a round. Katz also took advantage of the lull in the action to reload his Uzi. Bolan ejected the cartridge casing from his M-203 and fed another grenade into the breech.

''Your hand grenade seems to have made an impression on them,'' Katz commented as he took an egg-shaped bomb from his own belt. ''Maybe another one with discourage them from rushing the building.''

''Let's see what two will do.''

Katz lobbed his grenade outside. Another roving patrol arrived in a jeep, bringing reinforcements. The Executioner figured the new arrivals made a good target.

He fired the M-203 as Katz's grenade exploded. The first blast ripped a crater in the ground and tossed ravaged human bodies into the sky. Bolan's grenade struck the jeep, blowing apart the vehicle and the terrorists near it. Wounded and dead terrorists were strewn across the ground. Survivors retreated from the area.

''That ought to discourage them for a while,'' Katz remarked as he glanced at the ghastly debris outside.

''They'll be back.''

''And we'd better be ready for them,'' Katz said grimly.

''OH, SHIT,'' Carl Lyons growled when he heard the explosions and gunfire at the headquarters.

Lyons and Schwarz had covered the enemy barracks while the other Stony Man warriors dealt with their individual targets. The Able Team pair took out some unsuspecting sentries at the stronghold and met no other opposition. They then set about preparing for the terrorists at the billets.

Schwarz had brought his gear bag because it contained several Claymore mines, rigged to be detonated by radio receivers built into the firing mechanisms. Gadgets and Manning had developed this innovation with the help of Cowboy Kissinger. The mines could be detonated by a radio transceiver with a special ultrahigh-frequency signal programmed to match the receiver units.

The pair planted Claymores along the rows of tents and shacks and were still at work when the first explosion echoed far from the heart of the base. The sound attracted the attention of several terrorists, but the enemy still seemed unsure what caused the noise. Lyons and Gadgets managed to remain hidden among the shadows near the billets while the terrorists scanned the horizon for sign of a distant threat, unaware danger lurked much closer.

The eruption of violence at the HQ building changed the situation dramatically. Armed terrorists flooded from the tents and wooden dwellings. Lyons realized he couldn't avoid them for long, and he and Schwarz were too close to the barracks to set off the Claymores.

Burning wreckage cast harsh light across the compound, and they spotted Lyons. The commando opened fire with the H&K subgun and sprayed the terrorists with a sustained burst before they could point weapons in his direction. Two opponents fell, and others cried out in pain, wounded by the 9 mm missiles. Lyons dashed for the communications shed, firing his MP-5 as he ran.

"Bug out!" Lyons yelled, hoping Schwarz would hear him above the roar of weaponry.

Ironman dived for cover near the comm center, bullets ripping into the ground near his hurtling form as he rolled to the edge of the shack. He reached shelter as slugs punched into the wall and chipped wood chunks from the corner of the structure. Lyons returned fire, shooting around the corner blindly, unable to expose his head due to the intensity of the enemy salvo.

He didn't see that Schwarz had also opened fire on a group of terrorists near another row of billets. Gadgets darted to a line of sandbags set up for the terrorist defenses in case of attack.

Schwarz swung his MP-5 over the top of the bags and sprayed another volley at the gunmen, who were still unsure where the attack came from. Bodies tumbled to the ground, blood spilling from a dozen wounds. Schwarz ducked as enemy rounds plowed into the sandbags. Canvas split and sand leaked down on the Able fighter's head and shoulders. He took an M-26 fragmentation grenade from his belt, pulled the pin and lobbed the bomb at the advancing attackers.

He heard the grenade go off with a mighty roar, accompanied by the screams of those who didn't get clear of the blast. Schwarz realized that his position left him vulnerable to the same kind of attack. If the terrorists tossed two or more grenades among the sandbags, Schwarz wouldn't be able to gather them all up and throw them away before at least one fuse detonated.

He knew Lyons had also reached cover. There was no reason to hold back on using the Claymores. He took the radio transmitter from a pocket and pressed the signal key. The first set of antipersonnel mines exploded. The concave shape of a Claymore was designed to spray a wide pattern of shrapnel to take out as many of the enemy as possible. Tents and shacks were bowled over by the force of the blasts, and men were virtually shredded by the vicious wave of shrapnel.

Schwarz ducked low behind the sandbags. A severed arm hurled into the pit and landed beside him, a Makarov pistol still clenched in the lifeless fist. He pulled away from the grisly object and scrambled over the sandbags.

LYONS REALIZED Schwarz had found cover when the first round of mines exploded. He hit the transmitter key to his own remote, and the second group of Claymores blasted more billets.

Suddenly the door to the communications shack opened. Lyons glimpsed the figure who appeared on the threshold. He swung his MP-5 at the shape, but a boot connected with the subgun and kicked the weapon from his grasp. The attacker whirled with the motion of the karate roundhouse kick and unleashed his other leg in a powerful side-kick thrust that struck Lyons in the chest.

The Able Team captain staggered backward from the blow. He saw the blur of his opponent's hand as the terrorist slashed a karate chop at Lyons's face. The commando raised a forearm to block the attack and swung his own left hook to the guy's face. He saw Asian features as the fist sent the terrorist's head snapping backward.

Jiro tasted blood as he shuffled away from the big American. The Japanese Red Army killer was impressed by his opponent's strength. Yet he knew brute strength could be defeated by superior skill, and Jiro was certain no American or European could match his ability at martial arts.

The Japanese terrorist worked communications when not teaching classes in hand-to-hand combat, and he was in the building when the fighting had erupted. Unarmed, aside from his martial-arts skill, Jiro had waited until he could launch an effective attack against the big, muscular blond invader. He adopted a T-*dachi* fighting stance and waited for Lyons to make the next move.

The Able Team warrior recognized the karate stance and realized what the guy was doing. Karate was a defensive art, and Jiro wanted him to attack so the Japanese could counter and launch his own attack. Lyons didn't intend to play the game of life and death by Jiro's rules.

He reached for the Colt Python under his arm. Jiro immediately swung a kick at the American's forearm to try to prevent Lyons from drawing the big revolver, or kick it from his hand if the weapon managed to clear leather. However, Lyons didn't draw the Magnum—he'd feinted the move to lure Jiro into attacking.

He grabbed the terrorist's ankle and kicked his opponent's other kneecap. Jiro groaned as his leg buckled, and he began to fall. Lyons held on to the man's ankle, pulled hard and twisted the leg to send him spinning into the side of the building. The Japanese hit the shack in a graceless heap, and Lyons closed in swiftly to hammer a fist between Jiro's shoulder blades.

Jiro pushed away from the wall. His knee almost folded under his weight, and the pain traveled up his thigh to his groin. Lyons thew a left jab at the Japanese's head, but the man dodged the fist. Lyons swung a right. Jiro seized his arm, turned sharply and hurled his opponent over his shoulder.

The commando hit the ground hard, but he knew how to break his fall. He clenched his opponent's shirtfront with one hand and grabbed the guy's hair with the other. He pulled the Asian's head forward and rolled back on his shoulders to whip a knee into the guy's face.

Cartilage cracked in Jiro's nose. Lyons released the man's head and thrust a fist under his jaw. The blow sent the Japanese reeling, and Lyons quickly got to his feet. Blood oozed from Jiro's nostrils, and he realized he had to finish off his opponent quickly or the American would be the victor.

Jiro raised his hands in a threatening manner and threw a snap kick for Lyons's groin, who blocked the kick with a thigh. The Japanese swung a hand chop at the Able warrior's neck, but Lyons raised a forearm and blocked the attack. His other hand drove a hard punch to the terrorist's solar plexus. Lyons quickly hooked the crook of an elbow under Jiro's arm, pivoted and bent forward to hurl the Japanese over his hip in an adroit judo throw.

Before Jiro could recover, Lyons drew the .357 revolver from shoulder leather and pointed it at the man. The terrorist stared at the gun, his eyes rising slowly to Lyons's face. The big warrior smiled at his opponent.

"What the hell," the Able captain remarked as he returned the Python to the holster. "Let's finish it, pal."

Jiro nodded. The American was giving him one last chance to win the deadly contest. He was a man of honor. Jiro respected this. He screamed a *ki-ya*, charged, feinted a kick and thrust a spear-hand stroke for Lyons's throat, the kill shot.

Lyons parried the stroke with the heel of his left palm and simultaneously drove his right fist to the point of Jiro's chin, which knocked him back several steps. The Asian staggered like a drunkard, his knee buckled and his head bobbed in a dazed manner. Lyons stepped forward and hit the guy with a left hook. Jiro went down hard.

"What's going on?" Schwarz asked as he discovered Lyons kneeling beside the unconscious Japanese.

"Just tying up a loose end," he explained as he bound the terrorist's wrists with a plastic riot cuff. "Looks like we're kicking ass pretty good."

"Yeah," Schwarz agreed, "but it isn't over yet."

"Well," Lyons replied with a shrug, "no rest for the weary. Let's get back to work."

CHAPTER THIRTY-ONE

The three Phoenix Force commandos knew the cause of the original explosion that had triggered the battle. They'd heard the bang and seen the glare on the horizon. The enemy fishing boat headed for the Persian Gulf had been spotted by the USS *Narwhal* and blown out of existence.

The Stony Man trio also heard the tremendous and tumultuous upheaval at the heart of the enemy stronghold. The roar of explosions and the muzzle-flashes of constant gunfire at the center of the island revealed that the rest of the team was engaged in full combat with the enemy.

The terrorists at the pier and the generator center were also alerted to danger and prepared for an attack. Several men emerged from the boats in the cove, weapons in hand. Someone dragged a light machine gun from the hold of a boat and set it up at the aft deck.

Manning stood on a ridge far from the chemical plant with a clear view of the cove. He set the FAL assault rifle on full-auto and aimed at the advancing troops on the pier. The Canadian opened fire and nailed his closest opponent with a 3-round burst through the heart. He'd selected and taken out his next target before the first man fell to the ground.

The attack forced the enemy to retreat and seek cover. The men on the boat swung around the light machine gun, pointing it at Manning's position. They were slow and awkward because they tried to stay low to avoid presenting a clear target to the rifleman on the ridge. Manning expected the enemy to respond in this manner and realized they'd return fire with all the power they possessed.

He ducked low and crawled to a nearby barrel which he'd taken from the chemical plant. It had been empty until Manning set half a kilo of C-4 inside. The Phoenix demolitions expert set the timer to a detonator, rolled the barrel up the ridge and pushed it over the top.

The ensuing explosion ripped out the plank walkways to the pier and slaughtered the enemy gunmen, the force of the blast flattening the men on the deck of the boat. Burning debris and bloodied human remains rained down on the injured survivors.

While Manning dealt with the enemy at the harbor, Calvin James and Rafael Encizo took care of the electrical generator building. The Phoenix pair handled the problem in a simple and direct manner. James fired his M-203 launcher, and the explosion took out the guards with draconian efficiency. He and his Cuban partner closed in and mopped up, hurling fragmentation grenades at the structure.

Manning continued to fire his assault rifle at the survivors aboard the vessels in the cove. He kept the terrorists from launching a counterattack or escaping until James and Encizo arrived to back him up.

"Think they've had enough?" the black warrior inquired as he joined Manning and worked the slide action to the M-203 to eject the spent shell casing from the breech.

"Let's take out the remaining boats to be sure," the Canadian replied. He reached inside his gear bag and removed a Stony-M rocket launcher.

They fired rockets and grenades until every vessel in the harbor was reduced to floating kindling.

ELECTRICAL POWER throughout the island shut down when the generators were destroyed. The lights winked out inside the headquarters building, but the interior wasn't pitch-black. A flickering yellow glare from the fires burning outside the main house was reflected from the windows.

Bolan and Katzenelenbogen used the shadows to their advantage. They hid in the darkness while terrorist gunmen swarmed into the front room. The commandos opened fire with silenced weapons, cutting down the front-line attackers. The sound suppressors reduced the muzzle-flash, as well as the noise of the Beretta and Uzi, so the terrorists had trouble locating their opponents to return fire.

The Stony duo didn't give them time to fix targets. They took out the remaining terrorists, emptying their clips. Six bodies twitched on the floor as the Stony Man professionals moved forward, inserting fresh magazines as they approached a stairwell and a corridor. Footfalls and voices warned them that reinforcements were coming from both directions.

"I'll take the high ground," Bolan announced as he moved toward the foot of the stairs.

Katz took a grenade from his belt and pulled the pin. He popped the spoon and held the grenade in his fist for a short two-count before tossing it down the corridor. Bolan raised his M-16 and pointed it at the line of legs visible between the supports of a handrail at the upstairs hallway.

The Executioner fired, raking the lower limbs of the men above. Screams echoed from the upstairs, but the sound was drowned out by the explosion of the grenade in the downstairs corridor.

Billows of plaster dust and fragments of stucco boiled down the stairs. Three slain terrorists lay in the narrow hallway. The blast also blew open the doors to two rooms. A *keffiyeh*-clad figure emerged from one threshold with a Soviet-made submachine gun in his fists. Katz laid his Uzi along the forearm of his prosthesis and fired a short burst into the gunman's torso.

The man's weapon fell to the floor, and he slid along the doorway to die in an undignified seated position, legs splayed apart and head bowed like a skid-row drunkard sleeping off a binge. Another terrorist suddenly thrust an arm from the second doorway, a Makarov clenched in the fist. The gunner squeezed off two shots at Katz.

One bullet smashed into the frame of the Israeli's Uzi and sent the weapon flying. The second round struck Katz's prosthesis. The impact drove the mechanical arm back into Katz's chest with such force it knocked him off his feet.

The terrorist stepped into the corridor and looked down at the fallen Israeli, smiling as he aimed his pistol. Katz lay on his left side. His prosthesis was twisted in a crooked angle and blocked access to the Walther P-88 under his right armpit. The terrorist almost laughed when he saw Katz's left fist held a double-edged knife with a black metal handle.

The threat seemed absurd. As the terrorist prepared to squeeze the trigger, Katz pressed the lever at the quillon of the knife. A powerful spring launched the knife blade, sharp steel shooting out like a giant dart. It struck the terrorist in the solar plexus, the point piercing upward to puncture the chest cavity. Blood bubbled up into the terrorist's throat and dribbled from his open mouth.

The pain drove the man back two steps as he pulled the trigger, the Makarov firing a harmless round into the wall. He clawed at the blade lodged in his chest and tried to pull it free. Katz sat up, shoved the mangled prosthesis aside and drew his Walther P-88. The Israeli aimed the pistol and fired two shots. The terrorist collapsed to the floor.

"Yakov! Are you all right?"

"Nothing broken that can't be repaired," Katz replied as he got to his feet.

He examined the artificial limb. It was badly dented, and the trident hooks were stuck in place. The bullet was jammed among the gears.

Movement at the front door drew Bolan's attention. He swung his M-16 and pointed the barrel at two men who'd entered the building in a low crouch, MP-5 subguns already trained on the Stony Man warrior. They recognized Bolan even as he lowered the rifle.

"Some welcome, Mack," Lyons commented. "And we came to see if you need any help."

"What about the terrorists outside?" Bolan asked.

"As far as we can tell, they're already history," Schwarz answered. "The other three members of Phoenix Force are out there just in case."

"I thought they were still at the harbor," Katz remarked. "Obviously they took out the generators, but there's still the chemical plant...."

"They said there isn't any harbor anymore and the chemical plant is secured. James is going to head back there to stand guard just in case."

"Maybe the enemy is out of action here, too," Schwarz said.

Indeed, the building seemed to have fallen silent after the burst of violence only seconds before. Although all four men remained alert and continued to scan the area even as they spoke, there was no sign of danger.

"You two check upstairs," Bolan decided. "Yakov and I will check the rooms down here. Don't get overconfident, and watch out for booby traps, ambushes, that sort of thing. You guys know the drill."

The Able Team pair headed up the stairs. Bolan and Katz moved into the corridor, stopping abruptly when they saw a white cloth flapping on the underside of a rifle barrel. The gun extended from an open door to a room near the end of the corridor.

"Don't shoot!" a voice called out in guttural English. "I have a white flag. See? Don't shoot. I surrender."

"Toss the gun out!" Bolan ordered. "Then come out with your hands up. If you even think about going for a weapon, you're dead."

The rifle clattered to the floor. A man slowly stepped from the room, hands raised to shoulder level.

Bolan and Katz were surprised when they saw the man. He was stark naked.

"You see," Kaborya began, his face remarkably serene and serious for a man presenting himself in an embarrassing manner. "I carry no weapons. No reason to fear me. I removed my clothes so you would know I'm not hiding anything," Kaborya answered. "If you choose to make sport of me, so be it. However, I surrender and I demand the sanctuary and protection due me as a political refugee seeking asylum."

"Perhaps you belong in an asylum," Katz replied with a frown as he got a better look at the man's face. "My God. You're Kaborya, aren't you?"

"I have been known by that name for many years," the Palestinian admitted. "I remind you I can supply your government with vital information about Major Hawran and his operation here. Best if you let me cooperate. To do that, I must be alive."

"After spending all your adult life as a terrorist, you expect us to trust you now?" Katz asked with a disgusted snort. "I suspect deceptions and manipulations are second nature to you."

"I'm not nearly as mendacious as Hawran," Kaborya replied. "You'll find him back there with some of his Iranian monkeys and a couple of fellow Iraqis. Hard to say what they'll do when they realize they're cornered."

"Thanks for being so helpful," Bolan said dryly. He glanced at the doorway to the room Kaborya had emerged from. "Were you in there by yourself?"

"There were two Iranians with me," the Palestinian said with a shrug. "I shot them both in the back of the head with a silenced pistol. They would never have surrendered or allowed me to do so."

"And you didn't want to die for the cause?" Katz inquired.

"I'm a survivor," Kaborya explained. "And frankly I have no desire to die for Hawran's cause. He's already lost, and he's too stubborn to realize it."

"I'll go make sure he understands," Bolan said, turning to Katz. "Take nature boy into the hall and wait for the others to finish checking upstairs."

"Let's just cuff him, and I'll go with you," Katz urged.

"He might be the highest-ranking member of this conspiracy we'll take prisoner," Bolan insisted. "I want you to guard him and keep him healthy. With your prosthesis broken, the only weapon you can handle easily is a pistol. Better if you watch our boy and cover the front door."

"I don't like you going on alone," Katz said with a frown.

"It's a tough life."

CHAPTER THIRTY-TWO

The Executioner moved cautiously along the corridor to the crook in the L-shaped hallway. He glanced over his shoulder and saw that Katz had already escorted Kaborya from the area. He wondered if the Israeli had allowed the Palestinian to retrieve his undershorts before marching the guy to the front hall.

Bolan put his back to the wall as he moved closer to the corner. The corridor extended to the rear of the building. Major Hawran and a handful of his most loyal subjects were still there, according to Kaborya. The warrior knew he could be walking into an ambush the second he stepped from the corner.

He slowly eased his head forward and exposed only one eye to scan the corridor. The rear branch of the hallway was only eight meters long. No doors were located along the walls, but a barricade was set up at the end of the corridor. Three large tables stood on end, lengthwise.

Bolan spotted gun barrels, jutting between the tabletops. He immediately retreated around the corner as twin volleys of automatic fire snarled from the weapons. Bullets tore into the stucco walls and pelted the edge of the corner near Bolan's head.

The Executioner poked his M-16 around the corner and returned fire, a stream of 5.56 mm slugs slamming into the tabletops. The thick wood absorbed the bullets, and the terrorist gunmen once again blasted twin salvos at Bolan's position. The soldier withdrew from the edge of the corner once more.

The M-16 wouldn't do the job, Bolan realized. He discarded the rifle and drew the Desert Eagle, thrusting the barrel of the big pistol around the corner and opening fire. The powerful handgun roared and recoiled mightily in Bolan's fist. The Eagle weighed close to two kilograms, but the heavy frame helped handle the fierce recoil of the formidable .44 Magnum ammunition.

The big 240-grain slugs struck with penetrating force, punching through the heavy wood tabletops as if they were cardboard. One table fell forward and slapped the floor hard, a terrorist gunman collapsing on top of it, his chest and abdomen stained by scarlet blotches.

Bolan fired into the other tables, raising large splinters from the wooden shields. Tables toppled, and another terrorist fell into view. Both enemy gunners were out of the battle permanently.

The barrier was gone, and the warrior saw the double doors guarded by the slain men. He pulled the pin from a grenade and hurled the orb at the doors, the explosion reducing the entryway to rubble. Plaster and dust swirled from the first blast as Bolan threw a second grenade through the ragged opening. He heard the minibomb explode and charged forward.

A dazed figure staggered across the threshold. Bloodied and battered by the grenade blast, the man cradled his right arm in his left. Bolan drew closer and saw the guy's limb wasn't simply broken. The arm hung from a shred of skin and tattered cloth at the shoulder. The man's eyes rolled up in his skull as his knees buckled, and he dropped senseless to the floor.

The room within had been some sort of conference hall or war room. Chairs were scattered across the floor. A lecture stand lay lengthwise on the platform. The wall map of the world still bore the multicolored pins that revealed Hawran's targets.

Bolan moved to a door at the opposite end of the war room. He stood by the wall, clear of the door, Desert Eagle held up and ready. The warrior scooped up a chair with his empty hand and heaved it at the door. He dropped to one knee and cupped his palm under the butt of the pistol before the chair hit the door.

The door swung open on impact. No booby traps were set off, and no gunfire responded to the assault on the door. Bolan kept the .44 Magnum trained on the doorway and advanced slowly, still watchful of possible danger.

The next room was an office, which contained standard furniture but none of the enemy. Another door yawned open, and pale light from outside poured in through the doorway. The Executioner heard a car engine as he drew closer. As he moved to the door, a vehicle pulled away from the house and headed toward the airfield.

Bolan heard boot leather crunch plaster underfoot and turned to see a huge figure enter from the war room. A blur of movement distorted his view of the opponent as a chair hurtled toward him. The warrior tried to dodge it, but the chair hit him in the arms and chest, knocking him off his feet and sending the Desert Eagle spinning from his grasp.

When the Executioner hit the floor, the big attacker charged forward and bellowed with rage. Bolan rolled to his knees and drew the Beretta 93-R from shoulder leather. The attacker closed in and suddenly swung his foot, managing to kick the machine pistol from Bolan's grasp as soon as it cleared leather.

Mohandra towered over Bolan. He raised another boot and launched a murderous stomp, aimed at Bolan's head. The Stony Man warrior dodged the attack, and the foot slammed into the floor near his left ear. Bolan thrust both legs and kicked the Iranian in the hip. The man staggered from the blow, and Bolan rolled away and quickly got to his feet.

The Iranian attacked, hands aimed at Bolan's throat. The Executioner sidestepped the lunge and snapped a kick to Mohandra's abdomen, but a wall of hard muscle protected the Iranian from the full punishment of the blow. Bolan quickly grabbed the guy's wrist with one hand and the elbow with the other, then pulled the wrist and pushed the elbow. The effect increased Mohandra's momentum and sent him hurtling into the desk.

Bolan moved behind his opponent and stomped a boot to the back of a knee, following through with a karate chop to his nape. An ordinary man would have been put out of action by the combination of well-aimed blows. The Iranian simply grunted and swung a brawny forearm into Bolan's rib cage. The blow felt like a club and knocked the warrior into a wall.

Mohandra charged and threw a side-kick at Bolan's chest. The Executioner slipped clear, and the kick slammed into the wall, stucco and plaster giving way under the force of the blow.

The Executioner swung a left hook to his opponent's jaw and followed with an uppercut to the chin. Mohandra's head barely moved from the powerful punches. He retaliated with his own fist, the blow propelling Bolan into the desk. He tumbled over the top and fell to the floor. His head throbbed with pain, but he pushed himself up from the floor and got to his feet.

Mohandra suddenly closed in. He thrust his arms under Bolan's armpits and clasped his hands together behind the warrior's neck. He secured the full-nelson hold and applied pressure, determined to break his victim's neck like a twig.

The Executioner realized he had to act quickly or die. He reached back with both hands and found his enemy's head. Fingers pressed around the Iranian's skull, and Bolan jabbed both thumbs into his opponent's eyes. The terrorist cried out in pain as Bolan dug his thumbs deeper. Afraid the warrior would gouge out his eyes, Mohandra whirled and released his opponent.

Bolan was flung across the room, and slammed into a wall. The Stony Man warrior shook his head to clear it and turned to face his massive opponent. Mohandra held a hand over his eyes, still half-blind. The Executioner took advantage of the opportunity, rushed forward and kicked Mohandra in the groin as forcefully as he could.

The Iranian screamed in agony and lashed out at Bolan. The Executioner dodged the wild swing and delivered a roundhouse right. His fist smashed into the terrorist's nose hard enough to rock the big man on his heels. Bolan followed the punch with a heel-of-the-palm blow under the jaw.

A second later he stepped behind Mohandra and rammed a knee into his kidney. Bolan wrapped his right arm around the Iranian's neck and grabbed his own wrist with the left hand to secure the choke hold. The Executioner turned to plant a hip at the small of his opponent's back.

Mohandra struggled, but his exceptional strength finally failed him. The Iranian had been weakened and dazed by the punishment he'd already absorbed in the fight. Bolan twisted his trunk forcibly and heard something crunch in Mohandra's neck. He held his grip, forearm around the Iranian's throat and bicep jammed into his opponent's carotid artery.

Bolan felt the big man's body sag, but he didn't release the choke hold until he was certain Mohandra was dead. He finally lowered the corpse to the floor. The Executioner was breathing hard and his body ached, but he couldn't rest. Bolan crossed the room and retrieved his Beretta 93-R and Desert Eagle.

He looked outside and saw that the retreating vehicle had reached the airfield. The two men emerged from the rig. One crouched by the Land Rover while the other raced to one of the helicopters. Bolan stepped from the building and walked toward the field. There was no need to rush. The enemy wouldn't be going anywhere in the chopper.

MAJOR HAWRAN KNELT alongside the Land Rover, his Stechkin machine pistol filling his fists. His driver was an Iraqi officer and a trained combat pilot. Hawran assumed the role of guard while the driver hurried to the helicopter to start the engine.

Hawran stared out at the ruins of his stronghold. Fires burned among the wrecked vehicles and destroyed barracks. Buildings and tents lay in shambles. The grounds were dotted with the corpses of his followers. The major couldn't see the cove, but he realized the boats had certainly been taken out.

His plans had been demolished along with the base. Years of preparations and work had fallen into the ashes of defeat. For the major, this was the downfall of his life's ambition, the end of his world.

All that remained was a thin hope to flee and try to reorganize some time in the future. This seemed impossible, but Hawran knew there'd always be people who'd follow him as long as he pushed the right emotional buttons and masked his plans in the rhetoric that appealed to their feeble minds.

What most puzzled Hawran, as he stared at the carnage, was the lack of conquering forces visible among the ruins of his base. He would have guessed a hundred or more troops would have been needed to defeat his private army, yet he saw no evidence of a large attack force. It appeared that a small number of invaders had somehow taken on all his followers and won. Such a thing was impossible.

Wasn't it?

The pilot started the engine to the helicopter. The rotor blade turned one revolution before the vibrations rode along the metal carriage to the limpet mine Bolan had planted on the underside of the aircraft. The mine exploded and blew up the fuel tank, the

helicopter bursting into a miniature nova of white light
and flying metal shrapnel.

The force of the blast sent Hawran reeling. He
sprawled across the ground, stunned. He glanced over
his shoulder and stared at the flaming wreckage of the
chopper. Pain lanced his leg as if his lower limb were
on fire. Glancing down, the major saw that a long
metal splinter had stuck in his thigh. Bloodstains
formed around the projectile.

Hawran's head also ached, and blood trickled into
his right eye. He blinked to try to clear his vision and
reached for the metal shard. It was slippery with his
own blood, and he had trouble getting a firm grip on
it. He cut his palm on a sharp edge, but managed to
pull the tormenting blade from his flesh. Its removal
unleashed a flood of blood, and his thigh was washed
with crimson.

Hawran crawled to his Stechkin and retrieved the
machine pistol. He felt reassured by its familiar weight
as he dragged himself to the Land Rover. As the major gripped the door handle and started to open the
door, a bullet tore into the fabric at the backrest of the
driver's seat. The roar of a Magnum firearm bellowed from ten meters away, and Hawran whirled to
confront his opponent. The damaged leg gave way
under his full weight, and he fell to one knee. He
grimaced in pain as he looked up at the tall man in
black.

"Give it up or use your piece," Mack Bolan announced. He held the Desert Eagle in both hands.
"It's okay with me either way."

Hawran held his Stechkin low, muzzle pointed at the
ground. He realized he couldn't hope to raise the

weapon, aim and fire before the other man could shoot him. Maybe the first shot was an accident, and the big American had intended to hit Hawran and missed.

"My name is Karim Hawran," he declared in uncertain English. "I'm a field-grade officer in the Iraqi army. May I ask who you are?"

"Go ahead and ask," Bolan invited. "Last chance, Hawran. Drop your gun and raise your hands or you're dead."

Hawran forced a smile. "You don't object to murder?"

"Not murder," Bolan replied as he slowly lowered his pistol. "Justice."

Major Hawran figured this was his only chance to survive without surrender. He raised the Stechkin and began to squeeze the trigger. Hawran didn't see Bolan's big pistol move, but he glimpsed the muzzle-flash. The .44 Magnum round blasted into his chest and tore through his heart before he could fire his weapon. The Iraqi fell back into the Land Rover, the Stechkin slipping from his fingers. The thunderous report of the Desert Eagle seemed to echo repeatedly inside his head. It was the last sound Major Hawran heard.

FLARES LIT THE NIGHT SKY, the brilliant yellow and green lights informing Captain Lester of the USS *Narwhal* and the commanders of other naval vessels in the Gulf of Aden that the Stony Man commandos had accomplished their mission.

Kaborya and a dozen other prisoners were assembled near the airfield. Calvin James treated the wounded while Rafael Encizo and Yakov Katzenelenbogen stood guard. Gary Manning and Gadgets Schwarz helped Bolan remove the limpet mines from the remaining aircraft at the enemy field and the explosive rigged to the cannon inside the tent near Hawran's headquarters building. With the terrorists crushed, it wasn't wise to leave booby traps that might injure or kill friendly forces.

"Hal ought to be pleased with how this turned out," Carl Lyons remarked as he joined Bolan near the airfield. "We took out the terrorists, saved a few to testify in court and there are probably detailed records of their activities in those filing cabinets you saw in Hawran's office."

"Yeah," the Executioner agreed, "it's hard to argue with one hundred percent success. Brognola and the President will be glad to hear the news from us— the leaders in France and Great Britain will also be relieved."

"Blancanales and McCarter will be sorry to hear what they missed," Lyons commented with a grin. "Maybe they'll be luckier next time."

"Next time." Bolan nodded. He knew there'd be another mission. There always was. Terrorism, like evil itself, could never be totally eliminated.

Yet the next time was in the future. Stony Man forces had been victorious. Much blood had been shed, but many more innocent lives had been saved by their actions. Bolan savored this sense of satisfaction as he heard the gunships approach the island.

"U.S. Navy Bell UH-1D choppers and a great big Chinook," James announced as he watched the aircraft through a pair of binoculars. "Sure glad we won't have to swim home."

"Gentlemen," Katz added, "our taxis have arrived."

"I'll be so glad to get back to the Farm I might even accept a cup of that evil brew that Bear passes off as coffee," Schwarz declared.

"Oh, really?" Lyons inquired in a doubtful tone.

Schwarz thought for a moment and replied, "Naw. I guess not."

A storm is brewing in the Middle East and
Mack Bolan is there in . . .

THE STORM TRILOGY

Along with PHOENIX FORCE and ABLE TEAM, THE
EXECUTIONER is waging war against terrorism at home
and abroad.

Be sure to catch all the action of this hard-hitting trilogy
starting in April and continuing through to June.